The Hour of Death

Also available by Jane Willan

The Shadow of Death

The Hour of Death

A Sister Agatha and

Father Selwyn Mystery

JANE WILLAN

CROOKED
LANE

NEW YORK

Copyright © 2018 by Jane Willan

Published in the United States by Crooked Lane Books, an imprint of The Quick Brown Fox & Company LLC.

Crooked Lane Books and its logo are trademarks of The Quick Brown Fox & Company LLC.

Library of Congress Catalog-in-Publication data available upon request.

ISBN (hardcover): 978-1-68331-759-3
ISBN (ePub): 978-1-68331-760-9
ISBN (ePDF): 978-1-68331-761-6

Cover illustration by Teresa Fasolino
Book design by Jennifer Canzone

Printed in the United States.

www.crookedlanebooks.com

Crooked Lane Books
34 West 27th St., 10th Floor
New York, NY 10001

First Edition: October 2018

10 9 8 7 6 5 4 3 2 1

To Barbara, my tireless writing partner, for her endless encouragement, brilliant ideas, insightful editing, and Lutheran sensibilities.

Chapter One

When Sister Agatha slipped through the wrought-iron gate in front of Gwenafwy Abbey and started down the winding lane that led to the village, the sun had barely risen over the tower of Pryderi Castle. She smiled at the sound of the familiar click of the latch as the gate shut behind her. How many times over the years had she heard that gate catch and click as she headed down Church Lane on the short walk to the village? Gwenafwy Abbey, an Anglican religious order of the Church in Wales, with the mountain range of Snowdonia to its east and the Irish Sea a few miles to the north, had been her home for nearly four decades. She had grown up on a sheep farm just a stone's throw from the abbey and her earliest childhood memory was the gentle peal of the chapel bell calling the sisters to prayer.

She pulled out her mobile and glanced at it. The library meeting started at half eight, which meant she had just enough time to make the brisk ten-minute walk into the village of Pryderi and to the public library on Main Street. Pryderi, tucked into the heart of the heather-clad summits of the Clwydian Range, had sat at the bottom of a steep hill since before the

Norman invasion, as though one day it had tumbled down and then reassembled itself at the bottom. In contrast, Gwenafwy Abbey sat perched at the top of the same steep incline, as though graciously keeping watch over the comings and goings of the small community.

Although Sister Agatha lived and worked at the abbey, she and the other sisters spent much of their time in the small village with its cluster of shops, farmer's market, St. Anselm Church and the Buttered Crust Tea Shop. They occasionally dropped by the Saints and Sinners Pub for the hearty Sunday brunch and a pint, or on special occasions, when the nuns felt they needed a bit of fine china on starched white table cloths, they treated themselves to a formal Devon cream tea in the faded grandeur of the old Hotel Pryderi.

Stopping in the middle of the lane, she took a deep breath, feeling the cold air fill her lungs. She couldn't imagine living anywhere but North Wales. Even now, with the the sun barely breaking through the clouds, the Welsh countryside held its charms. Brown fields bordered by ancient stone walls formed squares like an unfurled quilt. Clumps of purple heather and flocks of white sheep meandered up to the edges of gray stone crofts whose chimneys plumed smoke into the morning sky. Looking down into the valley, Sister Agatha could just see the spire of St. Anselm Church, built in 1454 by the Normans, as it rose above the slate rooftops of the village. The tower of Pryderi Castle to the east cast its long shadow, while the River Pwy, which formed the western boundary of the village, glinted in the cold sunlight like a ribbon set on fire.

One could easily walk from the abbey to the castle by

following the length of Main Street passing the Buttered Crust Tea Shop, the public library, and St. Anselm Church and ending up at the castle drawbridge—all in about twenty minutes—if one walked briskly and with purpose.

Sister Agatha wrapped her muffler a bit tighter as she rounded a bend in the gravel lane. She stopped short, catching her breath at the devastation in front of her. The beautiful sloping meadow she had walked past almost every day of her life and home to sheep, wildflowers, and birds stared back at her, an ugly chaos of mud, rocks, and debris. A jagged hole the size of a small house gaped open. A backhoe, a forklift, a stack of pallets and other rubble littered the once tranquil meadow. At the far end of the property sat a large gray storage tank with the word *WASTE* printed on it in huge letters. To Sister Agatha, that tank was like a billboard advertising all that was wrong with the world. A garish orange-and-green sign glared back at her from the edge of the property: "DRM Development and Estate Planning."

She shook her head. *Progress.* To think that the lovely Welsh countryside could be ruined by greedy developers. Cheap houses quickly constructed without a care given to the infrastructure of the Welsh village or to the environment of the small farms struggling to survive.

After months of battle with the citizens of Pryderi, the construction company, DRM Development, had won, however—and the proposed housing complex was going forward. The villagers had argued that the housing development would change the culture of the village, straining local business establishments, paving the way for huge chain stores, which in turn would squeeze the life out of Main Street. Beautiful countryside that had been home to the flora and fauna of Wales destroyed to make way for car parks and concrete drives. The sisters of Gwenafwy Abbey were heartsick. For Sister Agatha, the destruction of the sheep meadow represented a worse tragedy. Everyone who had grown up in Pryderi knew that the tiny, sloping field was home to fairies. The sheep meadow was a fairy field. Sister Agatha, though a good Anglican, held fast to a few pagan traditions—as did her sisters—and she half-believed that on the occasional moonlit summer night, the fairies danced and sang. Wales was full of enchantments. One needed only to look carefully and listen. And not tromp over them with bulldozers!

Sister June, a solicitor in Cardiff before joining the abbey, had taken the lead in fighting the housing project and had managed to get a temporary halt of operations by citing that the development company did not comply with the village's Code of Ordinances. As hopeful as the sisters had felt when the digging stopped, Sister June warned them that it was only a temporary reprieve; big companies such as DRM Industries could easily hire the legal power to get an extension and continue work. But at least, Sister June had said in her matter-of-fact barrister voice, it would slow them down a little.

Sister Agatha had swelled with pride at last week's village meeting when Sister June, all five feet one inch of her, had neatly annihilated the arguments of the representative of DRM. Taking her place behind the microphone in the parish hall meeting, she had pointed out to the construction representative that the choice of Pryderi as a location for the housing development had very little to do with improving the economy of the small village but rather was concerned with lining the pockets of developers and politicians. She explained that the development companies were targeting villages like Pryderi because they were on the outskirts of national parks where real estate was lucrative. And as Pryderi sat seventeen miles east of Snowdonia National Park, it was outside government protection for development and therefore the perfect site for someone like DRM Industries to exploit. Sister Agatha and the others from the abbey had cheered the feisty and well-spoken Sister June as she put the developer in his place.

The next meeting of the village was this coming Monday, and Devon Morgan, minister for the environment, planning and the countryside, would be at the meeting to answer questions. And, some were afraid, to make a pitch for his upcoming campaign. Word had it that he was a hopeful for first minister of Wales. A typical politician, Morgan would never take a hardline in either direction—for or against building up the countryside around small villages such as Pryderi.

Sister June, who followed the news more carefully than the others at the abbey, warned that he was in the pocket of the construction companies. And now, this morning, standing before the horrible travesty of mud and destruction, Sister Agatha's heart sank. All seemed lost. *What were things coming to?*

As she headed down the hill to the village, the wind picked up and she was glad that she had worn over her habit her heavy woolen jumper from Sister Winifred. She reached into her book-bag and located the blue wooly hat that she had purchased in Killarney years ago and pulled it down over her short gray hair.

The sisters at Gwenafwy Abbey wore blue habits that reached to mid-calf and white aprons over their habits. In winter, they all made good use of Sister Winifred's hand-knit jumpers. Sister Winifred knitted endlessly, churning out receiving blankets for the newborns at the Wrexham hospital, mittens and hats for her many nieces and nephews, piles of mufflers for the jumble sale. A few Christmases before, she had knitted a Hogwarts scarf for each sister at Gwenafwy Abbey, and this winter, a new jumper for every nun, choosing the color that she thought best fit each individual personality—a peaceful azure blue for the Reverend Mother, tranquil green for Sister Matilda, and for Sister Agatha fire-engine red. Sister Callwen, always a bit sharp-tongued but generally spot-on, suggested it was to keep Sister Agatha from getting lost in the crowd.

She picked up her pace. It had been a busy morning. She had already said the morning office—matins, or morning prayer—with her sisters and followed it with a hearty Welsh breakfast at the long farmhouse table in the abbey's refectory. Then Sister Agatha had put in a productive hour cataloging a new shipment of books in the attic library. As the abbey librarian, she kept the other sisters supplied with every book they could desire—from romantic comedy to revisionist history, from theology to thriller. She also enjoyed a collegial relationship with the staff at the village library and met with them every Saturday morning to exchange ideas. She liked to keep current with the latest in library science.

She rounded the second bend in the windy road, aptly named Church Lane, to the village, and the spire of St. Anselm Church appeared over the treetops. Advent was well under way, and she found herself singing softly her favorite Advent hymn from the Anglican hymnbook:

> *Come, Thou long expected Jesus*
> *Born to set Thy people free;*
> *From our fears and sins release us,*
> *Let us find our rest in Thee.*

She loved Advent. Better than Christmas. Which most people didn't understand.

Advent meant far more than the four-week countdown to Christmas even though it usually began on the first Sunday in December. Most people thought it involved nothing more than the hanging of the greens or the lighting of the Advent candles. But Advent really meant expectation—the expectation of Christ's coming again. In the gray dreariness of December, when the sun set below the castle tower by late afternoon and the bitter wind rattled the windows of the abbey, Advent offered a welcome light in the darkness—one more candle added each Sunday to the Advent wreath in the chapel and to the one on the dining table in the refectory. Advent was a time of hope and grace, of looking forward to a better tomorrow and back to the rich traditions of yesterday.

This year, however, the expectation of Advent meant something even closer to the day-to-day than the arrival of the Christ child. It meant the arrival of something else far more tangible. An enthusiastic group of young nuns from a convent in Los Angeles were joining Gwenafwy Abbey in January—the first new sisters to join in a very long time—except for

Sister Gwenydd, who had arrived at their doorstep in a rather unconventional way—on the lam, fleeing because she thought she had accidentally murdered her boyfriend. It had all worked out in the end fortunately, and now she served as the abbey's incredibly talented chef as well as its newest and youngest member.

Suddenly a horn blasted and Sister Agatha jumped back, crashing into a gorse bush. A battered blue car roared past, spinning gravel as it headed up the hill away from the village.

Good heavens! She got to her feet and started back down the hill, pulling a sticky gorse thorn from the red wool of her jumper. What was wrong with people these days? Well, no time to dilly-dally. Her Saturday meeting with the other librarians started in less than ten minutes. After the meeting she hoped to entice Father Selwyn to join her for a mid-morning Welsh cake at the Buttered Crust Tea Shop. Father Selwyn, vicar at St. Anselm, had been one of her closest friends since primary school. Some people in the village had thought they had been more than friends when they were young, but then, at the age of twenty, Sister Agatha surprised everyone by taking orders at Gwenafwy Abbey. That same year, Father Selwyn had gone off to seminary.

She knew Father Selwyn would be enthusiastic for a morning stop at The Buttered Crust. The Buttered Crust Tea Shop was on Main Street in between the Pryderi Post and the Just-for-You Florist shop. It was the villagers' endless source of fresh scones, fragrant tea, and crusty oat cakes.

She crossed the stone footbridge over the River Pwy, pausing for a moment to gaze into the noisy brook, frigid water from the glacial peaks of Snowdonia gurgling in the center, ice crisping at its edges. She stepped off the wooden bridge and onto the cobbled stones of Pryderi's main street just as the sound of sirens split the air. Their high-pitched blaring shattered the peaceful morning. Clutching the brim of her blue wooly hat, she jogged down Main Street in the direction of the sirens and found the front entrance of St. Anselm Church blocked by an ambulance and two police cruisers.

Treven Preddy, owner of the Lettuce-Eat-Vegan grocery, stepped up to her. "It's not good, Sister," he said. Treven wore a parka pulled over his white grocer's apron. "Not good at all."

"Is Father Selwyn . . . ?" she asked. Her head felt light.

"No, Sister. Not the vicar," Treven said. "It's Tiffany Reese."

"Tiffany?" Tiffany Reese, a legendary church lady who organized the annual church jumble with tyrannical precision and conducted every Women's Institute (WI) meeting as though she were Speaker of the House of Commons, ruled as a daunting force in the St. Anselm parish. Her Welsh fruitcake was never dry, her solo on Christmas Eve flawless, her three-tiered lemon cake for the Ladies Devotional Tea always exquisite. Tiffany Reese was so perfect that almost no one liked her.

The Pryderi Women's Art Society held their annual Christmas gala in the church parish hall. It opened on the second Saturday in Advent. An imposing sign stood outside the church door advertising its opening at noon that day. Most of the women in the Art Society were amateurs at best, and although Sister Agatha supported anyone pursuing her craft, even she had tired of the endless watercolors of castles, sunsets over the Irish Sea, and baskets of kittens. Tiffany, the

9

recently elected president of the Art Society, had been dropping hints for weeks that her entry was no less than extraordinary. The year before she had won first prize for her painting. Her exquisite and detailed depiction of the "Red-Throated Diver" had stunned the villagers, who had stood mesmerized in front of it. Sister Agatha remembered that the local paper had described the painting as *Killian Mullarney meets Audubon*. She also remembered how last year she had stood there in the parish hall with the sounds of the art show going on around her, captivated by the depiction of the bird—its speckled back feathers, the red band on its graceful neck, and its snowy-white underbelly. For one moment she felt herself standing on the edge of the cliffs overlooking the Irish Sea.

Sister Agatha had been more than a little surprised that Tiffany Reese, whom Sister Callwen had once referred to as the greatest social climber since Cinderella, was so accomplished an artist. But then, Sister Agatha thought, people can surprise you.

At the sight of the two police cruisers, she automatically reached into her apron pocket for her detective's notebook and, when she found it wasn't there, sighed with regret. She had decided to stop carrying her notebook during Advent. It hadn't been her idea so much as the Reverend Mother's. Reverend Mother had reminded her that life at the abbey was a balance of prayer, work, study, and rest, not murder weapons, lists of suspects, and chasing down bad guys.

Sister Agatha was a devoted mystery writer—as yet, unpublished. She spent her spare moments writing, researching, and thinking about murder. That meant that whenever she wasn't in chapel with her sisters, or fulfilling her duties as the abbey librarian, or helping produce the abbey's award-winning organic cheese, fittingly named Heavenly Gouda, she feverishly wrote. And when the muse stayed absent, she immersed herself in all the classic murder novelists. Her hope was to glean ideas and skills from their protagonists. Between Agatha Christie's Poirot and Louise Penny's Gamache, she felt she was beginning to get her feet under her and had begun to think like an amateur sleuth.

Unfortunately, she had to admit that sometimes she did cross the line between writing about fictional murder and seeing herself as the actual detective. Consequently, she was rarely without her detective's notebook. Except today. She shook her head. Armand Gamache would never have been caught without the means to take notes. Even if it was Advent.

"Has Tiffany taken ill?" she asked Treven.

"Taken ill?" Treven raised his eyebrows and pulled his heavy parka around his substantial girth. "She's not ill, Sister. She's dead."

* * *

Sister Agatha pushed through the front doors of the church, waving off the young officer who started toward her. "It's all right, Parker," she said. She recognized him as Parker Clough, the officer who had arrested Sister Gwenydd that horrible day last summer at the Buttered Crust Tea Shop. She wasn't going to be slowed down by a young man who would arrest a nun in the middle of her tea. In her hurry, she took the stairs down to the parish hall two at a time, nearly falling, catching herself at the last second by grabbing the stair rail.

Although Treven had assured her that Father Selwyn was perfectly fine, she felt a surge of relief to see him standing there, prayer book in hand. Tall and balding, with a slight paunch that spoke of too many buttered scones and Glamorgan sausages, Father Selwyn chose to wear the traditional black cassock—when he remembered to iron it—and dog collar—when he could find it. (In the absence of his collar, he sometimes folded an index card and slipped it into his collar tabs.) Beloved by the Pryderi community and by the nuns at Gwenafwy Abbey, it was said that Father Selwyn could comfort those who grieved, encourage those who needed it, and ignore those who complained. The perfect skills required for a parish vicar Sister Agatha always thought.

Constable Barnes stood at the far end of the parish hall talking on his mobile. She was glad that he didn't look up when she came through the doors. He had made it clear in the past that he did not approve of her detective work, though she had practically saved his job for him over last summer's murder at the abbey.

Dr. Hedin Beese, coroner for Wrexham County, stood off to the side taking notes on an electronic tablet. Beese, just out of medical school, was far younger than Sister Agatha thought a doctor should be, but she had to admit that she had proved herself very capable. And unlike Constable Barnes, she kept an open mind.

Father Selwyn nodded to her as he opened his prayer book and knelt beside the body of Tiffany.

"Who called it in?" she asked, stepping next to him.

"Lewis Colwyn. He came down to the hall to check the thermostat at about six this morning. He's been filling in as sexton during school vacation." Two ancient boilers supplied heat to the entire church, and reliability wasn't their strong point. "He was very shaken. I guess he didn't turn the light on and almost stepped on her," Father Selwyn said. Lewis Colwyn was a popular teacher at the secondary school and an avid gardener on the side. He and Sister Matilda were fast friends, united by their love of plants. Sister Agatha knew that when he wasn't busy with his growing family, he was always helping out at the church.

Tiffany Reese lay slumped on the floor with her back to the wall, legs splayed out in front of her, as if she had fallen backward against the wall and slid down it. Her face, drained white, had a blueish-gray tinge around the nose, eyes, and fingertips. Her chin had fallen onto her chest. Her mouth was halfway open and slack. Both arms had fallen to her sides. A large diamond sparkled on her ring finger. Sister Agatha said a quiet prayer of her own as Father Selwyn began the prayers for the dead.

The church hall, usually cluttered with folding chairs, a few tables, and a jumble of equipment from the St. Anselm village daycare, had been emptied of anything that didn't relate to the art show. Rows of paintings displayed on the white walls, each with a small descriptive card underneath, represented a year's work from the Art Society women. The refreshments committee had pushed a long table covered with a lace cloth against the far wall. Sister Agatha could see piles of neatly arranged cocktail napkins, dessert plates, the WI silver service, and the huge church coffee urn.

She desperately wished she had her notebook and settled instead for a cocktail napkin. She pulled her paperback copy of *Murder on the Orient Express* out of her book bag to use as something to write on. It would have to do. She noticed that lying on the floor at Tiffany's right side was a teacup. The teacup was delicate—bone china?—and was broken into two pieces. She longed to put on latex gloves and examine the porcelain. Much as she loved being an Anglican nun, Sister Agatha sometimes fantasized about being a real detective. She imagined herself handing the pieces of teacup over to her second-in-command with a gruff instruction to "bag it." Coming out of her reverie, she instead retrieved the Sharpie from her jumper pocket and made a quick sketch of the scene on the cocktail napkin, noting the angle of the body, the exits to the room, and the position of the teacup.

What would Inspector Rupert McFarland do right now? Rupert McFarland, retired lieutenant at the Strathclyde Police headquarters in Glasgow, was a best-selling mystery writer and the host of the Radio Wales pod-cast *Write Now.* Sister Agatha never missed the weekly show. Every Sunday evening, Inspector McFarland tackled the toughest crime-writing dilemmas—from weak verbs to weak witnesses, questionable alibis to sloppy syntax. He had taught her more than her Master of Fine Arts in Creative Writing from the University of St. David ever had. She thought for a moment and remembered his advice just last Sunday night: *Don't let your imagination get in the way of hard facts. On the other hand, there is no detective work without imagination.*

Dr. Beese walked over and, saying an abrupt good morning to Sister Agatha, crouched next to the body, across from Father Selwyn. She continued tapping on her electronic tablet as Father Selwyn stood up, slipping the prayer book into his cassock pocket. Sister Agatha stepped back and swept the room with a piercing glance. Was this a crime scene with a dead body or was her imagination running toward murder without any facts? If Tiffany died of unnatural causes, then the crime scene had just been horribly compromised by the early morning visit of Lewis Colwyn. Sister Agatha imagined him tromping across the room in the dark on his way to the thermostat, which sat directly above the dead body, and nearly stepping on it. She shook her head and could almost hear Inspector McFarland's Scottish brogue, *Keep your crime scene secure, laddies! A crime scene without integrity is a crime scene without its day in court.*

"You didn't step on the body or anything did you?" she asked Father Selwyn

"Of course not."

"It's just that if this is a crime scene and you came plodding across it in your size-twelve brogues, well . . ."

"Crime scene!" he said in a loud whisper with a glance backward at Constable Barnes, still on his mobile. "We've no idea what happened here. You can't start calling it a crime scene."

"You never know," she said. "It seems suspicious to me."

"Everything seems suspicious to you."

Sister Agatha ignored him. She looked around again and made a few more notes on the cocktail napkin. The spot directly above Tiffany's dead body, where a painting should have hung, was empty. She noticed a small hole for the nail and, scanning the floor, saw it—a nail had rolled to the edge of the baseboard. She picked it up and slipped it in her jumper pocket. Underneath the spot where the painting should have been was a small placard reading "Melyn yr Ei thin," *Yellow Bird of the Gorse.* She took a snapshot of it with her mobile.

"Sister!" Constable Barnes' voice boomed across the hall. "What are you doing here?" Constable Heath Barnes sang bass in the St. Anselm choir, and although Sister Agatha liked him as a person and appreciated that he was a faithful member of the parish, she had her doubts about his competence when it came to crime. Especially murder. Constable Barnes started toward her. "The public is not allowed in here. A woman has died."

"I understand," she said. "But since I'm already here—could you tell me what happened?" She looked over at Father Selwyn, who widened his eyes at her, and then back to Constable Barnes, whose heavy face had turned from pink to red and splotchy. The sight of her snapping any more photos might tip Constable Barnes into the coronary he looked like he was about to have, so she slipped her mobile into her jumper and tried to set the scene to memory, noting that the teacup was broken almost perfectly down the center. She also remembered that every woman in the Women's Institute had a teacup with her name on it in the church kitchen. Everyone who used the church kitchen knew never to drink from a WI teacup: they were the sole property of the ladies. This teacup did not have a name. Did that mean that Tiffany had used someone else's? Or was she drinking tea at all? What if someone else had been in the room with her and had dropped the teacup?

"No, I cannot tell you what happened—except that the poor woman is dead," Constable Barnes said. "We won't know anything until Dr. Beese has finished. And please don't start your interfering. There's been no foul play as far as I can tell."

Sister Agatha tried not to roll her eyes, and she was almost successful. Constable Barnes never thought there was foul play no matter how foul the play looked. She resisted reminding him how wrong he had been the last time. He preempted her. "I'll thank you to not go jumping to conclusions just because of . . . well, because of you-know-what." Obviously, last summer's murder at the abbey was still a sore spot for the constable.

Dr. Beese stood and smoothed the front of her black skirt. "If I had to guess," she said, looking directly at Constable Barnes. "I would say a stroke or heart attack. Most likely a heart attack. But I will know more if there is an autopsy."

Sister Agatha began to write as quickly as she could, using the cocktail napkin placed on top of *Murder on the Orient Express* as her detective's notebook. "If there is an autopsy?" she said. "Surely this mysterious death requires a complete forensic autopsy. I was thinking . . ."

Dr. Beese cut her off. "There is no sign of foul play," she said. "At least not that I can see at this point. And it isn't that mysterious."

"Ligature marks?" Sister Agatha asked. "Injection sites?" Inspector Rupert McFarland had an exhaustive list of all the most probable ways that one's victim could die. She ticked them off in her head: *knife, poison, sword, a blow to the head, gun, garrote.* "Blood that has pooled and we can't see?" Sister Agatha had just finished reading a lengthy article on dual lividity and she was anxious to apply her newly acquired knowledge.

"No." Dr. Beese paused, her brow wrinkled. "At the risk of breaking confidentiality, Mrs. Reese was a patient of mine and had very high blood pressure. I had advised her to take care of her blood pressure because it made her susceptible to heart disease or a stroke. I don't mean to jump to conclusions, however." Dr. Beese opened her tablet, read for a moment, and then looked up. "Time of death . . . between nine and twelve PM last night."

"She must have stopped by the church to finish setting up for the art show," Father Selwyn said. He glanced at the clock on the wall. "Which opens in exactly two hours, by the way."

"Will you do a tox screen?" Sister Agatha asked.

"Why?" Dr. Beese looked thoughtful. "What are you thinking?"

"With no trauma to the body, one would consider death by poison. Just a thought." Sister Agatha's voice trailed off as she heard Constable Barnes snort.

"Interesting." Dr. Beese looked down at Tiffany's body and cocked her head. "Some poisons do induce a heart attack. But I don't think so in this case. I'm not sure I could justify sending off to Cardiff for a tox screen."

"There will be no tox screen and no autopsy," Constable Barnes said. "Unless the family requests it." He shot a withering glance at Sister Agatha.

Dr. Beese stuffed the tablet into her black holdall and snapped it shut. "I agree," she said, slipping on her coat and buttoning it. "The death is not suspicious. Mrs. Reese died of natural causes." She paused, and slinging the holdall over her shoulder, gave Sister Agatha a sympathetic look. "But I appreciate your concern, Sister. It's always good to stay open to possibility." They all watched as Dr. Beese turned and walked to the door of the parish hall, her heels clicking on the hardwood floor.

*　×　*

Father Selwyn and Sister Agatha climbed the stairs to Father Selwyn's study, occupied with their own thoughts. Sister Agatha went over the details of the scene. And Father Selwyn, she assumed, was processing the shock of a death in the parish. It wasn't every day that one came across a dead body in the parish hall. She watched as he put the kettle on the single burner. An electric log burned cheerfully in the grate. She settled into her usual spot—the squishy leather sofa that faced the fireplace. It was the kind of sofa that, once you had sat down, it was hard to get up from again. Still neither spoke. Father Selwyn heaved a sigh as he lowered himself into one of the wingback chairs that flanked the fireplace. He fingered his prayer beads, his face drawn as he watched the tea kettle.

She was glad to take refuge in Father Selwyn's office. It was a haven for her, and one of the few places where she found pure contentment—contentment as well as a steady supply of tea and cakes. The winter sun cast a beam through the stained-glass window, making a pattern of richly colored squares on the carpet. Overburdened bookshelves stuffed with everything from fishing journals to systematic theology lined the walls of the study. Comfortable, if slightly shabby, furniture sat invitingly in front of a small fire burning in the grate, and in the air was the slightest whiff of cinnamon. Cinnamon mixed with candle wax.

"Are you OK?" she asked.

"I am. I put in a call to Tiffany's brother, Kendrick. According to the housekeeper, he's out of town. And he doesn't pick up his mobile." Father Selwyn stretched and pulled the dog collar out of the tabs at the top of his cassock. "It's not as though I can leave something like this on his voice mail." The kettle soon began to sing, and she watched as he poured hot water into the ceramic pot on the small table between them, dropping in a few bags of her favorite tea, Welsh Brew. And then, sitting back down, looked at her thoughtfully but didn't speak. Father Selwyn was good at waiting and listening. He didn't have to keep up an endless stream of conversation like so many people seemed to these days.

"I managed to take a few more photos when Constable Barnes wasn't looking. Do you want to see them?" she asked.

"I do," Father Selwyn said. "Do you want a Welsh cake?"

"Yes, thank you. I've already missed my library meeting, so I don't suppose Reverend Mother will mind if I take time for tea." She handed the phone to Father Selwyn across the coffee table. "Scroll from the top." She bit into a Welsh cake and said, her mouth full, "You know what I'm thinking, don't you?"

"That Tiffany was murdered?" He squinted at the tiny mobile screen and then fished his spectacles out of his cassock pocket.

"So, you're thinking it too?"

"No. But I know you. I could see the wheels turning back in parish hall."

"Do you really think she died of a heart attack?"

Father Selwyn held up the mobile and looked at it. "I don't know." He leaned forward and selected a Welsh cake. "Bevan must have left these for us. That was thoughtful of him." Bevan was St. Anselm's indispensable administrative assistant.

"Has anyone reported her missing?" Sister Agatha finished her Welsh cake. This was just how Welsh cakes were supposed to be—crispy on the outside and crumbly with butter and sugar on the inside. "When she didn't come home last night?"

"Tiffany lives alone. No children, and her husband died ten years ago, at least."

"She's a pretty active member of the parish, right?"

He nodded. "Big time. Chair of the WI. Runs the Altar Guild. A member of the vestry."

"So she'll be missed." She waited while Father Selwyn sat munching the oatcake. "What? Tiffany won't be missed?"

"No. Of course she'll be missed. It's just that . . ." He chewed and swallowed. "Tiffany was kind of over-the-top. She had a way of offending. You know, alienating." Father Selwyn poured more tea into both their cups. "Tiffany was . . . how shall I say it? A little annoying. Pushy. Difficult." He sighed. "I'll admit it. She drove me crazy. Yet, she always got the job done. Our yearly jumble sale was never so successful as when Tiffany organized it. The WI runs like clockwork. The Altar Guild won a diocesan award for liturgical design." He put his teacup on the coffee table. "I hate looking at a screen. Do you mind if I print these?" Without waiting for an answer, Father Selwyn made several swipes and taps on the phone and then, a moment later, Sister Agatha watched as the four photos came churning out of the printer next to his desk. "I enlarged them too," he said.

"I'm impressed," she said. Father Selwyn was not known for his technical prowess.

"Bevan taught me." They both looked up at the sound of a knock on the door. Most people knocked and then just pushed in. "Come in," Father Selwyn said.

The door opened and Millicent Pritchard, whom Sister Agatha recognized as the young woman who worked behind the counter at the Just-for-You Florist shop on Main Street, stepped into the study.

"Sorry to bother you, Father," she said, giving Sister Agatha a weak smile. Millicent stood in the door of the study, her expression diffident, eyes wide-open. Thick brown curls tumbled from under a floppy felt hat. Sister Agatha's first impression was that Millicent was disheveled. After a second glance, though, she decided that "disheveled" didn't quite do it. It was more like a tornado of clothes had wrapped themselves around Millicent's fireplug body. And her entire wardrobe seemed to have come from the St. Anselm jumble sale. Well, nothing wrong with shopping at the jumble, Sister Agatha thought to herself. Most of the village shopped at the jumble at one point or another. Although perhaps they didn't layer on all of their purchases at the same time. Millicent tugged at the crocheted purple muffler swathed around her neck, its ends festooned with minuscule pink pompoms for fringe. "Is it true? When I came by with the Advent wreaths just now and I couldn't get in and I heard that Tiffany . . ." Millicent looked imploringly at Father Selwyn.

"It *was* Tiffany Reese, I'm afraid." Father Selwyn stood and moved across the small room in two steps to take Millicent's hand. "I'm so sorry. You were friends, weren't you?"

"Kind of. Yes. I mean, sort of."

Sister Agatha found that rather curious and reached for her notebook. Which wasn't there. She committed Millicent's comment to memory. In Sister Agatha's world, either you were friends or you weren't. None of this "sort of" business. "Do you always make deliveries to the church on Saturday mornings?" she asked.

"Um . . . Friday nights sometimes. Sometimes Saturday mornings. Sometimes both. Depends on my schedule."

"Did you come by last night with flowers?"

"Yes . . . I did. But . . . I didn't bring the Advent wreaths, just the altar flowers. So I'm back today. With the wreaths."

"Did you notice anything at the church last night? Perhaps in the parish hall?"

"No . . . I just went upstairs and put the flowers on the altar like always."

"Would you like to sit down?" Father Selwyn cut in, shooting Sister Agatha a sharp glance and gesturing to the wingback chair on the other side of the fireplace.

"Thank you, but I need to get back to the shop. Should I just put the wreaths in the sanctuary?"

"If you could. I think that would be fine." Father Selwyn was still standing, though he had released Millicent's plump hand. "Oh, wait. The Altar Guild wanted me to ask you something. What was it?" He searched the deep pockets of his cassock and, pulling out a yellow sticky note, read aloud. *"No more red and gold.* Wrong color for Advent." Father Selwyn looked at Millicent. "The color of Advent is purple—the color of penitence."

"Interesting. There aren't that many purple flowers available in the winter," Millicent said. She appeared thoughtful for a moment. "I guess there are, if you think about it. We grow a few in the hothouse. Canterbury bells, heliotrope, wolfsbane, dianthus." She paused. "It feels a little weird to me that you should be penitent before Christmas." Sister Agatha watched her even more closely.

"Well," Father Selwyn said. Sister Agatha could tell he was warming up to a teaching moment. There was nothing Father Selwyn liked better than to launch into a discussion of ecclesiology. "We are both penitent and joyful as we await . . ."

"Isn't wolfsbane poisonous?" Sister Agatha said, cutting Father Selwyn off.

"Sure, if you eat it," Millicent replied. "But lots of plants are poisonous if you eat them. By the way, do you know what will happen to the painting that Tiffany had entered in the show?"

An interesting question, Sister Agatha thought. She watched Millicent carefully as Father Selwyn explained that the painting was missing. Millicent seemed noticeably surprised.

"Did someone steal it?"

"We don't know," Father Selwyn said. "Anyway, it's gone."

"You liked Tiffany's art?" Sister Agatha asked.

"Of course," Millicent said, her voice suddenly a bit stronger. "She's quite talented."

"Are you an artist?"

"Me? Why do you ask?"

"There is a fleck of gold paint on the sleeve of your sweater." *Very Sherlock Holmes of me.* She experienced a tiny trace of smugness. *Even a bit Agatha Christie.*

Humility was not Sister Agatha's strong suit, and she took a quiet pride in the fact that she carried her literary hero's name. Although her actual name had been inspired by Saint Agatha of Sicily, a reputable Christian martyr in her own right—Sister Agatha now found herself equally inspired by Agatha Christie, a saint of the sleuthing and writing world. She doubted the Vatican would ever recognize her, though.

"What?" Millicent pulled at the sleeve of the slightly frayed brown cardigan that she had layered over a yellow turtleneck. "Oh. Yes, well, this used to be Tiffany's sweater. She sometimes gave me her things when she was done with them. So, I suppose this was one of her painting sweaters." She hesitated, as though she had more to say. But then she opened the door to leave. "I'll put the wreaths in the sanctuary. And no more red and gold." With that she slipped out and closed the door behind her.

Father Selwyn handed Sister Agatha the photos from the printer. "Millicent is an old soul," he said. "Shy, but very kind."

Sister Agatha spread the three photos across the table. She wished she could have taken a few more, but Constable Barnes was annoyed enough that she was even in the parish hall.

She leaned back and looked carefully at the first one—a snapshot of the empty space on the wall above Tiffany's head, the spot where her entry painting had hung. According to Treven, who was supplying the cheese and wine for the reception, the committee had finished setting up for the show. Every empty space on the walls held a painting—except one. The place directly above Tiffany's slouched and dead body was noticeably empty. "So where is the painting?" she asked Father Selwyn.

"Maybe she hadn't hung it yet?"

"I doubt it. The entire parish hall is set up with all the paintings that were entered. And if Tiffany was in the parish hall at ten PM last night and the Art Show judging was to start this morning, I really doubt that her painting wasn't already on display."

"That could be true. Or . . . it just wasn't hung up yet. Or she had taken it down for some reason."

"But if she had taken it down or not yet hung it, then it should be in the parish hall." She made a note to check the *Pryderi News* website for a photo of the winning painting from last year.

Father Selwyn leaned in to look at the other photos. Sister Agatha had taken a photo of the teacup lying on its side at

Tiffany's feet. Another photo was a straight shot of Tiffany slumped against the wall.

"Well, if she did have a heart attack, she could have easily been drinking tea and dropped it as she fell. One could imagine that she grabbed her chest and fell backward against the wall and then slid down," Sister Agatha said, checking her cocktail napkin of notes.

"There's no tea stain on the floor."

"Maybe she had just finished her tea and the cup was empty." Sister Agatha thought for a moment. "Or someone cleaned it up."

"But if someone cleaned it up, why would they leave the cup on the floor?"

"I wish I could dust the cup for fingerprints. Although it's not like I have access to the national fingerprint base." Again, she thought, the disadvantage to amateur sleuthing compared to professional detective work. Sometimes it was a bit of a cross to bear.

"Did Constable Barnes take the teacup with him as evidence?" Father Selwyn asked.

"No. Actually, I took it." To Father Selwyn's raised eyebrows, she defended herself. "He isn't collecting evidence because, in his mind, Tiffany died of natural causes. You heard him. Not even an autopsy."

Father Selwyn looked thoughtful as he concentrated on the photo of Tiffany lying slouched against the wall. "You can imagine her standing there, admiring her painting—or pondering where it was, if it had already disappeared—and then drinking the tea. Empty cup. Gripped by pain. Falling to the floor."

"Except the body was half sitting up slouched against the wall. Under the empty spot where her painting was."

"True. You would think that if you had a heart attack, you would kind of crumple down in the spot you were in, not move to the wall, lean against it, and then slide down. On the other hand, maybe you would. Maybe it came on slowly."

"Do heart attacks come on slowly?" Sister Agatha regretted not asking Dr. Beese for more information. "I'm thinking that this was a murder." She capped her Sharpie.

"What? So you think someone killed Tiffany Reese and stole her painting but first made her a cup of tea?" He leaned back in his chair. "Seems a bit far-fetched."

"If I could just rule out a few things, it would help. And some suspects might surface in the meantime." At the word *suspect*, Sister Agatha noticed that a look of slight hesitation crossed Father Selwyn's face, the tiniest crinkling of his brow. She waited, wondering if he had something to say.

Father Selwyn sat up and placed his empty teacup into the saucer. He stared at it for a moment, his lips in a thin line. "Well, don't take this too seriously. But at the deacons' meeting two nights ago I heard one of the women joke . . . or at least I thought it was a joke." He stopped as though he couldn't bring himself to say what he had heard. Sister Agatha waited.

"Well, anyway, Vonda Bryson is vice-chair of the WI and chair of our funeral dinner committee at St. Anselm. And she said . . . in a joking voice, mind you . . . that she looked forward to the day she could do Tiffany's funeral dinner."

Sister Agatha wrote "Vonda Bryson" on the remaining bit of cocktail napkin. "Anything else?" she asked, slipping the napkin between the pages of *Murder on the Orient Express.*

"Well, I hate to admit it, but we all laughed when she said it. I mean . . . I didn't exactly. Laugh, that is. But I certainly smiled."

"Does Vonda Bryson have a grudge against Tiffany?"

"Not that I know of. But as vice-chair she had to work side-by-side with Tiffany and that could make anyone a little stressed."

They both turned as Bevan Penrose knocked on the door frame and stepped in. "I need to tell you something, Father," he said quickly, looking from one to the other. "Perhaps you too, Sister. About last night."

Bevan picked up the empty plate from the coffee table. Sister Agatha noticed that he was forever cleaning up after Father Selwyn. The young administrative assistant was often seen following Father Selwyn around the church, gathering up dropped liturgical stoles, stray psalters, and the occasional fishing lure. The vicar was a zealous fly fisher.

"What is it?" Sister Agatha said.

"It's just that the church wasn't empty last night. Emeric was here practicing till late." Emeric Scoville was St. Anselm's organist. A music teacher at the village school, he often came by late to practice for the service on Sunday. Sister Agatha pulled the cocktail napkin out of the paperback and smoothed out the wrinkles. She uncapped her Sharpie. There was just enough room to write "ES" in the left-hand corner.

"The Constable called me a minute ago. He wants a list of everyone who has a key to the church."

Sister Agatha looked up. Perhaps Constable Barnes was taking a leaf out of her book and doing a little detective work after all.

"I told him most of the village have a key to Saint Anselm. Anyway, he said he talked with Emeric and Emeric told him that he left the church at eight o'clock, when he was done practicing the organ."

"But he didn't?"

"No. I'm sure of it. I rode by on my bike." Bevan picked up another used teacup, this time from on top of a stack of fly-fishing journals on Father Selwyn's desk. "I feel kind of bad, because when the constable told me that, I didn't say anything. I didn't want to get Emeric in trouble. But he was definitely in the choir loft practicing the organ."

"What time did you go by on your bike?" Sister Agatha asked.

"Nine-thirty or so. And the place was dark as pitch downstairs, but there was a light in the choir-loft window and I could hear Emeric—*Lift Up Your Heads, Ye Mighty Gates.*"

Sister Agatha nodded. Another absolutely favorite Advent hymn. "You're sure it was Emeric?"

"Who else would it be? And anyway, I saw that little scooter he rides parked at the side door. It was Emeric, all right."

"Did you see anything or anyone else?" Father Selwyn asked.

"No. Nothing."

"Would you say Emeric was playing loud or soft?" Sister

Agatha folded the cocktail napkin and glanced around for an actual piece of paper. Father Selwyn handed her an order of worship from the previous Sunday's service. She wrote in the margins. *Choir loft. 9:30 PM. Organist or really good imposter?*

"Oh, he was belting it out. You know how he likes to hammer down on the keys." Normally soft-spoken and reticent, when Emeric slipped on his organ shoes and took his place behind the console, he turned into a force to be reckoned with.

"So if there was a commotion of any sort in the parish hall, he wouldn't have heard it. Or at least might not have . . . if he was playing at the exact same time," Sister Agatha said.

"So why did he lie when the constable asked him if he was at the church that night?" Bevan asked.

Father Selwyn leaned forward, cutting them both off. "I'll talk with him. See what he says."

"One more thing. Lewis Colwyn called. His 'Gardens-All-Year' was supposed to meet tonight in the parlor. But he's had to cancel. His wife's ill."

"Gardening? In the parlor?" Father Selwyn said, his eyebrows raised.

"They don't really garden. They *talk* about gardening. And look at seed catalogs."

"Sister Matilda never misses. And I guess Lewis Colwyn is the Saint Francis of gardening," Sister Agatha said.

She was always a little puzzled by hardcore gardeners like Sister Matilda who spent the long winter evenings in the warming room and, while her sisters knitted, read, and watched Netflix, pored over seed catalogs. She even had her own gardening blog, titled *I Come to the Garden*. She and Lewis Colwyn were gardening soulmates and could often be found digging flower beds or weeding either at the church or on the abbey grounds. Lewis, who taught botany at the village school, was very involved at St. Anselm's.

Sister Agatha cast a sharp look at Father Selwyn as the door clicked shut behind Bevan. "It makes you wonder, doesn't it? Vonda Bryson makes a joke about Tiffany's funeral. Emeric Scoville lies to the police."

"Makes you wonder what?"

"Foul play. Murder." She shook her head. She thought of Father Selwyn as her crime-solving sidekick. But sometimes his refusal to see murder even when it was staring him in the face was exasperating.

"Why not wait and see what Constable Barnes comes up with?"

"Waiting for Constable Barnes is like waiting for the Second Coming. I might stop by and talk with Vonda Bryson, though."

"I'm sure she was joking."

"I'll be subtle. It's not like I'm going to walk in and accuse her of murder." Sister Agatha gathered the photos off the coffee table and slipped them into her book bag along with the ink-blotted napkin and paperback novel. She managed to pitch herself forward off the deep, squishy sofa and stood, straightening her red jumper. Sister Agatha had added leggings and fleece-lined hiking boots as well as the red jumper to her habit. The blue woolly hat replaced her usual veil and scapular.

"You know you look a bit like that boy in *A Christmas*

Story. The one whose mum gets him so bundled up he falls down in the snow and lies there like a turtle on its back."

"Do you think? Sister Callwen said I looked like one of Santa's elves that got caught in a gale-force wind. I don't know which is worse."

"A windblown elf in a habit. I like that."

"Anyway, I have my work cut out for me. I'll start with Vonda. I have just enough time to slip over to her house before heading back to the abbey. It could have been an offhand remark meant in jest. But you know what Hercule Poirot would have said."

"I'm afraid to ask." Father Selwyn took a sip of tea and looked longingly at the spot where the Welsh cake plate had been.

"Sweep away all extraneous matter, and you will see the truth."

"Ah, yes. 'And the truth shall make you free.'"

She squashed the blue woolly hat down over her short gray hair. "Miss Marple? *Murder at the Vicarage?*"

"No, Sister," Father Selwyn said, shaking his head. "Jesus. The Gospel of John."

Chapter Two

Walking up the flagstone path to the Bryson house, Sister Agatha felt a slight twinge of guilt for not being at the abbey where she should have been, working alongside her sisters. She quickly brushed off the guilt by reminding herself that a woman had possibly been murdered, and no one else seemed too interested in tracking down her killer. Except perhaps for Father Selwyn, who was generally on board with sleuthing or, as he put it, "making a few gentle inquiries." Vonda probably hadn't meant to announce that she looked forward to Tiffany's funeral, but she clearly disliked Tiffany and had a lot of contact with her. If nothing else, interviewing Vonda Bryson was a place to start. So instead of heading straight back to the abbey, as she knew she probably should have done, she found herself standing on the front steps of the Bryson house.

The large, comfortable two-story Victorian had cheerful curtains in the windows, shrubbery with colorful Christmas lights, and plastic toys in the front garden. Sister Agatha stepped over a skateboard on the front path to the door and smiled at a plastic doll buried to the waist in the frozen dirt of a flower bed. She had forgotten that Vonda had four boys in primary school. She paused for a moment before ringing the bell. She couldn't just walk in and ask Vonda Bryson if she had killed Tiffany Reese. She would have to be subtle. Lead up to it somehow. What would Agatha Christie do? Miss Marple often used deception to get information out of a suspect. Appearing to be a housekeeper or a tourist, anything but a snooping, amateur detective.

Sister Agatha pondered the idea of deception—a behavior certainly not recommended by the Book of Common Prayer, nor by Reverend Mother for that matter. On the other hand, desperate times call for desperate measures. Unable to settle on a good deception, she decided to leave room for the Holy Spirit and wait for inspiration to hit. She rang the doorbell.

Vonda Bryson didn't look anything like a vice-chair of the WI. Tall, in her late thirties with rumpled blond hair, she wore skinny jeans, an oversized man's jumper, and trainers like the kind Sister Agatha wore to the gym. No lipstick or makeup. Her eyes were red and puffy, and she clutched a box of tissues to her chest. "Sister Agatha?" she said. "Come in. Please."

Sister Agatha took care to hide her surprise that Vonda knew her name and smiled as she stepped into the house. It turned out deception was unnecessary. At least, not anything that she had to create on her own. "It's about the funeral dinner, isn't it?" Vonda said immediately as she ushered Sister Agatha into a pleasant, cluttered living room. A thick brown carpet, sturdy furniture, a fire in the grate. On the fireplace mantelpiece was a row of birthday cards bearing cheerful words about turning forty years old. An Advent calendar, held down by a plastic dump truck, lay open on the coffee table. In the adjoining dining room, Sister Agatha could see a huge bouquet of yellow calla lilies in a vase on the table. Vonda quickly scooped up a towering pile of folded boy's shirts and socks and dropped them into the largest hamper Sister Agatha had ever seen. "Here," she said. "Please. Have a seat, Sister."

"The funeral dinner?" Sister Agatha said, picking up a stray pair of black socks dotted with orange dinosaurs off the couch as she sat down. How could Vonda have known she was here to investigate her comment about the funeral dinner? Was she about to turn herself in? Sister Agatha felt her pulse quicken.

"I just heard." Vonda took a seat opposite in a large wingback chair. "They found her this morning? At the parish hall?" Her voice shook, and she plucked several tissues out of the box she was still clutching. "This is so awful. And in Pryderi. Things like this don't happen here. Of course, I'll do the dinner. I'm the chair of the funeral dinner committee and everything." Vonda blew her nose and then looked at Sister Agatha, who still hadn't spoken. "I thought the other sister—the young one, Sister Gwenydd—was in charge of the food? But I suppose one sister is as good as another. Oh . . . I didn't mean that the way it sounded. I just meant . . ."

Sister Agatha's mind snapped to attention. She remembered that Sister Gwenydd, the abbey's chef, had been helping out at St. Anselm's when they had a particularly large funeral dinner. Sister Gwenydd was new to the abbey and to religious life in general, and Reverend Mother thought it would be good for her to experience the day-to-day operations of a local church. She was the first young postulate in a decade to join, and the fact that she had not been terribly religious before she stumbled upon the abbey was nothing anyone wanted to quibble about.

"Yes," Sister Agatha said quickly. Even Miss Marple couldn't have planned it better. "Sister Gwenydd sent me." Sister Agatha felt her scalp tingle. An unfortunate reaction she always experienced when lying. Possessing a naturally honest personality was not an asset in a detective, though it wasn't such a bad thing in a nun. "You were friends with Tiffany, weren't you?"

"Well, I wouldn't say we were friends." Sister Agatha was suddenly reminded of Millicent's response about being "sort of" friends. Vonda paused, sitting back in her chair. "We worked together in the WI. She was president, I'm vice president. This is just horrible. They said she had a heart attack, which makes sense."

"It does?"

"Well, she was constantly stressed out. A real type A personality." She paused, taking a deep, quavering breath. "Although she seemed in such perfect shape. She ran, did yoga. Her house was perfect. She even had a specially designed artist's studio."

"You've been in her studio?"

"No. She wouldn't let anyone see it. She hosted the annual WI candlelight dinner. You know, for the officers. But we weren't allowed to see her studio." Vonda blew her nose again. "Did you come to talk about the menu?"

"Actually, I just came by to see if you were able to do the

dinner. I think Sister Gwenydd will want to figure out the specifics of the meal with you."

"Oh, okay." Vonda looked puzzled. "I'm surprised she didn't just text. That's how we did it last time. Last funeral, I mean."

"I stopped by myself because Sister Gwenydd felt a text was too impersonal considering you had known Tiffany so well." The tingling hit an all-time high.

"Wow. That's so nice." Vonda dabbed at her eyes with a tissue. "I mean, really nice."

Sister Agatha took a breath and fought the nearly uncontrollable desire to clutch at the top of her head. "Yes, well . . . Sister Gwenydd . . . is very thoughtful."

"Sister, may I tell you something?"

"Of course."

"I didn't really like Tiffany."

"Really?" She felt a wild urge to find the nearest cocktail napkin and start writing.

"Really. And now . . . now I feel terrible that she's dead."

"Well, sometimes it works that way. Just because you didn't like her doesn't mean that you wished her harm." *Or did you?* Sister Agatha thought.

"I said something horrible though. Last week, at the church, I said that I looked forward to . . . to . . . doing Tiffany's funeral dinner." Vonda's voice caught and her eyes filled with tears.

Sister Agatha felt sorry for the young woman and for one moment thought she might abandon her investigation altogether—offer some comforting words and then go back to the abbey where she belonged. *No, she thought, I've come this far.* She tried to look as neutral and nonjudgmental as possible.

"Well, honestly, who hasn't on occasion looked forward to a funeral?"

Vonda looked at her quizzically. "Well, I just thought . . ."

"I remember one very old and difficult nun at the abbey when I was first a postulate. She had taken quite a disliking to me, I thought. So when she died peacefully in her sleep a few months later—I have to admit—it wasn't an occasion of great sadness. So not feeling particularly sad over the death of someone isn't the worst thing." Throwing a party, now that was a different matter. And if you were the one who killed her, well . . .

"But I said out loud that I wanted to do her funeral dinner! I mean, how could I have said such a thing?"

"Well, why do you think you said that?"

"Oh, I was joking. You know. Pretty much." Vonda plucked a tissue from a box on the coffee table and blew her nose. "I mean . . . entirely, not pretty much. Of course I didn't want Tiffany to . . . you know . . . die." A gust of wind rattled the window. "I'm so sorry, Sister, can I offer you anything? Tea?"

Sister Agatha noticed that Vonda didn't make a move toward the kitchen. Not that she wanted anything, having just had tea with Father Selwyn. And anyway, she needed to get back to the abbey before anyone wondered why she had been gone so long. "Look. Vonda. We all say things we don't mean."

"But what if someone thinks I meant it? You know, overheard me. Lots of people were there. Even Father Selwyn."

"Well, I'm sure you have a good alibi for where you were last evening. At the time of the murder."

"Alibi? Murder? Why would I need an alibi? And why are you calling it murder? She had a heart attack, right?" Vonda's face had turned ashen.

"No—that's not what I meant. Unfortunate choice of words. I only meant, if you were asked, you could just tell whoever was inquiring where you were at the time of the death."

"You said *murder*." Vonda leaned forward, the box of tissue dropping soundlessly onto the thick carpet. Her eyes were wide and no longer tearful. If she was not truly surprised, Sister Agatha thought, she was doing a good job of faking it. "Are you saying it wasn't a heart attack? That someone killed her?"

"Yes. I mean *no*. I didn't mean murder. At all. I just meant *death*."

Vonda sat back but still stared at her, wide-eyed, silent. At least she had stopped crying.

"And if anyone wondered about your statement—a very innocuous statement meant in jest, of course—you could just tell them where you were last night." Sister Agatha paused and then couldn't help herself. "At nine and eleven PM."

"Well, I was here. Of course. At home. Watching telly."

Sister Agatha caught just the tiniest flicker of Vonda's left eye. A minuscule twitch that disappeared as fast as it traveled across her perfectly manicured eyebrow. "See? And that's all you have to say to people." Sister Agatha paused as Vonda continued to stare at her. "And your kids and husband were here? With you?"

"Well, no. Mark is away on business and the boys were at a sleepover. But I was here. All night."

"Well, then. You're all set. I'll tell Sister Gwenydd that you will contact her about the dinner," Sister Agatha said rising. "Are you going to be OK?" she asked, genuinely concerned and more than a little guilty. She hadn't meant to utter the word *murder*.

Vonda nodded. "I guess. I just wish I hadn't made that stupid joke." Vonda followed her to the door.

Sister Agatha turned around and faced her. "Look. We all make stupid jokes."

"Even nuns?" Vonda gave a rueful smile.

"Especially nuns." Sister Agatha gave Vonda a hug. And then pulling on her blue woolly hat she went out the front door and down the walk, careful to step over the skateboard. She really hoped Vonda was innocent, but until she checked out her alibi, she couldn't be sure. What was it that Inspector McFarland often said? *When you need information on a suspect, find their nosiest neighbor.* Vonda Bryson had said she was home all night watching telly. Sister Agatha knew just who to ask about that. She glanced at her watch. Only forty minutes until noontime prayer at the abbey. Well, if she hurried she could do the interview and make it back. *In for a penny, in for a pound.* And with that, she set off for the reference desk at the Pryderi village library.

*   *   *

Sister Agatha sighed, pulling off her woolly hat and ran her fingers through her short gray hair. Subtlety was not her strong suit. She had stupidly blurted out the words *murder* and *alibi* to Vonda. She wouldn't make that mistake again. Somehow, she had to find out if Vonda really was at home all evening last night. But she just couldn't saunter up to George Myers, library volunteer and across-the-street neighbor to the Brysons and start making make inquiries.

Taking a deep breath, she stepped up to the desk where George was scanning library books. After exchanging a few pleasantries about the onset of cold weather, she took a breath and launched into a question that would have made even Agatha Christie proud. "So, George," she said, glancing nonchalantly at the stack of fliers advertising the upcoming scrapbooking class. "Are you doing the annual tinned food drive for St. Anselm's?" She cringed at her small deception. Mild scalp tingling.

George snorted without looking up.

She took that for a yes.

"I've told Father Selwyn that this is my last year. Not a soul answers the door anymore."

"No one?"

"No one. Out all last night. Nothing. Everyone these days is out running around or is glued to their computer or watching telly. Shades pulled, houses all dark. I'll not do the door-to-door collection again. My last year."

This was too easy. "What about your neighbors, the Brysons? With the size of their brood, they must be at home nights. And have lots of tinned food on hand to donate." Sister Agatha wavered and then took the plunge. "You know, on Friday night, not even home then?"

"Are you kidding? That lot is never home. Always getting into that car and off they go—soccer, dance, music. And they don't even eat at home as far as I can tell. In my day, you sat down around the table every night."

"Times have changed, I'm afraid." Sister Agatha said. "So no one home all night?" She made her voice as casual as possible.

"Not so much as a light in a window. Went to bed myself at eleven. After telly, that is." George pulled a stack of books toward him and, opening the top one, ran the scanner over it. "There's a fine on that one," he said looking around. "And the borrower out the door without a backward glance." George grunted as he opened the next book and picked up his scanner. "You're right, Sister. Times have changed."

* * *

Sister Agatha was cold to the bone by the time she stepped into the large farmhouse kitchen of Gwenafwy Abbey just in time for lunch. Which reminded her—she needed to have a quick word with Sister Gwenydd before she contacted Vonda about planning the funeral dinner. She had walked as fast as she could up Church Lane and back to the abbey, resisting her strong desire to stop by St. Anselm's and discuss her thoughts about Vonda Bryson with Father Selwyn. She turned her head away when she passed the construction site with its ugly hole in the mud and machinery where a beautiful meadow had once grazed sheep. It was too painful to even look at.

As she neared the abbey, she could see the chapel steeple at the top of the hill. Just the site of the steeple, nestled between the tall yew trees, brought her a moment's joy. The abbey was truly beautiful. Medieval stone buildings encircled a small courtyard with the two wings of the convent surrounding its perimeter. On the west side, over the gate house, Reverend Mother had her private rooms. Above the east wing, the rest of the nuns of Gwenafwy shared rooms in a dormitory. The first floor underneath the dormitory housed the kitchen, the long dining room that the sisters called the refectory, and the warming room where the medieval monks, the original inhabitants of Gwenafwy Abbey, had kept a roaring fire throughout the winter. The sisters now used the warming room to relax during the evening—reading, knitting, binge-watching on Netflix, and engaging in bible study.

The attic library, the site of Sister Agatha's office and writing desk, was newly remodeled, with mullioned windows set into the blue-gray slate of the sloping roof. The outbuildings consisted of the cheese barn, a small stable, and a stone milking parlor grouped around the main buildings, along with the many flower and vegetable gardens tended by the nuns.

A stone shed at the edge of the orchard was used to store the Cadwaladr apples that the nuns harvested every autumn. The sheep barn for the new sheep sat nestled at the bottom of the meadow. A dovecote where a few wispy feathers still floated was next to the kitchen, and a crumbling tower overlooked the farthest northeast corner of the whole property— previously used as a medieval lookout in case of a Norman invasion.

Sister Agatha had been absent longer than she had planned when she left the abbey early that morning simply to attend a library meeting. Who knew she would end up examining a crime scene, interviewing a suspect, and checking out an alibi? Not bad for a morning's work if you are an amateur detective, but not exactly the normal Saturday morning for an Anglican nun. Especially as she was supposed to be giving up murder for Advent.

She hurried down the gravel drive and, cutting through the old farmhouse kitchen, ran down the hall and slid into her spot at the long farmhouse table, already lined on either side with the twenty sisters of Gwenafwy Abbey. She was prepared to explain why she had been gone all morning, but it seemed that no one cared. Not even Sister Callwen, her closest and best friend at the abbey who always knew when something was afoot, and not even Reverend Mother, who kept tabs on these things. Instead, they all wanted to hear about Tiffany Reese. Word had already spread that Sister Agatha had been at the parish hall, and they wanted to hear her opinion. Ever since Jacob, the beloved sexton at the abbey, had been murdered and Sister Agatha had brought his killer to justice, the nuns turned to her as their first informant on all things crime related. Of course, in the little village of Pryderi that wasn't much.

"Spill the beans, Sister Agatha." Sister Harriet said, passing the crock of steaming lamb stew down the table. Tall for a woman of eighty years, though still not as tall as Reverend Mother, Sister Harriet filled out her long, blue habit with little room to spare—a blue habit that often displayed a smudge from her charcoal drawing pencil. Sister Harriet had published to some acclaim a Sunday school curriculum composed of a series of graphic novels—all with a biblical theme and immensely popular with the primary school crowd. She had the broad face of a Yorkshire farmer, and her gray eyes flashed under the white band of her veil. "And don't leave anything out. It's been a dull morning and I want to hear every last little detail."

"Honestly, Sister Harriet," Sister Callwen said, neatly unfolding her napkin and spreading it on her lap. "A woman is dead. A member of the parish. Let's not treat it like a new episode of a BBC mystery series." Sister Callwen had been Agatha's companion and confidante ever since their first days at Gwenafwy Abbey. Her discerning brown eyes missed nothing, and her aquiline nose and high forehead hinted at a genteel ancestry. In contrast, Sister Agatha was quite a bit less refined, having spent her childhood working on the family sheep farm. Sister Callwen kept her blue habit spotless, her salt-and-pepper hair was always neatly tucked in her veil, and she always knew the proper thing to do and say. In her apron pocket Sister Callwen carried only three essential items: prayer beads from the Holy Land, The Anglican Pocketbook of Prayer, and a fresh, embroidered handkerchief. Sister Agatha's own apron pockets bulged with her Girl Guides knife, her detective's notebook (when she was allowed to carry one), her smartphone, the paperback mystery that she happened to be reading at the time, and a few spare sandwich bags from the kitchen to use as evidence bags. You never knew what you might come across in a day's excursions as a mystery writer and amateur sleuth. And of course, as an Anglican nun.

"Of course not." Sister Harriet said, unperturbed. "I didn't mean that, of course. I just meant—I want the whole story."

"We all do, Sisters. But let Sister Agatha eat first," Reverend Mother said. Though she looked as interested as Sister Harriet.

Before Sister Agatha could respond or take even a bite of stew, Lucy Pennoyer, the abbey's young artist-in-residence, spoke up. "Do you mean Tiffany Reese, president of the Art Society?"

"You know her?" Sister Agatha asked. Lucy, young and fresh-faced, with red hair and startling blue eyes, was a new arrival at the abbey. Not a nun, but a tenant. As part of an experiment by the sisters to generate added income for the struggling abbey, they had recently embarked on the adventure of becoming landlords. It was one of three new ideas they had to bolster their sagging finances. Their first idea was to increase their online presence in order to sell more Heavenly Gouda. This involved a plunge into social media as well as a new and improved website. So far, the response had been slow—a few "likes" and a couple of "shares." The second idea, sheep farming, seemed even slower to produce income, but that was to be expected. The sisters had invested in a small flock of Welsh Mountain sheep along with a part-time shepherd, a retired sheep man from the village named Ben Holden.

They planned to sell both wool and fresh lamb for profit and then use any excess at the abbey. Sister Winifred had big plans to spin her own yarn, and Sister Gwenydd thought home-grown, fresh lamb was just what her future cuisine needed.

Although the online cheese sales and sheep production were off to a slow start, the landlord idea was immediately lucrative. A monthly rent check for previously unused space made perfect sense. Reverend Mother had conceived the idea of turning the dovecote into a studio.

The nuns sometimes shook their heads at Reverend Mother's ideas, but everyone had to admit, she had seen the abbey through its worst times and she had always kept them on track. The starting center for St. Mary's College, she stood six feet one in her socks. She kept a basketball in her desk, which she tossed from hand to hand as a stress reducer, and a poster of LeBron James hung between a framed portrait of Archbishop of Canterbury Justin Welby and Barack Obama on the night of his inauguration. When Reverend Mother had a sticky bit of theology to sort out or a budget she couldn't seem to balance, she could be found making free throws at the hoop outside the abbey kitchen. Many nights the nuns would awaken gently from their sleep to the thud of a basketball hitting the backboard.

The sisters advertised the sunny room above the dovecote as an "artist's studio" in *Church Times, The Parish Circular,* and finally, on Craigslist. Sunny and cozy, the dovecote was the perfect artist's studio. In addition to studio space, the total package for the potential renter included a small dormitory room in the nun's quarters and three meals a day plus snacks. The sisters had labored over the photos and description for the advertisements and were pleasantly surprised at the almost immediate and enthusiastic response. They had settled on a young woman from Providence, Rhode Island, who had recently graduated from art school—the Rhode Island School of Design. There had been some disagreement on how much vetting of the final candidate should be done—Sister June advocating for a full background check while Sister Harriet thought a sample of her art was all that was needed. In the end, Reverend Mother talked with the young woman on Skype and a contract was signed.

Young Lucy Pennoyer had arrived at Gwenafwy Abbey the week after All Saints' Day, moving her easels, paints, brushes, and tiny dog, a miniature pinscher named Vincent van Gogh—he had lost a piece of his left ear in a fight with a poodle—into the studio above the dovecote. As far as the sisters could tell, the two had settled in nicely.

"I've met her," Lucy said, spooning lamb stew into an earthenware bowl and then reaching for a piece of warm bread. Lucy, thin as a rail, seemed able to eat endlessly and never gain a pound. Sister Agatha watched her with admiration and a twinge of resentment. *Youth is certainly wasted on the young.* "In fact," Lucy continued, her mouth full. "I was at last night's meeting." Chewing, swallowing. "Of the Art Society."

"You were there? Last night?" Sister Agatha said.

"Actually, late afternoon. As the guest speaker. They wanted me to talk about my art and my journey to becoming an artist. I told them all about my childhood of wanting to paint and about going to art school." Lucy paused and then added, "They seemed very nice."

Sister Agatha noticed a slight change in Lucy's voice and a tiny hesitation. Then it was gone. She made a mental note to follow up with the young artist. She wondered if the Art Society meeting went as smoothly as Lucy described. "When exactly was the meeting?" Sister Agatha asked.

"They asked me to get there at four o'clock. At that old church in the village. But the committee had been there all day it seemed. You know, setting up for the show and everything. They asked my advice on how to position some of the paintings. I've done a few gallery showings in school, so I felt I was at least a little helpful."

"That's the best part about leaving graduate school," Sister Gwenydd said, a recent graduate herself of the prestigious Leith's School of Food and Wine in London. "Before you graduate, it's like you're just a wannabe who knows nothing. Then you walk across that stage and suddenly people think you're an expert."

"Tiffany was killed about six or seven hours later." Sister Agatha pushed her bowl aside. "Did you notice anything unusual?"

"*Killed?*" Reverend Mother broke in before Lucy could respond. "Why do you think she was killed, Sister Agatha?" Reverend Mother took the basket of warm rolls from in front of Lucy and passed them down the table. "Sister Gwenydd, your fresh bread is a treat. As always."

"Well, it's conjecture, of course, at this point. Especially as there won't be an autopsy. Dr. Beese thought it was a heart attack," Sister Agatha said, taking a roll from the basket. Reverend Mother was right about the bread. It was wonderful. It could have been a meal in itself.

"Let me guess," Sister Callwen said. "A woman's tragic medical condition is now a murder that you need to jump in and solve?" She looked at Sister Agatha, her eyebrows raised.

"Isn't writing a murder mystery enough? Do you have to see murder everywhere?"

Sister Callwen had not quite recovered from Sister Agatha's recent brush with death when she solved the murder of Jacob Traherne, the abbey's beloved sexton. The table fell silent as all the nuns looked at Sister Agatha. Their glances then went to Reverend Mother. Reverend Mother was always a bit hesitant about Sister Agatha's interest in murder.

Reverend Mother cleared her throat. "Sister Agatha will certainly not jump into anything. There is no actual evidence to think it was anything other than a heart attack." She fixed Sister Agatha in her steady gaze. "Right, Sister?"

"Of course," Sister Agatha said, taking a quick sip of tea. "Right." A decided snort could be heard coming from the direction of Sister Callwen.

"I had hoped you would take the weeks of Advent to spend in prayer and contemplation, not chasing down murderers," Reverend Mother continued, "real or fictional. And I need you here. It's all-hands-on-deck to get ready for Christmas. Between the holiday jumble at Saint Anselm's, the potential uptick in sales of Heavenly Gouda, and the live nativity scene with Luther and Calvin, I need everyone present and focused. And it's not just Christmas. I am especially worried about the housing development. You can see that they have already started digging the first site. We can only pray to win some time if the weather turns bad."

The nuns nodded, several frowning. The threat of development in North Wales had been sobering, but when the nuns awakened one morning to the sound of earth-moving equipment in the meadow on the other side of Church Lane, things had gotten serious. The abbey, along with many in the village, planned to intensify their protest.

Sister Winifred leaned over toward Lucy. "Luther and Calvin are our pot-bellied pigs. The stars of the abbey's live nativity scene. Although I dare say this year we can have actual sheep as well."

"And don't leave out Bartimaeus," Sister Agatha said. She was very fond of the blind Shetland pony that the sisters had rescued from a petting zoo several years earlier. "He makes an awesome camel."

"Two pot-bellied pigs, a blind pony dressed up like a camel, and a few Welsh Mountain sheep." Sister Callwen sighed. "Now that's authentic."

"What we lack in authenticity, Sister, we make up in enthusiasm." Sister Harriet loved Christmas and wouldn't allow any nay-saying.

"Back home there are all these arguments and public outcry over nativity scenes," Lucy said. "Especially if they're placed in a public place like a town square. Is it really such a big deal?" She looked around. The room had fallen silent. Only the quiet clink of forks against bowls could be heard. "Sorry, but I've never been to church."

"Never. Not even once?" Sister Harriet asked.

"Our Girl Scout troop used to sell cookies in front of a mosque. It was the perfect spot. Does that count?" Sister Agatha watched as Lucy filled her bowl a second time. *Youth.*

"It certainly does *not* count," Sister Callwen said. "Going to a mosque is a very good thing, but not if you are there to *sell cookies*."

"Come by the kitchen this afternoon," Sister Gwenydd said. "I'll teach you everything you need to know about the nativity."

"The blind leading the blind," Sister Callwen whispered to Sister Agatha.

"Could we get back to our conversation about what happened to Tiffany Reese, Sisters?" Sister Harriet said. "I have poinsettias to arrange and take to the Care Center. I need to get moving."

Sister Agatha launched into a description of everything she had seen at the parish hall. The sisters had much to say about the teacup, the missing painting, and the possible ways that Tiffany could have died. Lucy was particularly disturbed about the disappearance of the painting. "I saw it yesterday. Stunning detail. Do you have any idea where it went? Would it have been stolen?"

"I don't know." Sister Agatha looked directly at Lucy. "It's simply gone."

"That's terrible," Lucy said. "I don't always like traditional nature paintings. But it had a spontaneous feel to it. I was impressed. Of course, she wasn't as modest as most amateur painters are. We must have heard twenty times that an art dealer in Cardiff wanted the painting for a show he was doing. She worked *that* into every conversation." Lucy selected another roll from the basket.

"Did you notice if that bothered anyone? Annoyed someone in particular?" Sister Agatha asked.

"No. People seemed happy for her. Proud, sort of, that one of their own was going to be in an art show. That's what is so tragic. A chance to be noticed by a well-known dealer is rare for most artists. It's your dream. Tiffany Reese finally gets the chance, and then she dies and her painting disappears." Lucy sat back in her chair, her blue eyes wide. "Sad."

"It *is* sad," Reverend Mother said, looking thoughtful. "And wrong." Reverend Mother had a strong sense of justice and was known for supporting the underdog. She looked down the long table to where Sister Agatha sat between Sister Callwen and Sister Matilda. "I am rethinking my earlier idea, Sister Agatha, that you should take a break from murder. We all have our calling. And when God beckons, one must respond. If you keep your inquiries gentle, I see no reason why you cannot do a little sleuthing. Just to see if things couldn't be set right for Tiffany. I'm not saying that I think she was murdered. But the disappearance of the painting seems suspect. Something is not right. And even though I won't pretend to have really liked Tiffany Reese, she certainly deserves better." Reverend Mother put a spoonful of stew into her mouth and chewed slowly. "Sister Gwenydd," she said, swallowing, and looking at her youngest nun. "I hope you never abandon your calling. This stew is superb."

* * *

The clock in the village bell tower chimed eleven times as the moon rose over the orchard. It had been a long Saturday, but finally, Sister Agatha could sit at her desk in the attic library with a teapot of steaming Welsh brew, her favorite teacup—the one she always used when she was writing—and a plate of Sister Gwenydd's ginger snaps. The ancient pipes in the walls had begun their comforting clanging, giving hope that they were about to pump out heat and steam in comforting bursts. Everything was in place for a long night of writing and thinking about murder. She poured the hot, fragrant tea into the teacup and leaned back to think. Didn't Inspector Rupert MacFarlane say that for every hour spent chasing down the criminal, a detective should spend three hours sitting and thinking?

The attic library was at the top of the world—or so it seemed to Sister Agatha—the rolling valley spread out below, the moonlight breaking through the clouds. The long room under the eaves had been recently remodeled by the sisters and turned into a functioning library. Sister Agatha loved her desk there in the third-floor attic library. An old teacher's desk rescued from the St. Anselm's jumble was positioned in front of the north window, which gazed out over the sweeping valley.

The desk was a place of refuge where she could be found busily working on her mystery novel—a private-eye detective story with a street-savvy investigator named Bates Melanchthon, who never darkened the door of a church but seemed to find himself in a lot of bars, brothels, and dark alleyways. While roaming the streets of London's East Side, Bates managed to bring to justice some of the worst criminals the city had seen. At least that was the plan. So far Sister Agatha had written feverishly to the middle of the novel and was deeply mired in a murder that had even Bates stumped. She expected the muse to return and a burst of inspiration to strike any day now.

Sister Agatha had always been a voracious reader, but only relatively recently had she embarked on writing. When each nun at the abbey turned sixty years old, the other sisters did whatever was needed to allow that sister to fulfill her lifelong dream—no matter what it was. Sister Harriet had hopped a plane to Rome and immersed herself in a study of sacred art at the Vatican. Sister Winifred left for the Shetland Islands and six weeks of weaving native wool. Sister Callwen, to everyone's surprise, made the journey to India and attended a yoga retreat at the Himalayan Yoga Center.

When Sister Agatha had said that she wanted to write a mystery novel, the abbey paid the tuition for her to pursue a master of fine arts in writing at the University of St. David. In the year since graduation, she had been working busily on her Bates Melanchthon mystery, spending all of her free time researching historical murders, reading forensic manuals, and perusing mystery-writer blogs. She tested out dialogue on her sisters and scribbled into her detective notebook every idea the minute it came to her—even if a brilliant thought did overtake her during Holy Communion.

Her desk in the attic was where she disappeared every evening after Compline to write late into the night, but it was also her work station. Sister Agatha's love of books and adeptness at using the Internet had made her the obvious choice for abbey librarian. She ordered books online, shopped in used bookstores, and consulted her colleagues at the tiny Pryderi library.

Although the year at St. David's had been an amazing time, the most valuable gift from the abbey, the gift that really said to her "we believe in you as a writer" was the desk in the attic. Sister Harriet had found the desk at the jumble sale and carted it home. The other sisters had refinished it and supplied an ergonomic desk chair. But it was Sister Callwen who placed the desk at the north window so that on a very clear day, she said, Sister Agatha could glimpse a silver ribbon glinting in the sunlight—the Irish Sea—and take inspiration from all the Irish writers who had made their way in the world writing. Late at night, when the moonlight was exceptionally bright, she could indeed glimpse the sea, and the spirit of George Bernard Shaw or Oscar Wilde or Maeve Binchy seemed to beckon to her across the waves.

She took a long sip of tea. A new investigation. Where to begin? Well, for starters, no more cocktail napkins—time to choose a new notebook from the stash in her desk. First things first. Inspector Rupert McFarland was quite a stickler about one's detective notebook. *"Your notebook is your best friend,"* he always said. *"Keep your notes shipshape in Bristol fashion at all times!"* For last summer's murder she had used a lizard-print, moleskin, slimline, pocket-sized notebook in a splashy orchid blue.

But this was a new day and a new murder, which obviously called for a new notebook. She opened the bottom desk drawer and considered her stash. Sister Agatha, generally very pragmatic about everything, did have to admit to one embarrassing weakness—she loved a new, fresh notebook. But not just any notebook—the expensive, cloth-covered, hand-bound ones that could be found at Smythson of Bond Street in London or the Stamford Notebook Company in Cambridge. She loved each watermarked page, every handmade binding, the carefully stitched spine that made just the slightest snap when first opened, the gentle aroma of paper and ink. Every page was gilt-edged and the covers were always of elegant cloth or smooth leather. Just opening a new notebook from Smythson's or Stamford's sparked her creativity like nothing else, and when she put her Sharpie to the first clean, empty page of a clean, empty notebook, the possibilities felt infinite. Luckily for her, Reverend Mother approved of the pricey notebooks as long as Sister Agatha didn't get too carried away. Reverend Mother believed that everyone—even nuns—should be allowed to indulge on occasion.

This particular notebook would need an Advent theme. Sister Agatha was a big believer in liturgical correctness—so nothing bright or perky. This murder had happened in Advent and one's notebook needed to reflect the somber mood of the season.

She thought for a long moment and then, reaching into the drawer, withdrew a recent acquisition—a lovely notebook, bound in purple lambskin, handcrafted in Bethlehem, with 192 leaves of Smythson's signature gilt-edged, cream-colored featherweight paper. Both practical and luxurious, the advertising copy touted, *"This mid-size notebook transitions effortlessly from your desk to your travel bag."* She hoped it would also transition from desk to apron pocket. Or, as it was winter in North Wales, from desk to oversized-red-jumper pocket. And purple was the perfect color for an Advent murder.

Sister Agatha placed the purple lambskin notebook on the top of her desk and uncapped a new Sharpie. Time to get serious. First, a description of the crime scene. She thought for a moment and pulled out her notes from a podcast from at least a year ago by Inspector Rupert MacFarlane. She remembered that he had a lot to say about the integrity of a crime scene and about collecting evidence. *"Once the lead investigator arrives at the crime scene, laddies, he is in control!"* She sighed. Inspector Rupert MacFarlane was very old school and his only fault—if he had one—was a bit of sexism. In his mind all detectives were men, and he frequently referred to them as "laddies." Sister Agatha had occasionally considered writing to Inspector Rupert MacFarlane about this one deviation from an otherwise flawless podcast. But so far, she hadn't.

She read her notes again and sighed again. Not only wasn't she the lead investigator—although in her mind, she certainly was—the official lead, Constable Barnes, had not even determined Tiffany's death a crime. Which was a crime in itself! Sister Agatha knew from her many podcasts that if Tiffany Reese was murdered, the crime scene itself would demonstrate it.

She remembered something the inspector had recently discussed. It had a funny name. Tapping her Sharpie on the notebook, she thought hard. *Lochard's Exchange Principle.* Inspector MacFarlane had gone on and on about it. She scanned the podcast notes. *"In every crime, the murderer brings something in*

*and he takes something out. Figure out what those things are and
you're halfway to a solved murder!"*

Sister Agatha sat back. Well, there was something that the
murderer might have taken out and its absence was obvious.
The painting. But what did the murderer bring in?

She smoothed out the ink-blotted cocktail napkin and then
began to transfer the information written on it into her purple
detective notebook. It might come to her if she just focused on
the information that she did have. *Small nail, broken tea cup.*
What else? She made a note to search the kitchen, which, like
most church kitchens, opened out to the parish hall. Who
knew how many people had walked through the kitchen by
now? In a real investigation, the perimeter would have been
cordoned off with yellow police tape and the public kept out.
She did realize that might have included her. Although Sister
Agatha didn't often think of herself as one of the public.

She gazed out the window at the night sky. As far as she
could tell, the painting was the only thing that had been
taken out. A burglar would have stolen the diamond from
Tiffany's finger, but only the painting was missing. Why? She
remembered that Lucy had said that an art dealer from Cardiff was interested in the painting. But dealers don't steal
paintings. Or do they? She made a note to check.

Taking a sip of tea and a bite of a ginger snap, she closed
her eyes and pictured the crime scene. Tiffany's body slumped
against the wall, arms at her sides, palms turned upward. Her
mouth slightly open. *What else?*

Sister Agatha reached into her jumper pocket and took out
the tiny nail she had withdrawn from the wall, then opened the

middle desk drawer and pulled out a sandwich bag from the stash she kept there. You couldn't be too careful with evidence. She dropped the nail in the bag and then tore off a piece of tape from the dispenser on her desk. She put the tape on the outside of the bag—just as Inspector Rupert MacFarlane had instructed—and carefully labeled it *#1 "little nail."* It was pretty obvious that it was a little nail, but the inspector had been very insistent about labeling evidence properly. She was determined to conduct this investigation meticulously. Her last murder case had been very catch-as-catch-can. More Stephanie Plum than Inspector Barnaby. Sister Agatha smiled. She definitely was more Stephanie Plum than Inspector Barnaby.

Opening the book bag that sat on the floor next to her desk, she lifted out a bundle wrapped in last week's copy of *The Church Times.* The broken teacup. She unwrapped the two pieces and, using a tissue, carefully placed them into another plastic bag, this one a quart-size ziplock that Sister Gwenydd used for freezing elderberries. She felt a pang of guilt for having removed such crucial evidence from the scene. But then, Constable Barnes had not declared it a crime scene and so nothing was off limits. And, she reminded herself, if no one else cared to collect evidence, then she was obligated to. Tearing off a piece of tape, she placed it almost reverently on the bag's right corner, and with her Sharpie wrote, *#2 "broken teacup."*

Without removing the cup from the bag, she fitted the two pieces together and carefully turned it over. *Wedgwood of Etruria & Barlaston Made in England Embossed Queens Ware.* She quickly googled it. A somewhat rare antique teacup, and expensive. Of course, Tiffany could never have used the porcelain mugs that everyone else in the church used. She had to have her own teacup, and the very same kind that Buckingham Palace had been drinking from for nearly a century. It also meant that Tiffany had made the tea herself, since she had used her own, special teacup. Sister Agatha laid the two evidence bags on the desk.

She closed her eyes as she imagined Tiffany Reese in the church kitchen. She had probably stopped by Saint Anselm's just to make sure everything was in order—in Tiffany's mind, only Tiffany could be trusted to do things right. Then, as she walked around, checking each painting, she decided she needed a cup of tea. Sister Agatha imagined her putting the kettle on and scooping tea out of the tea canister—no teabags for Tiffany Reese.

Sister Agatha opened her eyes and made a note to take a look at the tea in the church kitchen. She knew that Father Selwyn made his tea with tea bags. But then, he had been known to stir his tea with a number 2 yellow pencil. Eraser end, of course. Bevan, on the other hand, made tea with loose leaves, which he spooned into a silver tea strainer. She had seen him do it. And he insisted it was better. Sister Agatha was a teabag person. The nuns at Gwenafwy Abbey were divided down the middle. Sister Callwen, loose leaf. Sister Harriet, teabag.

So Tiffany Reese had made tea and walked back into the hall with her teacup. She had gone to her painting and stood there, no doubt admiring it. She sipped her tea and then had a heart attack? She staggered backward, leaning against the wall. She slumped down, falling to the floor. Her heart stopped. Murdered? That was the question. If nothing at all had been touched in the parish hall, Sister Agatha would have been less inclined to think that there was foul play. But the painting was missing. Lochard's principle. The murderer took something out. But what did he bring in? Whatever it was, it had killed Tiffany Reese.

Chapter Three

❧

The Monday evening village meeting to discuss the new housing development was about to convene, and already Sister Agatha could feel a growing animosity in St. Anselm's parish hall. Very few people in the village supported the idea of houses being built on land that had belonged to Pryderi sheep farmers for centuries and was thought by many to be a known fairy field. The Labor Party representative, Devon Morgan, was attending to answer questions.

By the time Father Selwyn slid into the chair next to Sister Agatha, the parish hall at St. Anselm's was packed. Every folding chair that the church owned had been set up in neat rows, and now villagers crowded into the back of the long hall, leaning against the wall, sitting on the table from last night's meeting of the diaconate. The paintings from the art show had been quietly removed by the Art Society ladies in deference to Tiffany, and there was no sign that a woman had been murdered in this very room. Sister Agatha looked around. The room smelled of furniture polish and floor wax. It could possibly be the most compromised crime scene in the history of crime scenes.

"Do we really want to sit in the front row like this?" Father Selwyn asked. "I feel a bit on display."

"We need to be right in front so we can make that slimy Devon Morgan as uncomfortable as possible."

"That's the Christmas spirit," Father Selwyn said, glancing around the parish hall, now full of villagers. "Although I can't argue that Devon Morgan is of questionable reputation. I don't know how he got appointed as minister for the environment, planning, and the countryside."

"He only wants to develop the North country with expensive houses for his own political benefit. All this nonsense about it benefiting the community and improving the economy is just poppycock."

"He has his sights set on first minister, which is how Carwyn Jones did it. He was minister for the environment and climbed his way pretty quickly to first minister."

"But I like Carwyn," Sister Agatha said. "He's a good Welshman. One of our oldest families. I can't believe he's allowing people like this Morgan fellow to be in charge of something as crucial to Wales as the environment." Sister Agatha glanced around and spotted Sister Gwenydd and Lucy coming in the back door. She waved them forward. Lucy was hard to miss. Her flaming red hair made her stand out in any crowd. She claimed to be Welsh, but she looked every inch Irish to Sister Agatha.

"Well, it certainly affects the whole area of the diocese of St. Asaph."

"Some are in favor of it though—you know, the fiscal benefit. A more progressive agenda."

"A more progressive agenda? Is that what you call tearing up an ancient pasture land to build expensive houses that no one in Pryderi can afford?"

Lucy and Sister Gwenydd claimed the two empty chairs that Sister Agatha had been saving for them. The rest of the nuns were scattered around the room. Sister June was up front near the podium. Sister Agatha was proud of her for representing Gwenafwy Abbey so competently. The president of the parish council took the microphone. He spoke for a few minutes about the housing development. Sister Agatha could tell he was trying to present both sides. In her way of thinking, there were not two sides. Not at all. Decided rumblings went through the audience.

Unenthusiastic applause broke out as the mayor finished his introductions and Devon Morgan, Labor Party representative, stepped up to the microphone. Sister Agatha, sitting next to Lucy, felt the young woman stiffen and sit up straight. She also noticed that Lucy leaned over and whispered to Sister Gwenydd.

"What?" Sister Agatha asked quietly.

"I know him. He offered me a ride the other night. At the Art Society meeting."

Sister Agatha took out her notebook out and made a note. Father Selwyn looked at her, eyebrows raised.

"I'll tell you later." She closed the notebook and turned her attention to Devon Morgan. Devon Morgan was tall and had reddish blonde hair, graying now but probably flaming red in his youth. He was expensively dressed, which wasn't the greatest idea for a politician in Pryderi. The villagers were sheep farmers, teachers, and shopkeepers. They distrusted anyone who displayed wealth—a wealth that they seldom saw. His expensive Mercedes parked out front with his driver waiting in it didn't help.

She listened, nearly grinding her teeth at Devon's polished presentation. She had heard that he stood for family values. In her experience, if you had to talk about your values all the time, you didn't have any. A good Welshman lived his values. She shook her head and Father Selwyn gave her a look. It was almost painful to sit and listen. She glanced toward the side door of the parish hall just in time to see Lewis Colwyn slip out. Well, good for him, she thought. We should all walk out and not listen to this drivel.

According to Devon Morgan, the new housing development would change nothing in the village or countryside and bring in loads of money. He was too charming for Sister Agatha, and perhaps for anyone in the room. He explained how seventeen new homes were planned to be built at the north edge of the village—in the field between the abbey and the village. "Let them build," he said, "and we will pave that pokey gravel road." Sister Agatha looked in horror at Sister June. Pave Church Lane? *Never.*

As it was, DRM Industries had made some exploratory projections, and according to Devon Morgan the results demonstrated that the housing development would be very good for the village economy. To her horror, she saw a few people nodding and smiling. The meeting continued, with Devon pushing hard his belief in the value of development to the prosperity of the local community. Sister Agatha wasn't buying it. A few others didn't either.

Devon smoothly turned any question of his political ambitions to a statement about how much he wanted a bright future for Wales. Murmurs of assent and dissent went through the room. He fielded question after question with deft, political charm.

"Do you feel like a cup of tea?" she whispered to Father Selwyn.

"Well, yes. But I didn't see any. I dislike a meeting without tea."

"Me too." Sister Agatha waited until the next round of applause—this time for Sister June—and she stood up and, slipping into the side aisle, made her way over to the kitchen door. She put the kettle on and then pulled out her notebook. She had seldom made tea in the St. Anselm kitchen, so she wasn't especially familiar with it. But like most church kitchens it was neat as a pin, with every drawer and cupboard meticulously labeled. Church kitchens were generally ruled over by a loving though tyrannical group of ladies who kept the place running like a ship in the British navy.

She noticed a cupboard labeled "Tea: WI Only!" and opening it, she found among the boxes of tea, creamers, silver strainers, and plastic stirrers a tall, ceramic tea canister. The label on it, printed in perfect calligraphy, read "Property of Tiffany Reese. Do not touch!" *Good Heavens!* No wonder the WI was having trouble attracting young people. Who would join if just making tea was such an issue? Probably too late to dust for fingerprints, Sister Agatha thought, lifting down the canister. She recognized the lavender-blue grape-leaf design on the white porcelain. It matched the teacup, now in an evidence bag and stashed in the library desk. But the teacup was lightweight and delicate, its edge thin and nearly translucent. The tea canister of the same design was heavy and sturdy, though nonetheless lovely, and it was almost completely full, in fact the ceramic top barely sat comfortably on the top. Sister Agatha made a note in her detective's book and then, setting the canister on the counter, she took a quick photo of it with her phone.

On an impulse and with a glance behind her, she found the drawer labeled "plastic bag" and, rummaging for a minute, withdrew the largest one she could find, a gallon-sized ziplock. With another look over her shoulder—she could hear Devon Morgan's smooth voice coming through the door—she upturned the tea canister into the bag and shook out all the tea. She replaced the canister in the cupboard just as the kettle began to sing. She would make Father Selwyn his tea, but certainly not from the tea found in the canister. It needed to be entered in her evidence log. And most important, tested for poison.

Sister Agatha stepped back and locked hard at the bag of tea. She assumed that it was both exotic and expensive—Tiffany Reese could hardly be expected to have drunk anything else. The question was how to find out if it had poison in it without dying first? Agatha Christie might be her only help here. Sister Agatha made two cups of tea—one for herself and one for Father Selwyn—using the Welsh Brew teabags she found in the cupboard labeled "Tea: Church Use Only." Good heavens, the WI and the church ladies had certainly squared off over tea. Pouring cream and sugar generously into the teacups and taking a sip, she shook her head. *Welsh Brew. Now that's real tea.*

* * *

The shadows had already grown long and the late afternoon air bitingly cold when Sister Agatha left the public library and her research on poisons to walk over to St. Anselm's church. She hadn't been able to discuss her latest thoughts after the meeting last night—she had hurried back to the abbey with the other nuns—and was anxious to recap the whole thing with Father Selwyn. Plus, she had rifled through Agatha Christie for all of her references to poison and had been unable to nail down any safe ways to determine if there was poison in the tea. But to her surprise, the tea was not exotic or expensive at all, it was indeed Welsh Brew. A workingman's tea. The cheapest—though in her opinion, the best—tea in all of the United Kingdom.

Sister Agatha had been given her own key at the library, along with a small desk and computer stashed in the corner of the reference section. She enjoyed the privilege of working at the village library and relished the collegiality of the other librarians. The library was a subscribing member of the WorldCat database. When she had first logged on to the 170,000 libraries across the world, she had been like a kid in a candy store—a kid about to go into diabetic shock in a candy store.

Today she needed to do some research for the abbey: a book on Karl Rahner, a mid-century Catholic theologian, for Sister Callwen's book group on the Eucharist; a journal on textile crafts for Sister Winifred, who was considering making a shift from knitting to quilting as the abbey was already entirely outfitted with scores of mittens, scarves, hats, and prayer shawls; and finally, for herself, a book on poison. She needed to know more.

* * *

"We have a lot to talk about," Sister Agatha said as she pulled off her blue woolly hat and plopped down on the sofa in Father Selwyn's office. If Father Selwyn was to be her sidekick, she really had to find a more efficient way to keep him updated. They had just recently started using Snapchat, but it wasn't going well.

"First, Vonda Bryson's alibi doesn't check out. Second, the tea in Tiffany Reese's tea canister is disappointingly nonpoisonous. And third, Devon Morgan is a snake in the grass."

The last of the bit of sunlight filtered through the stained-glass window, but a cheerful fire crackled in the grate in the pleasantly cluttered study. Also, there was the scent of cinnamon. She had always wondered if the tiny whiff of cinnamon, always present wherever Father Selwyn was, was because Bevan kept Father Selwyn supplied with plates of baked goods or because Father Selwyn used cinnamon soap. She had never asked. Inquiring about his soap seemed a bit intimate, even if they had been friends for nearly fifty years. But cheerful and pleasant as the study was, it failed to comfort her as it usually did. There were too many unanswered murder questions for her to relax.

Father Selwyn sat down in the wingback chair and, slipping off his size-twelve brogues, put his feet up on the ottoman. She noticed his socks didn't match. "I was hoping for something inspiring from you. But it sounds like you are as tired as I am."

"Sorry," she said. Usually Sister Agatha enjoyed her back-and-forth conversations with Father Selwyn, but today it seemed they were both a bit overwhelmed.

"Long week." Father Selwyn stretched out his long legs. Under his cassock he was wearing yoga pants. "And it's only Tuesday."

"Senior Yoga?" she asked. Father Selwyn led the older citizens in the village every Tuesday in a class Sister Agatha called "hot yoga for the old-age pensioner." Sister Harriet never missed it and could do the eagle pose like a twelve-year-old gymnast.

He nodded. "Generally, a little vinyasa restores me. But not so much today. A death in the parish hall. That horrible meeting last night." Leaning back, he closed his eyes. Sister Agatha waited. He was either praying or sleeping. The slight whiffling snore ruled out prayer.

She got up quietly, put the kettle on the electric burner, and placed a teabag in each of the two cups that sat at the ready on the little coffee table between them. Cream and sugar. No spoons. She sighed. It was number-two pencils again.

The meeting last night had been disheartening. The sisters had sat up late in the warming room discussing it. Devon

Morgan had come across as charming and intelligent. And he made a smooth defense of the building development. Sister June, who had worn her litigators' hat the whole evening, was adamant that Devon Morgan was not on the side of the small village and could not be trusted.

Sister Agatha tapped a key on the Remington Rand portable that Father Selwyn had left on the table next to the teacups. Probably the last functioning manual typewriter in the county. In the North. In all of Wales. Maybe in the entire UK. Father Selwyn claimed that a great-aunt, office secretary to the Dunlichity parish in the Church of Scotland and a daunting church lady in her own right, had bequeathed it to him, and that the typewriter regularly inspired his sermon-writing. Which was why his sermons leaned toward the Presbyterianism of the Scots. Although a deft typist on his laptop, for some reason on the portable he typed with only two fingers. And if you ever received a note from Father Selwyn, you needed to fill in the blanks on half the words because the letter *e* didn't work.

"How do you know Vonda Bryson is lying?" Father Selwyn sat up at the sound of the teakettle. He didn't seem to realize he had fallen asleep.

"Her neighbor," Sister Agatha said, not mentioning his snoring. "You know him, George Myers. He said she was out all night. At least until eleven, when he went to bed." She pulled out her notebook and opening it scanned the notes she had copied off the cocktail napkin. "Which means that she wasn't home the night of the murder and that she lied about it."

"Or maybe she just didn't want to tell you what she was

doing, which is a long way from lying about something due to the fact you committed murder."

"Of course. But it does make her a person of interest. People never lie unless they need to keep something secret."

"I'm not sure that's true. I think sometimes people simply lie. And it could be that Vonda is just being private, not secretive." Father Selwyn leaned forward and with two fingers typed a few words onto the Remington Rand portable. "There's a difference," he said, concentrating on the keyboard. "And anyway, didn't George wonder why you were inquiring about the whereabouts of the Brysons? Especially the day after a death so close by?"

"I was subtle."

"Sister," he said, continuing to stab rapidly at the well-oiled keys of the Remington. "You are the least subtle person I know. But then, lucky for you, George Myer is the least likely to hold back on a bit of gossip if given the opportunity to share it."

"Exactly. The question is, why was she lying? Even if it was simply to be private about something." Sister Agatha had to admit that the clacking typewriter sound was comforting. Not at all like her laptop keyboard. She had looked into buying a keyboard that made the same clacking noise that an old typewriter like the Remington made, thinking it might inspire her writing. The cost had deterred even her. Reverend Mother had reminded her that her vow of poverty was actually still in effect.

"It's hard to imagine Vonda Bryson killing anyone." Father Selwyn ripped the sheet of paper out of the roller and, after perusing it for a moment, slid it on the bookshelf to his right. "Sorry to be distracted but the bishop has asked for our annual membership reports. And I need to get information to Bevan to send off." He sighed. "The bishop's office is getting more demanding with Suzanne Bainton in charge."

Suzanne Bainton was the relatively new bishop of St. Asaph, one of the five dioceses of the Church in Wales. She had replaced a much beloved bishop, who had run the diocese in a pastoral manner, paying far more attention to church social events than to budgets and growth projections. The new bishop had taken the diocese in hand, and not everyone was thrilled with her leadership. Sister Agatha had an especially tenuous relationship with her. Probably because, during her last murder investigation, the Reverend Suzanne Bainton had been at the top of her list of suspects.

Sister Agatha watched as Father Selwyn finished typing. He leaned back in his chair and faced her. "Vonda Bryson doesn't seem the kind of person that would murder."

"No one ever seems the kind that would murder."

"True." They sat in silence, remembering that dark day not long ago when someone they both knew very well had, indeed, committed murder. The electric log in the fireplace glowed and crackled. Father Selwyn had recently replaced the small electric grate that had been in the fireplace of the St. Anselm's vicar's study since the late 1950s. The new log not only gave off heat but crackled like a real fire. Sister Agatha had thought it a bit foolish. But now she liked it. It was comforting. Maybe a fake crackling fire is no different from a fake manual typewriter keyboard. She watched as Father Selwyn poured steaming, fragrant tea into her teacup and then added sugar and cream exactly as she liked it.

"Vonda's comment about wanting Tiffany dead might have seemed like a joke, but you have to ask—was it? Or did it start as a joke and upon reflection the idea began to take shape?" She took a sip of tea. "A seed planted in a killer's mind?"

"Vonda Bryson hardly has time for murder. She has four boys under the age of ten and a husband who travels. My guess is that she spends her day checking homework, doing laundry, and making lunches."

"Which, as we all know," Sister Agatha pointed out, "would be enough to drive anyone to murder." Sister Agatha watched as Father Selwyn slid a sheet of paper into the roller and began to type again. He suddenly looked up.

"What did you mean, the tea was disappointingly nonpoisonous?" His eyes opened wide. "You didn't try it, did you?"

"Of course not. I'm not stupid." Sister Agatha didn't mention how close she had come to sampling the tiniest amount just to see if she experienced the smallest of symptoms. Not enough to harm herself of course, but enough to make it clear that there was poison in the tea. She had opted instead for carefully sifting for an hour through every last bit in the canister using a very fine strainer from the cheese barn, a bright lamp, and an old magnifying glass from Sister Matilda, who used it in her greenhouse to identify leaf mold. She had found nothing amiss. It seemed the only substance in the canister was Welsh Brew.

As she told Father Selwyn about her latest evidence

collection and examination, she pondered aloud about Tiffany Reese drinking Welsh Brew. "You would think she would go at least for Glengettie or something high-brow like Earl Grey."

"You never can tell about people. Just when you think you have them pegged, they surprise you."

"Maybe," she said without conviction, making a note to ask Vonda about Tiffany's taste in tea.

"I'm more worried right now about the housing development. Have you had any more thoughts about last night? About Devon Morgan?"

"No. Just that I don't feel optimistic about saving the meadow."

"I hope the village doesn't give up the fight. Devon Morgan seems crooked to me. In a very charming way."

"A politician. And not even a Welshman. Did you know that his family is from Ireland?"

"Sister, there is nothing wrong with being from Ireland."

"I'm not saying there is. I only meant that he's not Welsh." Sister Agatha took a dim view of anyone who wasn't Welsh. "No self-respecting Welshman would destroy a fairy field, that's all." She ignored Father Selwyn's gentle smile at her mention of the fairy field.

"How do you know he's Irish anyway?"

"You saw that red hair."

"Red hair doesn't mean you're Irish. Not anymore."

"Well, in his case it does. Red hair, blue eyes, pale skin. And anyway, I heard him going on about it on *North Wales Live*. How his ancestors left during the famine and emigrated to Wales to work in the slate mines and all. He plays the poverty card and I don't like that." She took one last long drink of tea and stood, slipping the purple notebook back into her jumper pocket and pulling on her blue woolly hat. She was grateful to Sister Winifred for designing the jumper with pockets large enough to stash her notebook, Sharpie, Girl Guides knife, and latest Agatha Christie. She looked around for her mittens, which Sister Winifred had also knitted to match her blue hat. "As disgusted as I am with Devon Morgan, I have other irons in the fire. Which I cannot ignore. In addition to Vonda Bryson, I think Lucy, our young artist-in-residence could be of interest as well. And anyway, I'm due back at the abbey for evening vespers."

* * *

Evening vespers had been emotionally stirring for Sister Agatha. The sisters had sung an Advent hymn that never failed to move her. "*O Come, O Come Emmanuel.*" The last verse was particularly powerful.

> *O come, Thou Day-Spring, come and cheer*
> *Our spirits by Thine advent here*
> *Disperse the gloomy clouds of night*
> *And death's dark shadows put to flight.*

As the last note lingered in the chapel, Reverend Mother had stepped into the pulpit and delivered a short but thrilling homily, as only she could, on darkness and light in the first chapter of Genesis. Following her words, Sister Harriet's impassioned voice read the haunting words of scripture as their benediction: *"And in the beginning when God created the heavens and the earth, the earth was a formless void and darkness covered the face of the deep."*

The chapel had been dark except for a few lights and several candles. *"And darkness covered the face of the deep."* She had never noticed that the story of the Creation had such spooky imagery. It gave Sister Agatha chills and made her think of murder. And with murder on her mind, she had hurried straight from the chapel to Lucy's art studio and knocked on the door.

Ever since talking with Father Selwyn that afternoon, Sister Agatha had wrestled with the idea that Lucy knew more than she was saying. Not that she was a strong suspect. Just a person of interest. However, the young woman had been with Tiffany not six hours before she died. And in the same place where her dead body was found. Something about Lucy gave Sister Agatha a frisson of doubt—a familiar feeling that she had learned during her last murder investigation not to ignore. Of course, she had to admit, nothing tangible about Lucy's behavior made her a potential suspect. But she was a newcomer to the abbey and you couldn't be too careful.

Sister Agatha knocked again and listened as Lucy, on the other side of the door, shushed her tiny dog's barking. "Do you have a minute?" Sister Agatha asked as the door opened.

"Sure. Come in," Lucy said. Sister Agatha stepped into the small work space and caught her breath as she saw the several canvases placed around the room.

"Don't look at my paintings, they're really preliminary." Lucy grabbed a sheet and tossed it over one before Sister

Agatha had gotten a close look at it. As far as she could tell, it was a group of people huddled together and looking down.

Sister Agatha ignored her and took a step forward, peering at one painting that seemed to be finished. It was a stunning portrait of Ben Holden, the abbey's sheep farmer, standing on the hillside above the orchard. Lucy had captured the essence of the old man perfectly. The way his one leg bent in at the knee, the slight crook in his back. His head lifted, eyes gazing with the look that Sister Agatha had often seen him have, though it had never registered with her until now. Ben looked as though he was always searching for a lost sheep. "Wow. I love this one. You're good."

"You sound surprised." Lucy said, pulling up a decrepit canvas chair and offering a matching chair to Sister Agatha.

"Not surprised as much as . . ." Sister Agatha couldn't finish her sentence. She *was* surprised. "It's just that I sort of thought you would paint more like the women in the Art Society."

Lucy smiled. "No. There's nothing wrong with their art. But I did go to art school. Which makes a difference. Or at least it should."

The ladies of the Pryderi Parish Art Society were as interested in perspective and shading as they were in tea and cakes, and Sister Agatha was glad Lucy had not thrown them under the bus.

"What did you want to talk about?" Lucy asked. She had pulled her normally messy red hair back into a ponytail. There was a smudge of yellow ochre on her left eyebrow.

"I was wondering if you could tell me about the Art

Society meeting. You know, did you observe anything that might have seemed out of the ordinary?" Sister Agatha opened the purple notebook and uncapped her Sharpie. "Tell me anything you think of. It doesn't have to seem important."

"Well," Lucy said, yanking out the ponytail holder, shaking out her hair, and then pulling it back all over again. Sister Agatha had watched other young women do this and found it annoying, but then, she had worn her own hair short for so many years that ponytails hadn't been an option. Lucy glanced out the small window over her table. The day had grown dark, and the little studio was cozy with the smell of acrylics and the warm colors of the paintings. Vincent van Gogh, with a sigh and a grunt, had curled up on the rug at Sister Agatha's feet. Normally she would have petted such a personable little dog, even taken him on her lap, but she didn't want to distract Lucy. She took a page out of Father Selwyn's book and waited. He was an attentive and focused listener and she had noticed that he always waited, silence never bothering him. She needed to work on her listening skills. Especially if the person she was listening to had something to say about murder. "I did a presentation at their meeting," Lucy said. "Like they asked for, you know, about my art. I do mostly portraits, though that's not at all trendy."

"What do you mean? Trendy?"

"I mean, in art school, portraits in oil aren't considered cutting edge. I tried forever to break out and do pop minimalist or . . . or something like Frank Shepard Fairey . . . or anything. But I kept coming back to portraits. So now, it's what I do."

"I know how you feel."

"You do? Do you paint?"

"No. I write. And for years, I tried to write the Great Welsh Novel, but I kept coming back to the murder mystery. In fact, the hardcore, gumshoe detective."

"Really? I'd think a nun would write characters like Miss Marple or Father Brown."

"You read mysteries?" Sister Agatha had to admit she was a little surprised. She had thought the twenty-something crowd didn't really care for the mystery novel. Maybe there was hope for the world yet.

Lucy grinned and, reaching under the table, dragged out a box of paperbacks. "I paid an extra fee at the airport to bring along my favorites—Christie, P. D. James, G. K. Chesterton, Evanovich. They're old friends. I couldn't leave home without them."

Sister Agatha was feeling better about Lucy every minute. "What about Louise Penny?"

Lucy's face lit up. "Are you kidding? I *love* Louise Penny. I want to meet a young version of Armand Gamache and marry him."

"Ah," sighed Sister Agatha. "Don't we all? Well, I don't want to *marry* him, of course. But I wouldn't mind sharing a chocolate latte and a licorice pipe with him." They both laughed, and then Sister Agatha brought the conversation back to where it had started. "Tell me more about the Art Society meeting. What was their reaction when you shared your story with them?"

"It was fine. Except . . ." Lucy paused, glancing out the window again.

"Except what?"

"Well, I could just be imagining this. Or reading something into it that isn't there. But Tiffany started off all excited about me being there—I mean, she was the one who invited me—but then, well, when she showed me her painting of the yellow bird—which really was beautiful—I offered some criticism. I'm only a few months out of Art School and for four years I've been critiquing art. And having mine critiqued. I forgot for a moment that I wasn't with my peers. Some of the paintings were good. Especially Tiffany's. But I think I was supposed to gush, and instead I gave her some pointers. It was really clear that was not what she had expected."

"No, Tiffany wouldn't appreciate criticism about her art. Or anything. No matter how constructive." Sister Agatha smiled just thinking about it. Tiffany would have assumed that she would be a mentor to the young artist. "So she didn't take an immediate shine to you. That's not unusual for Tiffany. She was mostly all about herself."

"It was more than that, to be honest. There was this sort of, I don't know, this vibe from her. Not at first, but at the end of the meeting."

"What do you mean? Vibe?"

"It's hard to say. I gave my talk, but before I had even finished Tiffany left the room and I could hear her on her mobile in the hall. It felt rude, but maybe it was an emergency or something. She sounded a little weird. Wound up. It's hard to say because I'd never met her before."

"What was she saying on the phone?"

"I didn't hear any actual conversation. Just the tone. There was definitely a tone. Almost . . ." Lucy stopped and thought for a moment. "Gloating. I know that sounds strange, but it just seemed that way."

"And then what, when she finished on her mobile?"

"Then she came back in and seemed fine."

"Anything else happen?"

"No. The meeting ended and I came home."

"Are you sure that's everything? I feel like there's more."

"No. That's it." Lucy looked directly at her. "You never answered my question."

"What question?" Sister Agatha closed her notebook and leaned forward to stroke the silky ears of the little dog.

"Why do you write about a gumshoe detective in the city and not a genteel woman from an English village? Or a bumbling priest?"

Sister Agatha thought for a moment. She realized that no one had asked her that question before. Reverend Mother had expressed some concern about Bates Melanchthon, her protagonist. He had the mouth of a sailor, a brutal left hook, and a decades' long absence from attending Mass. "Well, I live in a world where kindness and forgiveness are the order of the day. And as right and good as that is, sometimes it's nice to throw a punch first and ask questions later." Sister Agatha paused, impressed that Lucy didn't laugh or look astonished but instead simply nodded, her face thoughtful. "How about you? Why portraits? Even though they're not "trendy," as you say?"

Lucy sat silently for a long moment, staring at the oil brush in her hands. She looked up. "I guess I'm looking for someone. And I always think I might find them if I paint enough people."

"Who are you looking for?" Sister Agatha asked. Vincent van Gogh stood, stretched his tiny torso, walked over to Lucy, and then, with a grunt, lay down on top of her feet.

Lucy reached down to pet him, and when she looked up her blue eyes were bright with tears. She shook her head. "I can't tell you that," Lucy said. "I'm sorry."

"Don't be. Our art is personal. And not every little bit can be shared." She debated giving the young woman a hug but decided against it. Lucy seemed private. And as Sister Callwen was known to say, not everyone hugged at the drop of a hat.

Chapter Four

～

The next morning dawned cold and snowy. *At least the cheese barn is warm*, thought Sister Agatha as she looked around the room that bustled with activity. She loved her Gwenafwy Abbey sisters, but they were so infernally cheerful sometimes. Thanks to Sister Gwenydd, who had tuned her iPod to *Evensong for Advent: Nunc Dimittis in D Major* by the choir of King's College, Cambridge, music filled the room. Sister Agatha noticed that she had connected the iPod to a tiny Bluetooth speaker, which was about the size of a Welsh oatcake. It blasted the voices of the boy choristers as if they were in the next room. Advent music, a sudden winter storm pinging ice crystals against the window panes, and the common task of producing cheese seemed to have sent the sisters into a near frenzy of contentment and holiday joy.

But as she stood there, stirring the thickening wax and fiddling with the thermostat on the old range, Sister Agatha felt, instead of holiday cheer, her own personal slow boil of frustration—a mixture of boredom with all things cheese and a nagging stab of guilt for neglecting both her mystery novel and the real-life mystery that she faced—all this angst to the backdrop of her happy sisters and the King's College Boys' Choir.

She gave the vat of red wax a determined stir and went over the events of the last few days in her head. The murder of Tiffany Reese was now seventy-two hours old, and absolutely no progress had been made in the search for the killer. Tiffany Reese's funeral was tomorrow morning and half the village would be there. And although she did have some leads she needed to follow up, none of them seemed terribly encouraging. She needed to interview Vonda Bryson again, and she was still processing her conversation with Lucy. It hadn't really revealed much. The worst development of all: there would be no autopsy. Tiffany's brother, Kendrick Geddings, had been located—he had left on a business trip to Kenya the morning of Tiffany's death—and he had not consented to an autopsy. The body had been moved from the morgue to the funeral home, where it was probably being embalmed at this very moment, and so any potential evidence to be gleaned from the body would be gone—there would be no chance for a telling toxicology screen.

Sister Agatha felt discouraged even thinking about it. Inspector Rupert MacFarlane would have never allowed the body to have been embalmed without an autopsy. She could hear him now: *The dead will tell you things the living never could. Think of that corpse as your most revealing and crucial interview!* She shook her head. *Too late now.* And yet, she thought, looking around the cheese barn, *here at the abbey, the only crisis in people's minds was cooling wax;* a cold body in the morgue awaiting the embalmer didn't seem to bother anyone.

"Sisters," she said in the direction of the others standing at the long cheese table carefully brushing red wax across rounds of Gouda. "Time for a break, don't you think? A nice cup of tea perhaps? It'll give the wax time to settle down."

"Wax doesn't settle down like a flock of agitated sheep," Sister Callwen said, never taking her eyes off the round of Gouda that she was covering with slow, even strokes. "The wax has to be immediately brushed on, otherwise the cheese will dry out. And you've got to get that ancient stove to regulate the heat better or we'll never get the order ready in time for Saint Grenfell's Christmas Market. Wax that goes cold is of no help." They all knew that the wax had to stay hot while they brushed it on, then cool slowly, hardening around the cheese. Sister Callwen liked to say that cheese-making was both an art and science, and she loved the entire meticulous process, from the first starter culture to the last moment of ripening.

Sister Harriet walked over to the range and squinted at the thermometer. "The temp is holding at a hundred and twenty. Remember, Sister Agatha, it has to be hot enough to brush on the cheese, but not so hot that the vat explodes."

"Good Lord, it could explode? You never told me that." Sister Gwenydd wielded her brush like an expert and had hardly any wax spatters on her apron. When Sister Agatha covered the rounds with wax, she usually covered everything else with wax. Including her hair. Which was why she was now in charge of the vat. "That sounds dangerous."

"It *is* dangerous. Very. That's why we need a new stove in here so badly. And we could have a flash fire if we're not careful. Remember what happened to the Blackthorne Dairy three years ago?" Sister Callwen dipped her heavy brush into the pan of wax in front of her and began on the next round of Gouda. Blackthorne Dairy had nearly lost their entire production to a hot-wax mishap.

"I like the red wax," Sister Gwenydd said. Today was her first day working on a big order. "Is it red for Christmas?"

Sister Callwen's sigh could be heard across the room. "Gouda is brushed in red wax because it is a soft cheese. Very soft cheese is yellow or orange. A hard cheese would be in a black wax. And red is not an Advent color." Sister Callwen looked up from her brush. "Perhaps it's time to offer another cheese class for everyone."

Sister Agatha noticed that suddenly, the only sound in the room was the King's Choir. Sister Callwen's cheese class came with a lengthy quiz at the end and remedial work was required of those who didn't pass it. She glanced out the window and saw Reverend Mother hurrying across the garden toward the cheese barn. She had a look of pure joy on her face and a slip of white paper in her hand. In her rush, it appeared that she had forgotten to put on a hat and coat and the fast-falling snowflakes were covering her short gray hair and the blue jumper knitted by Sister Winifred. Reverend Mother didn't seem to notice that she was getting covered in snow and probably catching her death of cold. Sister Agatha frowned. Whenever Reverend Mother appeared that happy, something was afoot that would most certainly translate into a lot of work for someone. Sister Harriet called it her "Rodgers-and-Hammerstein look," and it was always a bit dangerous.

The door banged open and Reverend Mother fairly flew

in, bringing with her a gust of cold wind and a swirl of snow-flakes. "Sisters, I have the greatest news," she said, holding up the slip of paper and pushing the door shut against the cold. "Glad tidings of great joy!"

Sister Agatha cringed. This was possibly worse than she had thought. "What is it? An early Christmas present from the archbishop?"

"Almost as good," Reverend Mother said. "It's a cheese order."

"Good heavens!" Sister Harriet said. She had grabbed a tea towel and was brushing snow off Reverend Mother. "Is it really coming down that fast out there? I hope Ben is working on the walks and the drive."

"Is that all?" Sister Agatha said. "A cheese order?"

"An online order. Our first. At least since we started our big social media campaign. Listen to this, my sisters." Reverend Mother looked down at the page in her hand and read aloud. "A Mrs. Stevens in Pembrokeshire wants three rounds of Heavenly Gouda shipped immediately!" Sister Agatha watched as Reverend Mother dug her phone out of her jumper pocket. She thought she had seldom seen her so enthused. "I actually got the order off my mobile from our app. Then I printed it in the office."

"Well, that's good," Sister Harriet said, looking at Sister Callwen. "We can add three rounds to this batch if need be. We have just enough time, I think, to do it."

"Certainly." Sister Callwen said. "And well done, Sister Winifred. For getting us online. As you know, I was not a proponent at first, but this is wonderful." Sister Callwen, who still used a flip phone, picked up her brush and went back to making careful, sure strokes. "And it does make one feel rather clever—to be getting orders from an app on a mobile. Not that I plan to start using apps or anything."

"Reverend Mother? Is there something wrong?" Sister Agatha asked. Reverend Mother's face had gone from jubilant to ashen. She was staring at her phone.

"We've just gotten another online order." All the nuns stopped what they were doing and looked up. "Another order?" Sister Harriet asked slowly.

"Fifty rounds of Heavenly Gouda for a country store in London." No one moved or spoke. "And they've already paid. With a credit card." Reverend Mother looked up, speechless. Her phone vibrated and she clicked on the screen.

"Don't tell me," Sister Harriet said. "Please."

"Twenty rounds for the Wine and Rind Specialty Shop in . . . in . . ." Reverend Mother laid her phone carefully on the table, staring at it while the nuns waited. She looked up. "Dallas."

"You don't mean . . . Texas, do you?"

"Texas. Express shipping." The nuns stared at each other as the Reverend Mother's phone buzzed again. No one moved for a moment, then she slowly picked it up. "I'll get the others from the kitchen," Sister Callwen said, untying her apron. "The parish food baskets can wait. Sister Agatha, you find Lucy. We'll need every sister . . . or tenant . . . in the cheese barn before this is over."

* * *

The door to the dovecote-cum-art-studio was closed and Lucy wasn't answering her knock. Sister Agatha stepped back and thought for a moment. Lucy was always easy to find. She was either in her studio above the dovecote like she was last night when they talked or in her room in the dormitory section of the main building. Sister Agatha wondered if she was walking Vincent van Gogh across the orchard as she was known to do, but she couldn't imagine that the young woman was out and about in this weather. Sister Agatha called her name, knocked again, and then tried the door handle. No answer from Lucy or bark from Vincent.

She hurried down the steps from the studio and out the door to the dovecote. She checked Lucy's room in the dormitory— empty. Wrapping her parka around her, she headed out and started across the open meadow, stumbling a bit on the rutted frozen ground. Off to the east, she could see the abbey's flock of Welsh Mountain sheep huddled at the edge of the apple orchard. Ben stood in the middle of it with the flock gathered around him. She remembered him saying at breakfast that morning that he would start polling the young ewes. Sister Agatha, who had grown up on a sheep farm, explained to Sister Gwenydd that "polling" meant taking the horns off the females. The breakfast conversation launched into an enthused discussion of why the male sheep got to keep their beautiful curved horns and the females lost theirs. She noticed that Ben had left the room when the conversation turned from attitudes toward female horned sheep to female ordained priests. There was seldom a dull moment around the abbey breakfast table.

The snow let up and a cold wintry sun broke through the clouds. Over the hill appeared a lonely figure, scarf blowing and parka wide open. It was Lucy, waving frantically. The young American girl never seemed to care about the cold. She kept assuring the sisters that "Providence was much worse," but Sister Agatha couldn't quite believe any weather was worse than that on a Welsh highland five miles from the Irish Sea. But the young were hardy.

Sister Agatha waved back and began to hurry toward her when she saw Lucy turn and run in the opposite direction. Sister Agatha stopped and, cupping her mouth, shouted Lucy's name. Her shout died in the fierce wind. Had she even heard her? Then Lucy was running back toward her again, stumbling on the rough terrain of the field but not falling. As far as Sister Agatha could tell, the young woman didn't even slow down.

Sister Agatha felt a moment's annoyance, mixed with concern. What in the world could be so important that they were in an open field on a cold December morning, two weeks before Christmas? "Lucy," she shouted again. "What?" She watched as Lucy reappeared above the hill and waved both arms again, then turned and ran back down the slope, out of sight.

"Oh, good heavens," Sister Agatha said. She picked up the skirts to her habit and walked as fast as she could in the direction of Lucy. All she wanted was to get Lucy and herself out of the wind and back to the cheese barn, where no doubt chaos had broken loose as the twenty women of Gwenafwy Abbey tried to fill the biggest order for Heavenly Gouda they had ever hoped for. *Be careful what you hope for,* she suddenly thought.

Sister Agatha crested the top of the hill breathing a little harder than she liked to acknowledge, scanned the horizon for Lucy, then saw her kneeling next to a large wooden crate. Sister Agatha ran to her. Lucy was simultaneously sobbing and swearing as she tried to pry the crate open. A small whimpering came from inside.

Sister Agatha felt her blood run cold. Hiking up her skirts, she sprinted over to Lucy and the box. "Holy Mother, what's going on?" The wind whipped around them and the sun had gone back under the clouds. A snow squall blew up and pinged icy crystals against the crate. A sharp bark come from inside.

Sister Agatha felt a surge of anger. "That's not Vincent, is it?" Even as she said it, she knew the truth.

"Yes," Lucy gasped. "He's been missing since breakfast. I came out here, finally thinking he'd taken out after the sheep. And I found him here. In this horrible crate. Just help me." Sister Agatha saw that Lucy's fingertips had begun to bleed as she tore at the boards holding the crate shut. Maybe she had underestimated the young woman.

Digging in her apron pocket, she pulled out her Girl Guides knife and began to pry at one of the boards. In one part of the box only a few thin laths held it shut, as if whoever put the little dog in there had done it in a hurry. Getting one of the laths off with the knife, together they managed to yank off two or three other boards, and Lucy reached in and pulled Vincent van Gogh to safety.

Sister Agatha rocked back on her heels and watched as the young woman cradled the tiny, shivering dog as he squirmed and licked Lucy's face. She felt sick. What kind of person traps a dog in a crate, nails it shut, and leaves it out in an open field in the middle of winter? And on the grounds of the abbey? She could barely let herself think that no one had been on abbey grounds all morning except the nuns and Ben. Had it been an inside job? Impossible. She thought hard. They had all been so caught up in the activity in the cheese barn that perhaps no one would even have noticed if someone had come or gone in the past two hours. Maybe one of the sisters making the food baskets had seen someone. Or did the culprit take the dog while the nuns were sitting at the breakfast table arguing about horns on ewes? Of course, that also meant that Ben had an alibi. Or did he? He had left the dining room a good thirty minutes before anyone else.

"Come on Lucy," she said. "Let's get the two of you back where it's warm. The little pup will be just fine with a bowl of warm milk and bit of lamb stew." Lucy didn't move but just sat on the frozen ground, her face buried in the dog's fur. Sister Agatha waited a moment. "Come on," she urged. "Let's go. It's brass monkeys out here."

"Brass monkeys?" Lucy said, looking up at her.

"It's a phrase. 'Cold enough to freeze the . . .' Never mind. It's cold and we need to get inside."

"I shouldn't have come here," Lucy said. "I'm going home. First thing tomorrow, I'm getting a plane ticket back to Providence."

* * *

Ben Holden gave Sister Agatha a wordless nod as she closed the door behind her. She loved the sheep barn. Warm and filled with the fragrant smell of sheep and clover hay, it reminded her of her childhood and all the time she had spent following her father and brothers around the farm. Ben stood in the dimly lit interior, the sheep milling around him, quiet except for the soft sounds that a relaxed flock made. The sheep barn was more of a long, low shed at the far end of the meadow than it was a barn. The abbey had not used the old dwelling for nearly fifty years, but when the nuns decided to increase their revenue with sheep and to hire Ben to take care of the flock of Welsh Mountain ewes and their offspring, they made some repairs and repurposed the old building. Now it served as a warm spot out of the wind for the sheep. Ben looked up from the ewe he was inspecting—the ewes were all newly pregnant—and, letting her go, stood up. "Prynhawn da, Sister." *Good Afternoon.*

"Prynhawn da, Ben."

"Come to see the new ewes?" Ben gave the impression that he was an unsympathetic old farmer who saw animals as strictly for-profit, yet Sister Agatha wondered. Their welfare and even happiness seemed important to Ben. But then, his concern could be just to make sure they remained healthy and productive.

"Have you been out here all morning?" she asked.

"Aye. In and out. Why?"

"I just wondered if you saw anyone on the abbey grounds? I mean anyone you didn't recognize?"

"No."

As always, Ben was a man of few words. She watched as he dabbed ointment out of an old jar and rubbed it gently into the leg of a young ewe, all the while murmuring softly to the animal. Sister Agatha was having a hard time envisioning Ben shutting a tiny dog into a crate and leaving it out in the bitter cold to die. She sat on a bale of sweet-smelling clover hay and watched as Ben moved from lamb to lamb. She had liked Ben from the time they hired him. He reminded her of her own father and brothers as they worked the sheep when she was a child.

"By the way, Reverend Mother was wondering, is Lucy's dog bothering the sheep any?"

"Nay. But I don't like a dog that doesn't earn its keep." Ben moved on to the next lamb.

"Has the dog been a problem?"

"Nowt so far. But I've told the lass to keep it away from the ewes. I don't want anything disturbing them."

"Has she done that? Kept it away, I mean?"

"Aye." He let the ewe go and stood up. "I looked at the old pony and I think we need to get the veterinary out."

"You do?" Bartimaeus was the blind Shetland pony the sisters had brought home from a petting zoo in the village a few years back. They didn't like the way he was being treated, and when they complained to the owner of the zoo, he told them callously that it didn't matter, as "the moth-eaten old thing was about to be put down anyway." The sisters had taken Bartimaeus home with them, coaxing him to follow them up Church Lane with bits of apple. He had been living out his golden years at the abbey ever since, fat and happy. But lately he had begun to fail. Sister Agatha knew she was ignoring the inevitable—that he was perhaps getting to end of his long life.

"Aye. Don't worry. I'll give the old boy an extra bit of warm mash. It will set him right in this cold weather."

"Thanks, Ben." Sister Agatha tucked her scarf around her neck and slipped out into the cold. She couldn't imagine Ben hurting the little dog. On the other hand, who else could have done it?

The wind picked up as Sister Agatha walked across the meadow back to the abbey. The large sheep meadow was neatly sectioned off by stone fences that had stood sentinel for the past century at least, built by the early inhabitants of the abbey back when it was a monastery run by Cistercian monks. They were true farmers, she thought, picking her way across the frozen ground. Their entire livelihood, from the food they ate to the clothes they wore, was produced by the sheep, the gardens, and the other livestock. Was that not a better time, she thought to herself? *Well perhaps not.* No wi-fi, central heating, or Netflix. No interlibrary loan or aspirin or comfy yogapants. No. Not a better time, but perhaps, she had to admit, a time more authentic to the calling of a religious order.

The shadows were growing long and the words to the psalm read in chapel that morning came to her: *Truth shall spring out of the earth; and righteousness shall look down from heaven.* There was something about the season of Advent that called one back. Back to the real reason they gathered as an abbey. As a community. She wrapped her scarf tighter and made her way across the garden, now in snowy drifts. The lights were on in the cheese barn and that meant that the sisters were hard at it. Although she really wanted to climb the steep steps to the attic library, where she could think through this puzzling event, she didn't. She turned instead and walked to the cheese barn. The Wine and Rind needed their Gouda.

* * *

Sister Agatha sat down on the bench at the kitchen table. Normally Wednesday was the day of the week on which she got caught up. Not today. She had rescued a kidnapped dog, talked with Ben, helped in the cheese barn. Add to that all the other things she had managed to accomplish—cataloging books in the abbey library, packing food baskets, and meeting with Sister Matilda in the greenhouse for a book discussion.

Sister Matilda had partnered with Lewis Colwyn, botany teacher and avid gardener, to teach a winter gardening class at St. Anselm's. They had been burning the midnight oil to get the class planned, and that afternoon they had called upon Sister Agatha to help them with curriculum resources. Sister Matilda and Lewis were up to their elbows in potting soil and starter bulbs when she met them in the abbey greenhouse for a conversation about potential classroom resources. Usually a conversation about books was her favorite thing, but this evening she had been tired. The conversation must have continued long after she left them because she just saw Lewis' car pull out of the abbey drive.

She reached across the table for the tin of gingerbread that Sister Gwenydd always kept at the ready. Just as she was removing the lid, the door to the kitchen opened and, with a gust of cold wind, Lucy stepped in. It was unusual to see the young woman anywhere other than slipping into her studio or walking the little dog. But then, she had spent most of the day helping the sisters in the cheese barn, so maybe she was feeling more at home. "Looking for a late-night snack?" Sister Agatha asked. "I can offer you gingerbread and tea, if you wish."

Without smiling, Lucy pulled off her mittens and brushed snow out of her red hair. She sat down at the table and, unzipping her purple ski jacket with one hand, reached into the tin of gingerbread with the other. "I love gingerbread. But not tea so much. At home I drink only Starbucks. But thanks for the offer."

Sister Agatha shook her head. All Starbucks and no tea sounded dreary indeed. "How are you doing?" she asked. "And where's the puppy?"

"He's in my studio. Reverend Mother had Ben put another lock on the door and so I took the chance and left him alone."

"Are you really heading back to Providence?"

"I guess not. I texted my mother and she said I should stick it out. That everything is an adventure and Vincent van Gogh wasn't hurt and it would all work out. My mother is like that. Always positive."

"Not a bad trait to have in a mother."

"I suppose." Lucy finished off her slice of gingerbread and took another out of the tin. Sister Agatha intuited that Lucy had something she wanted to say. She would force herself to wait her out. As Rupert McFarland often advised, *Sometimes being quiet with a suspect is best. If you keep talking, all you may ever hear is yourself.*

"I went for a walk on the beach," Lucy said, her mouth full. The sisters at Gwenafwy Abbey spent many hours each summer enjoying their close vicinity to the Irish Sea, and on a warm, sunny day, a walk there made for a pleasant afternoon outing. But not in December. Although the snow had stopped and the sun had broken through the clouds, it was still bitterly cold.

"Reverend Mother let me drive the van. That way I could

take my easel. I needed to get away. Think about things. And paint."

"And did you? Think about things and paint, that is?" Sister Agatha put the kettle on. This could be a two cups of tea night.

"Not really. First of all, it was way too windy for me. I started off by just walking, but then I met up with this woman who was painting. She was incredible." Lucy bit into a piece of gingerbread. "I mean amazing."

At least walking in frigid weather had gotten her mind off the gruesome kidnapping of her dog. "An artist? On the beach?"

"Yeah, all set up with an easel." Lucy waited while Sister Agatha took the teakettle off the stove and poured the teapot full. "I guess I could have some tea. It might be nice. You guys don't do a lot with central heating, do you?" Without waiting for a response, Lucy continued. "I loved it. I mean, I'm not into painting nature. But the Welsh coast is so spectacular. Anyway, we spent the whole time talking about art."

"Who was it?" Sister Agatha poured out the tea into her own cup, adding sugar and cream to her own.

"Her name is Millicent. Millicent Pritchard." Lucy picked up the tin and looked into it. "I hope Sister Gwenydd doesn't mind but we've cleaned her out of gingerbread."

Chapter Five

~

Early the next morning, Sister Agatha walked up to the Bryson house for the second time in a week. She had slipped into the village that morning with the excuse of needing to run an errand for Sister Gwenydd. Which was true. In a sense. Sister Gwenydd did say she was out of cilantro, and Sister Agatha was more than happy to make a quick run to the Lettuce-Eat-Vegan to purchase some. And interview a suspect on the way home.

The toys that had cluttered the lawn last time had disappeared and been replaced by new ones. She recognized a Batman action figure, a Sponge-Bob Square Pants, and an old Tonka truck. Loud shrieks and shouts reverberated from inside the house. She could hear a television blaring and a dog barking. She rang the doorbell, and this time it wasn't a tired, red-eyed Vonda who met her but a tired, surprised Vonda. Although still a bit disheveled, she was wearing linen pants, a silk blouse, and heels. Behind her two small children chased each other around the living room. Apparently, the brood was back.

"Sister," she said. "Come in. I wasn't expecting anyone."

As Sister Agatha stepped into the vestibule, she saw a young teenage girl whom she recognized from Father Selwyn's confirmation class, sitting on the couch, reading to a much quieter child. The other two stopped running long enough to wrestle each other to the carpet over a toy. "I'm about to step out. The sitter is here."

"Oh, sorry to interrupt. I just wanted to talk for a moment."

"OK. Sure. I have a minute," Vonda said, waving her into the kitchen. The room was equally cluttered, though clean. Clean dishes rested in the dish drainer and the table held a tray of tea things. Sister Agatha sat down, and after hesitating and looking at the clock, Vonda did too. "Are you here about the funeral dinner? I would say that Sister Gwenydd and I have it pretty much set."

"No . . . it's not that." Sister Agatha was suddenly completely at a loss as to how to proceed. Could she just blunder in as she wanted to, asking Vonda where she was the night of the murder? Or would she have to take a subtler approach, which Father Selwyn had made abundantly clear did not fit her personality? She decided to go with subtle—or at least as subtle as she could manage.

"I was just doing some asking around about Tiffany. To gather information about her for Father Selwyn's eulogy." Sister Agatha felt her scalp tingle with her lie.

"Oh really? You do that for him? Well, I suppose there is a lot I don't understand about how you do things, you know, how the church works." Tiffany took a seat at the kitchen table. "What do you want to know?" She glanced at the clock again.

"The last time we talked, you indicated that you didn't

really like her." She wanted so badly to just come out and say it. *I know you weren't at the house watching telly the night Tiffany died. Where were you?* But only a real detective could proceed that heavy-handedly with a suspect. Inwardly, Sister Agatha sighed. At the end of the day, she was a nun. Not Bates Melanchthon or Inspector Barnaby or even Stephanie Plum.

Vonda picked a dish towel up off the table and twisted it in her hands. Shrieks of laughter erupted from the living room. Vonda didn't seem to hear it. Sister Agatha had noticed that young parents seemed a bit deaf when it came to the noise their offspring made. Especially in church.

"Well, if you want the truth, no. Not particularly. I certainly didn't want her to die—but I didn't like Tiffany, if you are asking."

"Was she ever rude or hurtful to you?"

Vonda gave Sister Agatha a sharp look. "Will that be in Father's eulogy?" She went on, "Tiffany took 'rude' and 'hurtful' to a whole new height. So yes. But then she was like that to everyone."

Sister Agatha glanced around the kitchen. A bright-green canister sat on the counter. She had almost forgotten. "What kind of tea did Tiffany drink?" she asked.

"You want that for the eulogy? Well, OK. That's easy. Radiance Infusion from Harrod's. It's the most expensive tea Harrod's carries. At least that's what she was always telling us at WI. I buy our tea at the Tesco, so I wouldn't know."

"Did you like it? Her tea, that is?"

"Never had it. No one touched Tiffany's tea or her teacup."

"One last question, was there anything that you did like about her? You know, for the eulogy?" Sister Agatha added quickly.

"Well, I admired her."

"You did?" Now it was Sister Agatha's turn to be surprised.

"Tiffany had a certain way about her that I wish I could have." Vonda paused and gestured around the cluttered house. A house that Sister Agatha had to admit that, though chaotic, held a warmth and family-feel that seemed genuine. "Tiffany was perfect—hair, clothes, house. And while doing all that, she was an accomplished artist. And what have I done? I never finished school. I love my four boys and my husband, of course. But I haven't done anything other than soccer practice and church work in a decade." Vonda slumped in her chair and looked imploringly at Sister Agatha. "Tiffany might have been insufferable and generally obnoxious. But she had a life. She *did* something."

* * *

Sister Agatha found that she had a lot to think about on her walk back to the abbey. She had finished the conversation with Vonda no closer to where she had been the night of the murder. For once Sister Agatha found herself happy that she was not a real detective. Sitting there at Vonda's kitchen table, she had realized that getting a suspect statement out of Vonda was not the only important thing. Bringing some encouragement and cheer to a young woman who was doing an impressive job with her family and church was important too.

She had stayed for a while with Vonda, praising her work at St. Anselm's and telling her how wonderful she indeed was. Being a wife and mother was underrated these days, and frankly, she couldn't see anything more worthwhile. Or demanding. Or, as she shut the door behind her on the loud chaos of the children, more thoroughly exhausting.

Thinking back on her conversation with Vonda as she climbed Church Hill, Sister Agatha was glad that she hadn't pushed her any further but was still concerned that she had gained no new information. She couldn't shake the feeling that, although she possessed no concrete evidence, Vonda was somehow involved in the death of Tiffany. She knew it was a long shot. But concrete evidence was overrated. The detective's instinct was important. *Or so Inspector Rupert McFarland was often saying.*

But she had to determine where Vonda had really been that night. She resolved to figure it out, and she had a lot of library work to accomplish. But now she had to get back to the abbey. The sisters were planning a long afternoon of baking for the St. Anselm's Christmas jumble. A murdered woman, a kidnapped dog, a lying suspect, a stack of uncatalogued books. And she was going to spend the afternoon making Welsh cakes and Monmouth pudding. This would never have happened to Armand Gamache.

* * *

The afternoon sun was slanting through the attic windows when Sister Agatha finally got back to her duties as librarian. She pulled a box of books, newly acquired though gently used copies of *The Interpreter's Dictionary of the Bible*, across the library table and began to unload them. She planned to spend the rest of the afternoon making spine labels. Setting the books out in order and lining up her supplies, she realized that the image of Vincent van Gogh trapped in a crate out in the field haunted her like a bad dream. What kind of depraved person steals a puppy, puts the little thing in a box, nails it shut, and dumps it out in a field? *A horrible person. A dangerous person.* And the bigger question, *why?* Why steal the dog? A murder in the church and two days later a dognapping at the abbey. Were they connected?

She felt fairly confident that it wasn't Ben. He was abrupt and crusty, but kind. And he seemed to have a compassionate heart for animals of all sorts—even dogs who didn't earn their keep. True, he had no alibi. But she knew something about Ben that no one else knew. She knew what he liked to read. And a person's choice of reading material, in her mind, was not only personal and confidential, it was an excellent indicator of their personality. Their integrity. Who they really were as a person. Ben read romance novels. And not the steamy, graphic kind. He preferred the more gentle, idealist stories of a hero rescuing a heroine. Any man who read *Moonlight and Magic* or *Love at the Villa* would not viciously hurt a little dog. She was sure of it.

Slipping on ear buds, Sister Agatha tuned into Inspector Rupert McFarland's latest podcast "Collecting Evidence." She needed something to occupy her mind while making the spine labels. If someone had come onto abbey grounds, gone up to Lucy's apartment, and stolen Vincent van Gogh, wouldn't they have left some sort of evidence that they had been there? She listened carefully to Inspector Rupert MacFarland's entire thirty-minute podcast and then started it over and listened again.

With the spine label task completed, and her inspiration to track down the intruder high, she neatened up the library work table and then headed down the stairs. Her mind was racing. Who did this and why? And the bigger question, did it have anything to do with the death of Tiffany Reese just two days ago in the village? And what did the perpetrator take away, and what did he leave behind? It was time to collect some evidence.

* * *

Sister Agatha pulled her woolly hat down over her ears. The sun had dropped below the yew trees and the wind had risen. Armed with a tape measure from Sister Callwen's sewing box, an old toothbrush, three plastic sandwich bags, and a pair of salad tongs from the kitchen, she felt ready. She stuffed all her evidence-gathering items into the pockets of her red jumper along with the purple notebook and set forth. Inspector Rupert MacFarland recommended latex gloves, but her fur-lined leather gloves from last year's St. Grenfell jumble would suffice. It was just too cold for latex.

She started off thinking about where the intruder might have come in. It was likely that he or she drove, as only the nuns made the walk back and forth to the village. And what self-respecting criminal is without a car? And anyway, yesterday had been absolute brass monkeys. No one would have strolled up Church Lane. Unless, of course, the person didn't need to arrive at the abbey. What if he/she already lived here? Sister Agatha banished that thought from her mind. She refused to believe the dognapping was an inside job.

She made her way down the long drive to the Church Lane where the perpetrator's vehicle would have entered Gwenafwy Abbey property. Walking through the wrought-iron gate and stepping onto the lane, she saw immediately a lone tire tread in the frozen mud. Someone had driven up over the berm and left a gouge next to the gravel drive. She followed it back down the gravel drive to the abbey, but it disappeared.

Sister Agatha imagined the person turning into the drive and then perhaps cutting the engine and rolling to a stop in the drive, so as to not attract attention. Stealthily pulling a wooden crate out of the back of a car. Cutting across the brown frozen vegetable garden to the dovecote at the back of the main buildings. All of this would have had to be done quickly, as the person would have had no way of knowing how long the sisters would remain at breakfast.

She stopped short. How did the person know the sisters *were* at breakfast? Or that the dog was in the artist's studio at the top of the dovecote? Or that the dovecote had been turned into a studio space? *Only if he had been spying on the abbey for quite some time.* Sister Agatha shivered. Or if he or she was a member of the abbey. No. *Impossible.*

Taking out Sister Callwen's tape measure, she walked back to the edge of the road and measured the tire track, noting its exact width and depth, and jotted down the information in her notebook. She would measure the tires of the abbey's aging minivan and make a comparison, but even at a glance one could see this was a smaller tire. She went out onto Church Lane and stood in the middle of the road in front of the abbey gate. An old stone wall ran along the gravel road from the entrance of the abbey all the way down the steep hill to the village, less than a mile away. Across the patchwork of fields were the rooftops of the shops, the spire of St. Anselm's, and, at the edge of the village, Pryderi Castle. Sister Agatha shook her head. *We don't build things like that anymore, she thought. More's the pity.*

That was when she noticed the flecks of blue paint along the stone wall closest to the gate. Removing the toothbrush from her pocket, she brushed as many of the flakes as she could get, which was only a few, into a plastic bag. Most of them stuck to the old toothbrush so she tossed that into the bag as well. Tire treads and blue paint. Did the perpetrator swerve out of the drive after doing his dastardly deed, peel out and therefore leave tracks in the frozen dirt, and in his haste to get away sideswipe the stone fence? Stuffing the baggie and tools back into her pockets, she walked briskly back down the drive and nearly plowed into Lucy and Vincent van Gogh. The tiny dog was fearlessly facing the wind and seemed quite happy to be out and about. But then who wouldn't be, dressed in tartan plaid?

"He looks quite sporting," Sister Agatha said, smiling at Lucy who had scooped up the little dog in her arms, as she seemed often to do.

"Did you see the boxes?" Lucy asked her, an edge in her

voice. Without waiting for an answer, Lucy gestured ahead. "Come with me." She hurried along as Sister Agatha followed her past the cheese barn to the attached stable at the back where Bartimaeus was kept and Ben had his workshop. She swung the door open and pointed. In the corner next to Ben's workbench was a stack of crates identical to the one the little dog had been trapped in. "They're his. Ben's. Sister Gwenydd gets kitchen supplies in them. She said Ben keeps them and uses them out here." And as if perhaps Sister Agatha still didn't get it, Lucy turned to her and said, "He did it. He nailed Vincent into the box and dumped him." And Sister Agatha had to admit, romance novels or not, it didn't look good for Ben.

Chapter Six

⁓

Sister Agatha slid into the back booth at the Buttered Crust Tea Shop. She liked Friday mornings at the tea shop. There was the usual commotion, noise, and clinking of teacups, all of which somehow increased her productivity and allowed her to get some work done on her novel. Wednesday morning was her morning to write, to get away from the abbey to the back booth of the Buttered Crust where she could really focus— and have all the tea and Welsh cakes she wanted. She usually combined it with a trip to the public library to check on something for the Abbey library or the post office or at Lettuce-Eat-Vegan for Sister Gwenydd. Today she was picking up an interlibrary loan book for Sister Harriet—*Graphic or Manga: Everything You Need to Know.* Sister Harriet was working on the Sunday school curriculum using graphic novels for young adults. Sister Agatha wasn't sure, but she thought the topic was bible stories with a scary twist. God knew there were plenty of those.

She opened her computer and stared at the latest activity of her protagonist detective, Bates Melanchthon. He had most recently cracked the case of a double homicide and was in the process of tying things up. The problem was she had read over her story late last night and found a glaring clue that she had overlooked and that would unfortunately prove the murderer's innocence. She poured a cup of tea from the teapot on the table. *Oh well,* she thought, making a few notes on the napkin next to her, *there is no murder out there that a good cup of Welsh Brew couldn't solve.* Just as she began to type, Father Selwyn slid into the booth.

"I thought I would find you here," he said. He looked up and called out to Keenan, the young waiter, "A pot of Glengettie please, Keenan. With a cranberry scone."

"Always good to see you, Father," Sister Agatha said, smiling.

"The muse treating you well today?" he asked.

"Not bad. I'm kind of in the weeds. Morning mass go OK?"

"Awesome. As always."

"Big crowd?" Early mass at St. Anselm's wasn't known for its record attendance. Especially on a wintry morning.

"Sister. *Where two or three are gathered . . .* You know what our Lord said."

"In other words, no one?" She took a sip of tea and went back to typing.

"Actually, two. And interestingly, Tiffany's brother was there. Kendrick Geddings. I haven't seen Kendrick sitting in a pew for years." Father Selwyn smiled as Keenan placed the tea and scone in front of him and then frowned as he looked up. "Incredibly sad for him, I would imagine. Tiffany was the last remaining relative in the family. The funeral is this Saturday."

"Now that will be a big crowd." Sister Agatha figured most of the village would be at Tiffany's funeral.

"Bates Melanchthon making progress?" Father Selwyn asked, changing the subject.

"Not really. It's hard to write about a fictional murder when a real murder has just taken place in your own parish hall." She closed her laptop and filled him in on the dognapping, evidence collection, and follow-up conversation with Ben Holden.

"Poor Lucy. Is she packing up to leave, do you think?"

"Not at all. She's made of sterner stuff. Welsh by birth, you know. Despite that red hair and being adopted by Americans. It makes a difference."

"What does?"

"Being Welsh. We're a strong people."

"Oh, right. Of course." Father Selwyn sat back. "Well, I hope she stays. She seems clever and resourceful. A good sort. Reminds me of someone I know. But I can't put my finger on who." He poured more tea and added sugar and cream to both cups.

"You know the young woman who works for the florist? She was in your office on Saturday."

"Millicent Pritchard?"

"Right. Well, Lucy ran into her the other day. Apparently, they hit it off. I felt like the fact that she connected with a girl her own age who was also an artist has helped her feel more like staying, even with the whole dog thing happening."

Father Selwyn took a sip of tea. He listened intently as Sister Agatha filled him in on the encounter between the two women. "Seriously? A painter? Didn't she tell us specifically she wasn't a painter. That's odd."

"What do you think it means?"

He shrugged. "Who knows? Maybe she doesn't think of herself as an artist. Just someone who does it as a hobby."

"According to Lucy, she's brilliant."

"Yes, but I doubt Millicent thinks of herself as brilliant. However, that does point to a connection to Tiffany. Perhaps Tiffany gave her art lessons. Especially if she is painting birds like Tiffany did."

Sister Agatha took a bite of her oatcake. "That doesn't sound like Tiffany Reese. I'll talk with Millicent."

"What do you think of Ben Holden? He a tough old guy, but I can't imagine any farmer doing that to a dog. Trapping it in a box? In a field in the middle of winter?" Father Selwyn shook his head.

"I mostly agree. But whoever did it used a packaging box from the abbey kitchen. I guess Sister Gwenydd gets kitchen supplies in them and, when she empties them, gives them to Ben."

The bell over the door jangled and Sister Agatha looked up to see Bevan Penrose come in. He made his way toward them. Even from across the room Sister Agatha could sense that St. Anselm's administrative assistant was on a mission. He slid into the booth next to Father Selwyn. "I thought you would be here," he said, nodding to Sister and frowning at Father Selwyn's cranberry scone. He glanced down at the post-it notes in his hand. "Lewis Colwyn just called. He wants to know if they can use the kitchen for Winter Gardening."

"Of course, but why does Winter Gardening need the kitchen?"

"They have refreshments halfway through, I guess. So, they want the kitchen." Bevan pulled up the next post-it note. He hesitated.

"What?" Father Selwyn asked.

"Well, the constable called about the parking detail for the Reese funeral and said that if I saw Sister Agatha I should tell her . . ." Bevan's voice trailed off. He looked down at the paper in his hand, "and . . . I'm quoting . . . 'if you see the Sister, tell her that she can stop running around like she's Jessica Fletcher on *Midsomer Murders*.'" Bevan looked up. "It's gotten back to the constable that you've been asking around about Tiffany Reese."

"Good heavens," Sister Agatha said, opening her notebook. "Jessica Fletcher is on *Murder She Wrote* not *Midsomer Murders*. Doesn't he know the difference between Angela Lansbury and John Nettles? No wonder he can't solve the simplest murder." She uncapped her Sharpie. "And anyway, I am *so* not Jessica Fletcher. She was old and a retired English teacher. I'm much younger and a *nun*. A world of difference."

Bevan glanced at Father Selwyn and then they both studied the tabletop. Without looking up from her notebook, Sister Agatha continued. "And I still can't believe that he didn't do an autopsy with a tox screen. Anyone who has read a single Agatha Christie mystery would know that certain poisons can make it look like someone has had a heart attack."

"Do you really think someone would kill Tiffany Reese?" Bevan asked.

"Someone? More like several someones," Sister Agatha replied. She watched as Bevan reached out and took the last bite of cranberry scone off Father Selwyn's plate.

"You know you're not supposed to be eating these," he said popping it in his mouth.

Father Selwyn fixed Bevan with a direct look. "Those of you who have not sinned cast the first stone."

Bevan swallowed and grinned. "I'm not off all processed carbs. You are."

Sister Agatha stood up and pulled her hat on. "You two can sit here and talk about scones all you want. I need to pay a visit to our local florist."

* * *

Just-for-You Florist on Main Street sat directly across from Buy-the-Book bookstore and was only a few shops down from The Buttered Crust. Sister Agatha stepped through the door and immediately inhaled the wonderful fragrance of fresh flowers. Out on the sidewalk it was a brisk winter day, but here in the shop a lush tropical paradise. This was also how she felt when she walked into Sister Matilda's greenhouse at the abbey. Which reminded her, she needed to track down several books at the public library for Sister Matilda and Lewis Colwyn's winter gardening class. She looked around and saw Millicent through the door of the back room arranging a large vase of holly sprigs and red ribbons. Sister Agatha slipped past the counter and knocked on the frame of the open door.

"Millicent?" she said. "Do you have a minute? Sorry to disturb you."

Millicent turned toward her and smiled shyly, wiping her hands on a paper towel. "One sec. Do you mind waiting up front at the counter? My boss doesn't really want customers back here."

Sister Agatha had no choice but to retreat to the front of the store. She had hoped for a private word in the back. She thumped her heavy book bag down on the worn wooden counter and looked around. The shop was filled with Christmas-themed flowers, plants, and decorations. She shook her head. Was it only the religious world that recognized Advent? Millicent came out of the backroom and stepped behind the counter. "What can I do for you, Sister?"

If Millicent had the predisposition to kill someone, she certainly didn't look like it. Her round face was flushed and smiling, her eyes bright. She seemed a bit more put together than that day in Father Selwyn's office, although then she had just heard of Tiffany's murder—enough to throw anyone off their game. Her green florist apron covered a new feat of layering: a white button-down shirt that looked like it had once belonged to a fairly rotund man on top of a fuchsia T-shirt. A brown ribbed corduroy skirt—Sister Agatha didn't realize they still made those—and burgundy tights with hiking boots.

"Well, I wondered if you had a moment to talk with me about Tiffany Reese?" Millicent's cheery demeanor faded, but only for an instant.

"Of course. That reminds me, I need to start working on the flowers for the funeral."

"Well, I was just wondering . . . since you were there at the church so early to deliver wreaths on Saturday . . . and you had been there the night before . . ." Sister Agatha realized that she should have worked harder on her reason for why she was asking, "if you saw or heard anything?" Lame interrogation by any standards, but a start.

"No, why? Constable Barnes already asked me about it the day after Tiffany died."

"Well, you know . . . in an investigation . . . one cannot be too thorough." There, that sounded a little better.

"An investigation? Constable Barnes didn't say he was investigating. He told me she died of natural causes—like a heart attack or something."

"Yes, well. I'm just looking into a few things. You know, tying up any loose ends before the funeral." Sister Agatha realized she had gotten way too comfortable with lying. Her scalp was barely tingling. Not good.

"Oh. Well. Sorry, but I didn't see anything."

"Did you hear anyone in the church kitchen?"

"No." Millicent looked at her directly. "I was upstairs." Eyes clear and her expression open. According to Inspector Rupert MacFarland, a lying suspect never maintains steady eye contact. Either Millicent Pritchard was telling the truth or she was a very good liar.

Sister Agatha decided to change tack. "Were you and Tiffany close friends?"

"No. Why?"

Sister Agatha noticed a tiny flicker of Millicent's left eyebrow, and a red flush began just above the neckline of the fuchsia T-shirt. She was dying to whip out her Sharpie and make a note. "I was just thinking that you might have known why Tiffany was at the parish hall that night."

"Because she was setting up for the art show?" Millicent said.

Millicent had regained all her composure and was now looking at her like she had two heads.

"Right, of course." Sister Agatha smiled and tried her best to sound casual. "What did you think of Tiffany's art?"

"I loved it." Millicent glanced at the small clock sitting on the counter. "If you don't mind, I have to get back to my Christmas arrangements."

"One more thing. You said you weren't an artist that day in Father Selwyn's office. But you are, aren't you? An artist."

"I dabble. Nowhere as good as Tiffany Reese." And with that, she turned and walked into the backroom, this time shutting the door firmly behind her.

* * *

George was indeed behind the desk at the library, but he was obviously busy. A tall, slender man in his mid-forties wearing an expensive gray suit stood talking with him. They seemed to be friends. Sister Agatha noticed that the expensive-suit guy carefully straightened things as he talked, squaring the blotter with the corners of the desk, absentmindedly lining up George's pens and pencils in a perfect row, placing the pamphlets on reference books in a precise stack. George didn't seem to notice. Their conversation had turned from laughter to library business—the new fund-raiser to add a wing in the children's section. After a few moments, expensive-suit guy turned and, with a nod to Sister Agatha, hurried out the door. He seemed to be a person with a purpose, not like the usual Friday morning crowd of mothers and toddlers gathering for story hour or the seniors' book group.

"Bore da, George," Sister Agatha said. *Good morning.*

"Bore da, Sister," he replied.

How could she draw George out without making him question her motives? She needed to ask if he had spied on his neighbors enough to know where Vorda had gone on the night of the murder. Was she at the church, or not? It was a little tough to launch gracefully into a question revealing one's nosiness. How would Stephanie Plum handle this? Miss Marple? Her mind was a blank, and then suddenly George started talking.

"You know who that fellow is, don't you?" he asked, nodding toward the library door. Without waiting for an answer, he told her. "Kendrick Geddings. The wealthiest man in Pryderi is my guess."

"Really?" Sister Agatha said. Richest man in Pryderi really wasn't saying that much, but George seemed impressed. Sister Agatha thought for a moment. The name rang a bell. *Tiffany's brother.* Father Selwyn had mentioned that he was at morning prayer. He had left for Kenya on the morning Tiffany's body was discovered. A phone call from Constable Barnes and he had turned around and flown back. Not too surprising that he was wealthy. Tiffany always looked as if she had money.

"On the library board." George said, scanning a book. "Wanted my opinion he did. Not many of that kind who would care what the senior volunteer at the library thinks, but he does. A sharp businessman. With him on the library board, we might just get our new wing."

"Oh? Well, I'm glad we have some interested citizens who care about the library." The truth was the public library was always in a budget crisis.

"I would think so." George pulled another book off the stack and, opening its back cover, scanned it. "There is a bit of gossip about his sister though. The one that died at the church." George shook his head. "A sad business."

Sister Agatha lifted her eyebrows but didn't speak. Everyone knew that gossip was the bread and butter of village sleuthing. She didn't want to interrupt him and miss whatever tidbit might be coming her way. George seemed to take her silence as encouragement to keep talking.

"Locked into a big estate fight with her, he is. The old battle-ax—not to speak ill of the dead. I heard she wanted everything. Even though the mother's will named both siblings equally. Or so I've heard. You can't trust everything you hear."

"Where did you hear it?"

"Parish council."

Father Selwyn might have more information, she thought to herself. Again she desperately wanted to whip out her notebook and take a few notes, but she had written MURDER across the front of the purple notebook and it looked a bit off-putting.

"And now that Tiffany has died . . ." She left the sentence open, hoping George might feel inspired to fill in with the rest of parish council gossip.

"So you can bet, Mr. Geddings there inherits the whole shebang now that his sister is dead. May she rest in peace."

Sister Agatha tried to look casual, but a sudden death in the middle of an estate fight where the murder victim had been a major beneficiary was just too much to take calmly. She needed to get back to Father Selwyn and ask him what he knew about Kendrick Geddings. She turned to leave and then realized that George was still talking to her.

"I was asking what you were wanting? Checking out a book?" he held up his scanner, his eyes questioning.

"Oh. I was checking in about the food drive. For Father Selwyn." The smallest of scalp tingling. Maybe there was hope for her ethics yet. "How's it going?"

"Not bad. I collected from the Brysons across the street. Three times I stopped by, and finally they were home. And you know what they gave me? Three tins of beets. Can you believe it? That is not what I call Christian generosity."

"Well, every little bit helps." Although Sister Agatha was always annoyed at the many tins of beets and creamed corn they received at the food pantry. And half of those tins were dented.

George leaned forward and said in a low voice, "But I did figure out where that young Mrs. Bryson goes of an evening." He gave a wicked grin. "Want to know?"

All of her training as a nun screamed no and all of her training as an amateur detective screamed yes. She said a quick prayer for forgiveness and croaked, "Tell me."

"The Bump and Grind out on the A7. Saw that red Volvo

the young wife drives in the parking lot. Twice now. On my way to the Tesco, of course."

Sister Agatha knew the Bump and Grind to be the locals' nickname for a bar off the highway. She wasn't sure of its real name because absolutely no one called it by its real name. It was known for seedy country music and cheap drinks. Not exactly a place the sisters would frequent. They preferred the much more tasteful and quiet Saints and Sinners Pub in Pryderi. And even then, just for the occasional Sunday brunch.

"Only one reason to my mind why a mother of four would be going to the Bump and Grind." George gave her a knowing glance.

"What would that be?"

"To meet someone, of course."

Sister Agatha said nothing, but personally she had to agree. Although the thought of it made her sad. She needed to find out exactly who Vonda Bryson was meeting. And was that where she was on the night of the murder? As she left the library she realized that Inspector Rupert McFarland was right. If you stop talking and start listening, you really will eventually hear something interesting.

* * *

Sister Agatha settled into her desk in the attic library and glanced out the window. The moon was rising above the apple orchard. Friday night at the end of a long day. She needed to work through her notebook and figure out what was what. Inspector Rupert McFarland always said that a good detective kept up with the paperwork—*Don't let your notebook go to seed,* he would emphatically repeat, *or you'll find yourself a day late and a dollar short.* The whole investigation felt like a complete jumble of information at this point, with nothing pointing to a killer. She decided just to work through each suspect one at a time.

Vonda Bryson. She was lying about her alibi and had been spotted engaged in behavior that was questionable perhaps, but not murderous. Going to a local bar—for whatever reason—did not make her a killer. However, it made her suspicious. And it could explain why she wasn't able to provide a truthful alibi. Who would admit to a nun that they were at the Bump and Grind on the same night her husband was out of town and kids at a sleepover? It didn't take a detective to figure that one out. But perhaps the manager of the bar would be willing to verify Vonda's whereabouts on the night of the murder, and then she could take her off the suspect list. Sister Agatha hoped so. She like Vonda and hated the thought that she might be the one who had killed Tiffany.

Ben Holden. Could it have been Ben who kidnapped Vincent van Gogh? Sister Agatha shivered just thinking about it. There was no evidence that it was Ben. The stack of crates didn't prove anything. Anyone could have grabbed one of the crates and used it. The whole dognapping incident was unnerving and had set the abbey on tenterhooks. Sister Agatha was convinced it was related to the murder, although she had to admit she had no idea how. But one thing she decided that she did know: it wasn't Ben. She drew a line through his name. He was officially off her list.

Millicent Pritchard. Sister Agatha liked the young woman—she seemed horribly shy and insecure to her. However, she thought, leaning back, shy and insecure wasn't Lucy's opinion of Millicent. Lucy viewed her as a highly competent artist and an interesting person. It seemed as though when standing on the beach with her easel, she was a different person than when she was in the village. Why? And what connection had she had to Tiffany? Had she admired her as an accomplished artist? Did she reach out to Tiffany and was rebuffed by her? Tiffany would not necessarily have chosen someone like Millicent as a friend unless there was something in it for her. Perhaps Millicent somehow stroked Tiffany's ego. So why lie about it? Sister Agatha made a note to find out exactly where Millicent was on the night of the murder.

Emeric Scoville. According to Bevan Penrose, Emeric was at the church at the same time the murder took place. Although, because he was all the way up in the choir loft with the organ going full blast, he might not have been aware of anything going on in the parish hall. So why did he lie about being there? Did he simply freak out when questioned by the constable? Sister Agatha knew that when questioned some people do simply lose it even if they are perfectly innocent. Or did the church organist have something to hide? She wrote in the purple notebook next to Emeric's name: *lying and at the crime scene the night of the murder.*

Kendrick Geddings. Interesting. There was absolutely nothing to link him to the murder. However, any detective worth her salt would add him to her suspect list. Engaged in an estate dispute over what appeared to be a huge sum of money and then the only other beneficiary ends up dead. Leaves for another country the morning after his sister's murder. Sister Agatha underlined his name in her notebook and added, "Ask Father Selwyn."

She tossed her Sharpie onto the desktop. Nothing really made sense. Lots of mild lying and a smattering of questionable behavior. Nothing pointed directly to murder. But then, in a murder investigation nothing ever did, until the end, and the end only came when enough hard evidence had been uncovered. Right now she was short on hard evidence but long on speculation and intrigue, and everyone knew that speculation and intrigue never solved anything.

Sister Agatha sighed. It was late. Time to pack it in. Evensong seemed like a long time ago and the nuns rose early. She needed to get to bed. Opening her top desk drawer, she slid in the purple detective's notebook. That was when she saw it—a single piece of paper, folded. She picked it up and scanned it. It was an article reprinted from the *Los Angeles Times*. The headline across the top read "The Big-eyed Children: Epic Art Fraud." *Art fraud?*

Forgetting her fatigue, Sister Agatha sat up straight and began to quickly read the article. She read with increasing interest the story of Margaret Keane and her husband who posed as the "real" artist. His wife did all the painting while he took the credit, along with all the money and fame. The really disturbing part of the story was that he imprisoned her in a sort of "art slavery," holding her captive by the use of seclusion and fear.

Sister Agatha finished the one-page article and sat back.

Someone had come up to the library, opened her desk drawer, and put the copy of the article inside. Who and why? She slipped it back into the drawer, then thought better of it. Folding the print-out twice, she slid it into the purple notebook and put the notebook back into her jumper pocket.

As she left the library that night, for the first time ever, Sister Agatha looked over her shoulder before turning off the light. Someone had been in her desk and left her a message. *In every crime, the murderer brings something in and he takes something out.* She closed the door and hurried down the stairs.

Chapter Seven

⁓

"She's a lounge singer at the Bump and Grind. Works Friday nights." Sister Agatha looked around Father Selwyn's study and breathed deeply. She had come into the village on an early Monday morning to check in with Father, but also to pick up supplies for the cheese production. It had been a frantic and exhausting weekend of cheese making at the abbey, with only a few hours off for prayer and meals. Here, things were peaceful. The electric fire burned in the grate. Sunlight was streaming through the stained-glass window, making patterned squares of color on the carpet. Someday she really was going to ask him about the cinnamon.

Father Selwyn poured hot water into the teapot and the fragrant aroma of Glengettie drifted up. A jumble of fishing tackle, sinkers, and fishing flies lay on the little table. On top of it all were Father Selwyn's sermon notes. He often tied flies while pondering that week's lectionary.

"You're kidding!" Father Selwyn said. "I thought you were sure she was meeting someone there? Which surprised me a little. Though it happens more often than you think."

"I *assumed* that was what she was doing. But then I thought about it. A romantic dalliance just didn't seem like Vonda. How would anyone with four small children have time for an affair?" Sister Agatha didn't know how anyone with four children would even find time to take a shower. "I went on the website just to do a little research and there she was. Vonda may not know this, but she's on the Bump and Grind Facebook page. A photo of her standing at the microphone. Lots of jet-black hair, a sequined top, really belting it out. Someone should peg her for the church choir." Sister Agatha poured out two cups of tea. She added extra cream and sugar. They both needed it, in her opinion.

"Vonda Bryson. A lounge singer at the Bump and Grind!" Father Selwyn shook his head. Taking the teacup from her, he sat back in the wingback chair.

"I figure it must be some kind of middle-aged mom sort of thing."

"Well, good for her."

"Why do you say that?"

"Because it's harmless and maybe she needs it. I mean, she's barely forty years old and she has four boys and a husband who's never home."

"Her stage name is Jasmine. So probably if you go there to see her, you'll have no idea it's Vonda Bryson, vice-chair of the WI."

"Well, we all need to let loose occasionally. I fly-fish. You write murder mysteries."

"I think that's a little different, don't you? I mean Vonda puts on a red sequined dress, a black wig, and belts out country songs while her husband thinks she's at the church doing committee work."

"Harmless. And if I were home all day with four children under the age of ten I might be a lounge singer at night too." Father Selwyn paused. "Or something like that anyway."

"I'm not judging her. In fact, I wouldn't mind catching Vonda's act if Reverend Mother wouldn't mind. Unfortunately, she's very particular about where the convent minivan is parked, and the Bump and Grind might not reach her high standards."

"So Vonda is off your suspect list if she was at the Bump and Grind Friday night?" Father Selwyn picked up his tea and looked at her over the brim.

Sister Agatha sighed. "Afraid so. Which leaves me down a suspect with no clear prospects for the murder." She stirred her tea and took a slow sip. "What do you know about Kendrick Geddings?" she asked. "I've heard that he and Tiffany were in a huge argument over their late mother's estate."

"Well, yes. Parish gossip."

"What are people saying?"

"That Tiffany wanted more than her fair share. But I don't know that there was any truth to it. Although . . ."

"Although what?"

"Well, in my experience, family members can be ugly following a death. Always about the estate, the inheritance. And they are often individuals you would never expect to act in such an . . . an ungracious way."

"Is Kendrick being ungracious?" Ungracious wasn't exactly murderous.

"No. Not at all."

"But then, what does he have to be ungracious about? The only other person named in the will is dead. Think about it. Inheritance is certainly a motive for murder."

"But did Kendrick have the means to get into the church and kill someone? It sounds a little preposterous." Father Selwyn took another sip of tea and, picking up a small remote, made the electric fire kick out moreheat. Sister Agatha noticed that he also made it crackle a bit louder. She shook her head. *Technology.*

"There's only one way to find out," she said. "Ask him."

"Ask him what? If he killed his sister?"

"No. Ask him where he was on Friday night." Sister Agatha paused. "I know he flew to Kenya the next morning. But Tiffany was killed around ten PM Friday night. That would give someone plenty of time to get to the airport in Cardiff. The only tricky part is to get an alibi without offending him or letting him know that you want an alibi."

"Good luck with that. And I think you're barking up the wrong tree with Kendrick. What else do you have? Anything?"

Sister Agatha filled him in on the mysterious article that appeared in her top desk drawer.

"Good heavens! Who do you think put it there?"

"It has to be someone with access to the abbey, but I've asked all the sisters and they say they didn't do it. And anyway, if one of them wanted me to read an article, they would have just given it to me, not hidden it in my desk. The only other person who would have access to the library is Ben Holden, and I can't imagine he would sneak around leaving things in my desk. And he would never open my desk drawer. He's very discreet."

Father Selwyn shook his head. "I have no idea." He picked the article up off the coffee table where Sister Agatha had left it. "I remember this scandal. She did all the work and the husband took the credit. And no doubt the money."

There was a knock at the door and Lewis Colwyn stepped in. Sister Agatha was a little surprised by his demeanor. His hair looked like it hadn't been washed in several days and his eyes were bloodshot. Had Lewis been sick? A terrible cold had been going around. Whatever it was, the middle-aged teacher, a favorite at the school and church, certainly wasn't his usual put-together self.

"Sorry to interrupt, Father Selwyn," Lewis said. "But I need to get into the kitchen and I seem to have lost my key." It was only then that he seemed to realize that Sister Agatha was even in the room. He nodded abruptly to her.

"Good to see you, Lewis. I've been enjoying your gardening blog—and I don't even really like plants. Unless they're chopped up and tossed in a bowl."

"Glad to hear someone's reading it," he said. "Bevan's gone home for the day and he's the only one who hands out keys. So unless you can give me yours, I can't get into the kitchen."

"Well, I can't give you mine because I may need it." Father Selwyn stood up and opened his top desk drawer. "However, I should have an extra."

"Thanks," Lewis said, nearly grabbing the key as Father Selwyn handed it over to him.

"Everything OK?" Father Selwyn asked.

"Yes, of course. I just wanted to clean that floor before anyone comes in." Lewis pulled the door shut behind him.

"It's just that everything has gotten weird—a dog is kidnapped, a mysterious article is left in my desk, a respected mom and church lady is moonlighting as a lounge singer, another young woman is a brilliant artist but denies it. And worst of all, a woman is dead and I can't figure out who killed her. Or even how she died." Sister Agatha stood up and looked around for her mittens. "I have to figure this out. And soon. But right now, Reverend Mother wants all of us at the abbey to deliver our annual Christmas gift to the residents at the Pryderi Care Center."

"What are you giving them this year, more knitted prayer shawls?"

"No, this year Sister Gwenydd headed up the committee and we have gone . . . a little more . . . shall I say, contemporary."

"Oh?" Father Selwyn sat up.

"We pooled our money and got them a giant flat-screen TV for the recreation room. And a year's subscription to Netflix, Brit box, and Hulu."

*   *   *

Sister Agatha left St. Anselm's and finished her shopping, buying two packages of rennet and several culture starters. The nuns ordered their cheese-making supplies through Let-Us-Eat-Vegan, which was more than glad to stock anything for the abbey. Stuffing everything into her book bag, she began the climb to Church Lane. As she left the village behind her, she couldn't help feeling as if the investigation had ground to a halt and that she was leaving the murder behind as well.

Vonda was no longer a person of interest. So that was one suspect off of her list. The dognapping was frightening, but she had no idea who could have done it. Millicent was lying about being an artist and was in the church the night of the murder, but that hardly made her the murderer. Emeric Scoville had lied about being in the church at the time of the murder. Or maybe not. The organist was well known for losing track of the time when he was practicing, and it could actually be that he really didn't hear anything up in the choir loft. She really needed to interview him. Emeric was so busy, like any church organist right before Christmas, that he was almost impossible to find. She made a mental note to stop by choir practice the next night.

Maybe the constable and medical examiner were right—this wasn't a murder at all. But what if it truly *was* murder? Then the killer was out there and might kill again. And finally, the mysterious article left in her desk was intriguing but far from illuminating. She was at a loss right now, but she would not give up. Maybe she just needed to dig deeper.

What would Inspector Rupert McFarland say? In a recent podcast, *The People We Love to Hate,* he had talked about how family members kill other family members. Could Kendrick and Tiffany be a case of sibling rivalry carried too far? Throw in the high stakes and emotional toll of an estate settlement and perhaps it had been enough to push Kendrick over the edge. Sister Agatha's mind raced as she plodded up Church Lane. What was the relationship between Kendrick and Tiffany? Were they terrible rivals or supportive siblings? Had they had to fight for every scrap of love in the family? Were they pitted against each other by obsessive parents or were they loved equally? And, in the end, as the parents grew old and died, which sibling did the lion's share of the caretaking?

She stopped again as she reached the top of Church Hill. Kendrick Geddings was a well-respected businessman in the village who had ties all over the North. Would he risk losing everything to murder his own sister? She thought for a moment, and Inspector McFarland's heavy Scottish brogue came to her: *Never underestimate a person's motive for murder. It can be as complicated as the discovery of a sordid love affair or as simple as the discovery that someone took the last piece of chocolate cake.*

Chapter Eight

~

The Girl Guides' Big Lunch in St. Anselm's parish hall was off to a roaring start. In fact, Sister Agatha was pretty sure that the parish hall hadn't seen this much activity on a Tuesday noon in a long while. According to Father Selwyn, the Bysowch Barod Cymru (Girl Guides in Wales) was launching a national campaign to bring people together in communities by sponsoring an event they called The Big Lunch. She looked around, taking in the chaos, conversation, and laughter filling a room where, less than a week ago, a dead body had lain slumped against the wall.

Just about everyone who owned a business on Main Street had been invited, along with the sisters from the abbey and the village police. She noticed that Constable Barnes had declined and sent his young deputy, Parker Clough. She recognized a few teachers from the school and one of the bus drivers.

Sister Agatha was a longtime supporter of the Girl Guides program in Wales, having been a Girl Guide herself. At age twelve, she had attended the Diamond Jubilee in Eisteddfod at Gregynog Hall, where over two hundred Girl Guides had gathered to greet Princess Margaret on her visit there. It was an experience Sister Agatha had never forgotten. Now she supported the Girl Guides as often as she could. Father Selwyn and Macie Cadwalader, the young female vicar at St. Grenfell, ran the St. Asaph Girl Guides together. She watched as the two of them tried to bring some order to the madhouse of Rainbows, all in uniform and thoroughly enjoying themselves.

Each invited guest had been instructed to bring their favorite food to share. And the Rainbows had wisely decided to invite Sister Gwenydd, who had brought along a huge roaster filled with lamb stew and an enormous tray of Christmas cookies. The guests sat at small tables scattered throughout the room, while the Rainbows poured tea, passed along plates of food, and generally ran around. It was bedlam, but Sister Agatha had to admit, quite fun. Apparently, after eating, the guests at the Big Lunch would be treated to a concert of Rainbow singing followed by a skit about healthy eating.

She found herself at a small table across from the young police officer Parker Clough. The young man had been at the crime scene and, in fact, was the same one who had arrested Sister Gwenydd the previous summer. Sister Agatha had just about forgiven him for putting handcuffs on one of the sisters. He was, after all, just doing his job. She observed him as he chatted with one of the Rainbows who stood next to the table. He was listening intently to her recitation of all the badges sewn on her uniform sash. Sister Agatha was impressed with his careful attention to everything the little girl said while complimenting her on her achievements—all the while trying to eat a plate of lasagna. And Officer Clough, who probably had a desk full of paperwork waiting for him at the police station, acted as though the seven-year-old standing in front of him was the most important person in his world.

"That's a lot of badges," he said to Sister Agatha when the little girl finished her recitation and shot off to join the other Rainbows. "She'll make deputy someday."

"You're good with children, Officer Clough."

"I come from a big family. The oldest of six. All sisters. And I think they were each in the Girl Guides at one point or another."

"So you grew up living with women?"

"I did. It's probably what drove me into the police force—the academy was almost all male the year I joined. Of course, there are a lot more women now." He took a bite of salad. "Which is a good thing," he added, his mouth full.

"I grew up with all brothers," Sister Agatha said. "And now I live in a convent with twenty other women. I wonder if that's what drove me to the convent?"

Officer Clough smiled and then cast an eye around the crowded room. "It's hard to believe what was in this room a week ago."

"I know." Sister Agatha responded, remembering Tiffany's body stretched out on the floor, the medical examiner taking notes, and Father Selwyn giving last prayers. "Is the constable looking into her death at all?" Sister asked.

"No. It's a closed case according to our office."

"Yes, of course." Sister Agatha thought that the young

man had more to say, but she wasn't sure how to pull it out of him. "What do you think, Officer Clough? In your professional opinion?"

He looked up, his eyebrows raised. Chewing and then swallowing and taking a long sip of tea, he still paused but finally said, "I'm not a detective, Sister. And Constable Barnes is very thorough. If it was murder, he would have pursued it as such."

Sister Agatha liked it that the young man showed loyalty to his boss, even though she knew his boss to be entirely wrong. "Well, of course. But there is room for error in any decision, is there not? Not that the constable was wrong, as such. But if you were the constable—as I am sure you will be someday— what would you offer as an opinion?"

"Well." He looked around again. "There was an earlier incident. And . . . it made me think." He paused. "I tried to get the constable to follow up on it. But you know how busy the office is right now." He stopped and took a drink of tea. "I don't think this is confidential because it was printed in *The Pryderi Post,* and so anyone who likes to read the police log could have read it."

Sister Agatha nodded. *The Pryderi Post* was the village's newspaper, not known for its accuracy to detail. She felt for her detective's notebook in her apron pocket but decided to let it stay there. Best not to have people see her madly scribbling in a book labeled MURDER. It could put a damper on the Rainbows' Big Lunch.

"Anyway," Parker Clough went on. "We had a domestic

call a few weeks ago to Tiffany Reese's house—the neighbors called it in—reporting a commotion next door."

"A commotion? What kind of commotion?"

"Screaming, shouting. We showed up, and it was Tiffany and her brother Kendrick. You could hear the yelling before we got out of the cruiser. Mostly obscenities at that point. I think the argument had been going on for a while. Domestic situations usually start off pretty calmly. Or they can. But as the fight or the disagreement builds . . . well, it escalates. And let's just say, bad things can happen."

"Did you feel that something bad was about to happen?"

"With a domestic call, you go in prepared for anything. Anything from verbal insults to blood."

"Was there blood?"

"No. Not at all. If there had been, we would certainly have made an arrest. But . . ." The young officer broke off.

"But what?"

"Usually when it's a man and a woman, you automatically figure that the man is the aggressor." Sister Agatha thought Officer Clough looked especially uncomfortable.

"And in this case?"

He leaned forward, casting a glance around for any stray Rainbows or village members who might be listening.

"So as we headed up the walk to the porch, the house went totally silent. I figured that they had noticed the cruiser and were taking a step back. You know, in order to look better when we came in. But suddenly, I had a bad feeling, and we just went in without knocking. It's a good thing we did."

He shook his head and leaned back. "It was Mrs. Reese. She had her hands around her brother's neck and had him backed up against the wall. He had turned blue and was collapsing. If we had gotten there two minutes later, he would've been dead."

*　*　*

"He refused to press charges. Even though what she did was basically strangulation. Or attempted strangulation." Sister Agatha was sitting across from Father Selwyn in his study. She had to admit, he looked knackered. Hosting a Rainbow Big Lunch was not for the fainthearted. Macie Cadwaladr had just left after staying to help clean up the parish hall. The event had been a huge success—great food, lots of opportunities to get to know one's neighbor, a concert of Girl Guides singing—a few of the songs Sister Agatha had remembered from her own years in the Girl Guides. But maybe the most important part of the lunch had been the conversation with Officer Clough. Kendrick Geddings had just moved to the top of her list of suspects.

"I can barely believe it," Father Selwyn said. "Yet you would be surprised how many of our best church families are living with domestic situations that are violent."

"But I never think about men being abused by women."

"It certainly happens. Maybe more than we think." Father Selwyn looked both thoughtful and disturbed. "My question is, was this the first time? Did it start out a simple argument that escalated into dangerous behavior? Or had Tiffany done this to her brother before?"

"According to Officer Clough, Kendrick told him that it had never happened and that they just had a big argument that got out of hand."

"Which could be true." Father Selwyn leaned back. "On the other hand, who knows. I've heard that before—*This is the first time. It'll never happen again.* This could have been the culmination of a long-simmering unhappiness between the two of them. I do know for a fact that she was challenging the will. I hate to say it, but the Geddings inheritance was a major topic of conversation at Senior Yoga yesterday."

"What did you hear?"

"Mostly that Tiffany wanted more than her share and that Kendrick was about to cave."

"If he was about to cave, then that could change things."

"This was gossip. I hardly think Senior Yoga participants are privy to the actual terms of the will or to the legal proceedings."

"What do you know about Tiffany and Kendrick's relationship?"

Father Selwyn blew out his breath. "Not much, really. Tiffany was very involved in the parish—as you know. But Kendrick, not at all. He lives in Wrexham and I seldom see him in Pryderi. I've worked with him on the Animal Shelter Board—he has a great love of animals and their welfare. I liked him. Although it's hard not to like a person who is devoted to rescuing unwanted dogs and cats. I also know he is a passionate runner. But that's about it. I may find out more tomorrow. I'm meeting with him to discuss the funeral service." Father Selwyn poured tea into her cup and then into his. "Why? What are you thinking?"

"I'm just wondering why a man in as good a shape and as athletic as Kendrick would allow a woman to shove him against a wall and nearly strangle him to death."

"You mean, why didn't he fight back?"

"Yes. Or something."

"The stigma, perhaps. Maybe he didn't want to physically hurt a woman. Or he didn't want it to get out that this was happening. Or . . ."

"Or what?"

"Or she really did overpower him. Tiffany was a big woman, very physically fit. And although Kendrick is a runner, he might have lacked the power to fight her off successfully. If you think about it, pound for pound, she outweighed him. Maybe he *was* her victim."

"And so, when he had the chance, he killed her. By some means that wouldn't involve brute force, and when she wasn't expecting it. And it would solve two problems for him—he would get rid of both an abuser and the only other beneficiary of the will in which he was named."

She waited for Father Selwyn to argue with her, but he didn't. Finally, he spoke. "What's your plan?"

"Find out where Kendrick Geddings was the night of the murder."

Chapter Nine

On her way home from St. Anselm's, Sister Agatha had stopped by the library to check the Wildcat database and to give some thought to a potential meeting with Kendrick Geddings. The sticky part about being an amateur sleuth was that you just couldn't walk up to a suspect and demand their alibi. Her fictional detective, Bates Melanchthon, had a much easier time of it by using all sorts of tactics. None of which would have met with the approval of Reverend Mother.

Sister Agatha sighed and leaned back in her desk chair. The screen in front of her was asking for her password. She slowly typed *SherlockHolmesmeetsArmandGamache,* her favorite daydream—the two detectives hanging out together in a pub sharing a pint, comparing notes. She sat back and waited, watching the screen. The Internet could be slow in Pryderi on a Tuesday afternoon.

The Pryderi library was small, but it was well used by the village and was lively with patrons at the moment. Her eye fell on the bulletin board, and she noticed that several of the fliers and posters were outdated. In a public library where most workers were volunteers, details like updating the bulletin board went neglected. No one had taken down the fliers advertising events for nearly a month. One caught her eye.

All Creatures Great and Small Late-Night Race: Run to help the Pryderi Animal Rescue. Friday, December 10. Start time 9 PM at the Animal Shelter. December 10th was the night that Tiffany was killed.

According to the flier, the race looped around the village and ended at the Saints and Sinners pub for some "post-race carbohydrates." Sister Agatha couldn't imagine running at all, let alone running at night. What was wrong with people? Why not just take a sensible walk in the middle of the afternoon? These days everyone went to extremes. Sister Harriet doing something she called "Hot Yoga," and now the people of Pryderi, running at night.

Sister Agatha caught her breath as her curiosity rose. Hadn't Father Selwyn said that Kendrick was a runner? And that he had served on the Animal Shelter board? Had he been at the Late-Night Race? Taking out her notebook, she began to write. Chances were good that he had been part of the race. Maybe even planned it. But did he run in it? And would that have taken him through the evening?

Turning back to the computer, she clicked out of the World Cat database and clicked onto Google. Entering *Late-Night Race Pryderi* resulted in an article from the online version of the Animal Shelter's newsletter. The lead article was a thank-you to everyone who participated and congratulations to the top five runners. She sat back. Kendrick hadn't just run in the race; he had won it. There was a picture of him sitting at the Saints and Sinners pub with a group of other runners, raising a pint in one hand and holding up a medal with the other.

He looked pretty happy, she thought, for someone who had just killed his sister. The race had started exactly one hour before Tiffany was murdered. Although the coroner said approximately ten PM, she knew that was a guess at best. Could Kendrick have run the race, gone back to the church, murdered Tiffany, then joined his mates five blocks down the street at Saints and Sinners?

She stood up from the computer desk and, gathering up her book bag, headed out the door. There was only one way to find out. Do what any self-respecting amateur detective would do. Make up a big story, stick to it, and see if you can get some information out of someone.

* * *

Michael wiped down the bar with a damp cloth and thought for a moment. It was mid-afternoon and the Saints and Sinners was almost empty. "No, he didn't come in with the others. I do remember that much pretty clearly."

"How do you remember?" Sister Agatha asked. It turned out that she didn't even have to make up a big story. Or any story at all. She had more than a passing acquaintance with the Saints and Sinners barman Michael, and he might be willing to talk with her. They had met the summer before when she investigated the death of Jacob, Michael's boyfriend. No big made-up story required. "Wasn't there a big crowd here?"

"There was. But he had won the race, you know. So all his mates were asking about where he'd gone off to. It was quite a rowdy group and they got drunk pretty fast. Anyway, when he came through the door they all started cheering for him and offering to buy him a pint. You know, for winning first place. But also, I suppose, because the fund-raiser had been a big success."

"Any idea what time he came through the door?"

"Ten thirty. On the dot."

"On the dot? You noticed?"

"I was hoping to get off early so I was watching the clock. No such luck though—I ended up closing."

"How long did Kendrick and his mates stay?"

"Until we kicked them out—right after last call."

Chapter Ten

Sister Agatha slid into the back booth. She had just finished an early morning meeting with the village librarians and had stopped by The Buttered Crust Tea Shop. Today's discussion had been interesting—how to interest teens in using the reference section. The librarians ended the meeting with the conclusion that they had no idea how to interest teens in using the reference section, but it had still been a riveting discussion. The meeting had ended a bit early—the people for the Thursday Morning Story Hour for Toddlers were pouring in, and she felt the urge to leave. She desperately needed a moment to think and no place was better for that than The Buttered Crust Tea Shop.

She opened the purple notebook and paged through her notes. She needed to find out from Kendrick himself if he would admit to the time lapse between ending the race and showing up at the pub. But how? She seemed to remember that Father Selwyn had said he was meeting with him about the funeral this morning—right now, in fact. She couldn't exactly crash the church office and start questioning Kendrick about where he had been the night of the race. She imagined herself as Bates Melanchthon. He would put it plainly to the suspect. "And where were you, sir, between finishing your race at ten PM and entering the Saints and Sinners Pub at ten thirty? Please account for those thirty minutes, if you will." In her mind, she could just imagine the suspect crumbling under Melanchthon's steely gaze and blurting out that he'd been at the church, killing the victim. *Crime solved.* She looked around The Buttered Crust. In her world, no opportunity existed to put the screws to anyone. And getting a confession out of Kendrick just wasn't going to happen. Even if he was guilty. Which she was almost totally certain he was. She picked up her mobile and texted Father Selwyn:

At Buttered Crust. R u meeting with KG?
A moment later her cell pinged. *ys. why?*
Ask him where he was between 10 and 10:30
    Friday.
What? how?
You'll think of something.

Sister Agatha opened her notebook again and, turning to a new page, wrote: "remaining suspects—*Millicent and Emeric. Possibly closing in on Kendrick.*" She spent the next half-hour going from her notes on the murder of Tiffany to the baffling double homicide that was puzzling Bates Melanchthon. She realized that she was really making no progress on either murder, fictional or real. It was a relief to close her notebook, when her mobile pinged: *Order my usual. Leaving the church now.*

She called over to Keenan. "A pot of Glengettie tea and a cranberry scone, if you will, Keenan."

"Father Selwyn joining you?" he asked, walking over and giving the table a swipe with his cleaning rag.

Sister sighed. In a village as small as Pryderi, it was hard to do anything on the quiet. "Yes. Father Selwyn is coming over from the church. He'll want his Glengettie." Keenan ambled off without saying anything.

A few minutes later Father Selwyn slid into the booth. "Did you get me my . . . ?"

"It's coming." She looked at him with eyebrows raised. "What did you find out?"

"Well, first of all, I want to say that sleuthing and pastoral care of the bereaved really do not go hand in hand. That being said . . ." he looked up. "Thank you, Keenan."

Sister Agatha watched while he poured tea into his cup and, adding cream and sugar, took a sip, then set the cup into its saucer. He broke the cranberry scone in two.

"So I wasn't keen on just outright asking, Where were you on the night of your sister's death?" Father Selwyn took a long sip of tea. "But, I didn't have to bring it up at all. He talked about it openly." He paused. "This is bordering on the confidential, but he did say that he felt terribly guilty that he was enjoying himself at the race and pub while all the while his sister lay dying from a heart attack on the floor of the parish hall not four blocks away. And then that he got on a plane early the next morning and left the country. He seemed very remorseful. Genuinely so."

Father Selwyn picked up a large piece of cranberry scone.

"I love it when it's full of cranberries like this. Nothing beats The Buttered Crust for baked goods." He popped it in his mouth.

"Did you ask him if he went straight from the race to the pub?"

"Believe it or not, I did. It came out sounding a bit funny. I mean, he probably wonders why I needed to know. But anyway, I asked. And he didn't hesitate. He said he did. They finished the race and drove right to Saints and Sinners."

"He said he went with the friends he ran with? Straight there?"

Father Selwyn nodded, his mouth full of scone. Sister Agatha watched as he took a long drink of tea. "His exact words were, 'And to think, we drove past the church on our way from the race. All I could think about was celebrating with my mates.'"

"According to Michael, Kendrick arrived at Saints and Sinners a full thirty minutes after the other runners got there." Sister Agatha opened her notebook and uncapped her Sharpie. "If I could place him at the scene, I would say it is time to go to the constable." She leaned forward and lowered her voice. "Here's what I think happened—he ran the race, which ended in the parking lot of the primary school. He left the school in his own car—not with his running buddies—then stopped at the church on his way to the pub and killed Tiffany, then continued on to Saints and Sinners. Where he apparently had a lot to celebrate."

"He did all this without anyone noticing?"

"What's to notice? Tiffany had every reason to be in the

parish hall late at night as the art show was the next day and she was president of the Art Society. And if anyone saw Kendrick Geddings stop at the church and go in, what would they think? That her brother was lending her a hand—probably." Sister Agatha made a note in her notebook. "I wish I had some way of knowing if he was seen going into the church."

"I keep telling the parish board that we need a security camera at the main doors."

"Would Emeric have noticed? According to Bevan, he was up in the choir loft the whole time."

"I doubt it. I can ask him."

Sister Agatha stood up and began gathering her things into her book bag. "Text me when you find out. I'm out of here. I can't be late for cheese."

Chapter Eleven

"Emeric said he heard a voice that sounded very much like Kendrick Geddings in the parish hall the night that Tiffany was killed."

The constable shifted in his seat behind his desk and shuffled some papers. "Died. You mean the night Tiffany died. There is still absolutely no evidence that Mrs. Reese did not die of natural causes."

Sister Agatha and Father Selwyn had hurried over to the police station as soon as Father Selwyn had talked with Emeric. Sister Agatha happened to be at St. Anselm's to borrow a few shepherd's crooks for the abbey's live nativity scene. She had talked briefly with Father Selwyn, and they had decided there was too much evidence—even though circumstantial—against Kendrick Geddings to not bring in the constable. And this final piece of evidence should convince him to investigate the case as a murder. But so far, the constable was less than convinced.

"Is this the same Emeric Scoville," Constable Barnes said,

"who told my deputy that he was nowhere near the church that evening, that he had left hours before the lady died?"

"It seems he withheld that . . . piece of information . . . for personal reasons." Father Selwyn said.

"He lied to the police for personal reasons? What sort of personal reasons?"

"Truthfully, I don't know." Father Selwyn and Sister Agatha looked at each other. They had wracked their brains as well as pressured Emeric to tell them why he had lied to the police. If he had been in the building, why didn't he just say so? But he wouldn't tell them. For Sister Agatha, it verified exactly what Rupert McFarland always said: *Everyone has a secret. Some secrets are just more interesting than others.*

"But Constable, wouldn't you agree that the important thing is that he has come forward now?"

"First of all, he hasn't come forward. I see a nun and a vicar in my office, not the church organist. And second, if he lied to the police, how do we know he is not lying to the clergy?" He looked at Sister Agatha. "Are you clergy, Sister? I mean, technically?"

At the same moment Sister Agatha said, "Yes," Father Selwyn said, "Not really." They looked at each other. "It doesn't matter," she added quickly. "What matters is that Kendrick Geddings was at the scene—a fact that he has hidden—and has been challenging the will in which the victim was the only other beneficiary."

She left out the part about Tiffany nearly strangling Kendrick, as she wasn't sure young Parker Clough was supposed to share that piece of information and didn't want to get him in trouble with the constable. "Don't you think it is time that you investigated Kendrick Geddings?"

"Investigated him? Why? Your proof that he was at the scene is based on a very shaky source and you are forgetting that there was no sign of a murder. So the event you are talking about is a poor woman collapsing from a medical emergency—an emergency that, according to the coroner, was a heart attack. I'm more interested in why Emeric has suddenly decided to incriminate another person—a well-liked individual in the village."

Sister Agatha noticed that the constable wrote *E. Scoville* across the top of his desk blotter. It might have been the first time she had ever seen him take notes.

Constable Barnes stood up. "Look, I appreciate your interest in this case." Sister Agatha noticed that he was looking at Father Selwyn, not her. "But it's nearly Christmas. Let's put aside all this talk of murder and death at least until after the holidays. Surely there is enough going on at the church and the abbey this time of year to keep you both busy. Without seeing murderers hiding in the holly." And with that, the meeting with the constable was over.

* * *

It was standing room only at St. Anselm's on the morning of Tiffany's funeral. Sister Agatha had arrived early and chosen a pew in the very the back of the church. From that vantage point she could see each person as they entered the church and sought out a seat in the pews. So far, most of the village had arrived. She watched as friends and family quietly entered—shedding coats and scarves as they walked down the long middle aisle looking for a seat in the already crowded pews. Tiffany, well known throughout the parish as a result of her involvement in the WI, the church, and all her civic groups, would have had a well-attended funeral under normal circumstances, but the fact that she might have been murdered added to the intrigue and to the size of the crowd.

Sister Agatha wanted a seat where she could see everyone, and the back pew was the best she could do. She wanted to run through her list of suspects in her head as people walked in. As Inspector Rupert MacFarland had said, *Don't neglect the funeral, laddies! A murderer loves to make an appearance at his victim's funeral.*

Sister Agatha watched as Father Selwyn entered from the vestry and took his seat behind the pulpit. The bishop, Suzanne Bainton, sat in the front pew. Sister Agatha was amazed again at how put-together Suzanne Bainton was. Tall, impossibly thin, with perfectly styled hair and expensive clothes, Suzanne Bainton was so beautiful and sophisticated that she looked nothing like clergy. Sister Harriet had once remarked that the bishop might have been a runway model who had gotten lost on her way to Paris and ended up in seminary.

Father Selwyn told her that the bishop wanted to participate in the funeral and so she would be doing the benediction and one of the readings. When Sister Agatha questioned why Suzanne Bainton should even attend the funeral, he had frowned slightly before telling her. Apparently, Tiffany's brother had given very generously to the St. Asaph diocese—a gift in memory of his parents. The gift had been large enough that it had impelled the bishop to leave her office and come to the funeral to pay her respects to Kendrick's sister. *It must have been a lot of money,* Sister Agatha thought. She had never known the bishop to show up for anything in the village. Sister Agatha didn't truly disapprove of the idea of Suzanne Bainton coming to the funeral, it was just that such behavior was so typical of the bishop. She was always thinking of money and budgets, revenue and connections. It seemed wrong somehow. The last bishop had been far more interested in the people of the parish, not the finances. On the other hand, when he retired, the diocese found itself in something of a financial mess. To her credit, Suzanne Bainton had sorted it out. *Take the good with the bad,* as Reverend Mother always said.

Sister Agatha tuned back into the funeral and listened as Father Selwyn read from the Book of Romans: *For whether we live, we live unto the Lord; and whether we die, we die unto the Lord: whether we live therefore, or die, we are the Lord's.*

Ah, she thought, leave it to the Apostle Paul to hit the nail on the head. She looked around some more, craning her neck to see the front pew. Could Inspector Rupert MacFarland be right? Did the murderer show up for the funeral? If so, that meant he or she was in the room right now.

Kendrick Geddings was sitting in the second pew with the few out-of-town family members. They were older by at least one generation than Tiffany or Kendrick. Kendrick seemed deflated, the wind knocked out of him. Sister Agatha had seen him when he came in the church, and he seemed genuinely distraught. But maybe he was distraught over the fact that he had killed his sister, not because she was dead. Sister Agatha felt a small pang of guilt over having such an uncharitable thought while sitting at a woman's funeral. But she couldn't just slip off her detective hat that easily, and Kendrick had had both the means and the motive to kill. She did notice in the funeral bulletin that all memorial gifts were to go to the animal shelter in Pryderi. And she had heard from George when she was at her last library meeting that Kendrick had given a huge gift toward the library capital campaign. Would someone so generous murder his own sister for the inheritance?

Sister Agatha watched as Millicent came down the center aisle—late—and looked around for a seat in the back, but, unable to find one, drifted forward. She finally slid into the conspicuous third pew. Millicent, as usual, was swathed in layers of clothes, only this time they were not fuchsia or purple but mostly gray and black—though she had draped an emerald-green scarf over her shoulders, giving her the appearance of a florescent swami. Millicent did not look as distraught as one would expect considering that she and Tiffany had been friends. In truth, Sister Agatha thought, she looked bored.

Father Selwyn continued with the liturgy, his deep voice filling the nave with the stirring words from the Book of Isaiah: *"The spirit of the Lord God is upon me, because the Lord has anointed me to comfort all who mourn."*

He continued in his rich voice until the first part of the liturgy was ended and the congregation rose to sing. Emeric launched into a stirring rendition of *For All the Saints,* and Sister Agatha felt the familiar sense of joy sweep over her. Not joy because a woman had died. And certainly not joy because she thought of Tiffany as a saint. Far from it. But a quiet joy because of the hope that the hymnwriter expressed.

For all the saints, who from their labors rest . . .
there breaks a yet more glorious day,
the saints triumphant rise in bright array.

The hymn began perfectly, but then the impossible happened. Emeric hit a wrong note. A jarringly wrong note. He quickly recovered and went on, but Sister Agatha looked up from her hymnbook just in time to see Father Selwyn glance into the choir loft. Emeric Scoville was such a stickler for perfection when it came to his playing that to hear him mess up was a bit of a shock. Was his mind on other things? Murder, perhaps? Sister Agatha desperately wanted to whip out her purple detective's notebook, but she resisted. Even she knew that a book with the word MURDER in big letters on the front wasn't exactly appropriate at a funeral.

The door that led from the sanctuary down to the kitchen opened and Sister Agatha watched as Vonda Bryson slipped through and took a seat in a side pew. Vonda had obviously been in the kitchen preparing the funeral dinner for Tiffany. Again, Sister Agatha wanted nothing more than to open her notebook and uncap her Sharpie. Again, she resisted. She wondered how Vonda was feeling. She had taken Vonda off the suspect list now that she had determined that the young mother was at the Bump and Grind the night of the murder. Looking at her sitting in the pew, Sister Agatha felt for her.

Vonda, pale and shaken, was staring at the page in the hymn-book, but she wasn't singing. Perhaps she was remembering her offhand remark about Tiffany's funeral dinner—the dinner that she was now preparing only a week later.

Sister Agatha turned her attention back to Father Selwyn who, she thought, in his black cassock and white surplice, brought an image of stability into the midst of a distressing death. She turned around at a slight disturbance behind her. Lewis Colwyn had stumbled while walking down the aisle in search of a seat. Unable to find a place to sit, he tried to crowd in with the Murdoch family, who finally squeezed together to make room for him in their pew. Sister Agatha wondered about the absence of his wife. Until recently, they had always been seen together, laughing, talking. They seemed to enjoy simply being together. But lately, his wife had been absent. Maybe that had something to do with Lewis' unkempt appearance. Perhaps things weren't so great at home.

Father Selwyn read again from the Book of Common Prayer. And then Suzanne Bainton rose and led the congregation in prayer. Both she and Father Selwyn descended the steps of the altar and stood next to the casket, now covered with the funeral pall. Sister Agatha listened to the ancient words of the commendation:

> *Into your hands, O Merciful Lord,*
> *we commend our sister, Tiffany,*
> *in the sure and certain hope*
> *that, together with all who have died in Christ,*
> *she will rise with him on the last day.*

And then, with the bishop walking behind him, Father Selwyn led the casket out.

* * *

From where she stood in the graveyard, Sister Agatha could just see the top of the big crane that had been moved to the construction site. The procession to the cemetery had snaked halfway up Church Lane to the small graveyard that overlooked the village. The sorrow of the moment seemed even worse because of the proximity of the construction site.

Father Selwyn spoke the final words of committal and the interment was over. Tiffany Reese had been laid to rest. As the mourners turned and walked back to their cars, the cold wind picked up and clouds covered the sun. Sister Agatha felt weighed down by one truth—she was nowhere near to solving Tiffany's murder.

The Gwenafwy Abbey sisters had decided just to walk back to the abbey as they were already so close. When they reached the wrought-iron gate, Sister Callwen asked Sister Agatha why she wasn't wearing her blue wooly hat on such a cold day. It was then that Sister Agatha realized she must have dropped it at the cemetery. She hated to lose her favorite hat, so she turned back, telling the others not to worry but to go inside and get warm, she needed a bit more of a walk anyway.

The cemetery was deserted by the time she reached it, and she planned to retrace her steps in her attempt to find her hat. But she stopped short at the entrance. Kneeling next to Tiffany's open grave was Lewis Colwyn. Uneven, wailing sobs shook his body. She stood and watched for a moment, unsure of what to do. Spotting her hat lying at the foot of a particularly interesting gravestone that she had stopped to examine on the way out, she picked it up and jammed it over her short, gray hair, without moving her eyes from Lewis. She hated to walk away and leave him there alone, but it seemed a very private moment, and to interrupt and offer him comfort would have been invasive. She turned and slipped back out the gate and headed up Church Lane, wiping tears from her own eyes.

* * *

Sister Agatha headed up the steep stairs to the library—the books for Sister Matilda and Lewis Colwyn's winter gardening class had come in and she wanted to get them labeled. Saturday afternoons at the abbey were usually quiet and she had high hopes of getting a lot accomplished.

Halfway up the stairs, she found herself thinking over the stirring words from the noontime prayer:

> *And God shall come down like rain upon the mown*
> *grass,*
> *as showers that water the earth.*
> *And the righteous shall flourish, and there shall be*
> *an abundance of peace*
> *so long as the moon endureth.*

Usually the sisters didn't observe noontime prayers. But it was something special that Reverend Mother was doing every day during this last week of Advent. Today's reading, Psalm seventy-two, read in Sister Harriet's lilting voice, had drawn her in: *An abundance of peace, so long as the moon endureth.* On late nights at her desk, watching the moonrise had become her norm. It was as if she and the writer of the psalm shared an understanding of what was important in the world—the constancy of the moon's nightly rise and the desperate need for an abundance of peace.

She also felt preoccupied with thoughts of Tiffany's funeral, including the sight of Lewis Colwyn sobbing at the grave. Had he and Tiffany been friends? She didn't think so. She had asked Father Selwyn about it, and he just said that tragedy affects different people differently. Maybe Tiffany's death triggered some old grief in Lewis. Sister Agatha wasn't convinced, but she didn't have anything better.

Reaching the top step realizing that she really needed to get back to the gym—her mobile pinged. She dug it out of her jumper pocket and, stepping into the library, read it. *If Reverend Mother can spare you, I could use some help. Emeric's been arrested. FS.*

* * *

Father Selwyn and Sister Agatha pulled up behind the police cruiser that was parked in front of Emeric Scoville's small bungalow. By the time she had made it back down the library stairs and located Reverend Mother, Father Selwyn had already turned into the abbey drive in his 1968 BMI Mini. After a quick consult with Reverend Mother and the other sisters, who were about to start the hanging of the greens, she had climbed into the tiny car and they had sped back to the village and Emeric's house. Emeric had frantically called Father Selwyn to say that the constable was searching his house and threatening to arrest him. Sister Agatha knew Father Selwyn felt a little guilty. They had gone to Constable Barnes about Kendrick, and now it was Emeric who was under suspicion.

Parker Clough nodded to her as she hurried past on her way up the cobblestone walk to the house. He was digging up the flower bed in the front garden. His face was stoical, but his eyes betrayed his concern. Something was wrong here. She remembered that Parker's youngest sister took piano lessons from Emeric, as did half the children in the village. She followed Father Selwyn through the front door, where they found Emeric slouched on a worn loveseat and Constable Barnes sitting across from him. The constable was perched on a chair far too small for his large frame. From the sound of it, officers were searching the house, and through the kitchen window she could see two other officers pulling up plants in the back garden.

"What's going on?" Father Selwyn asked, ducking his head under the doorway as he stepped into the small front room. The bungalow was an old council house that had been built right after World War II. It had three tiny rooms and a kitchen. Sister Agatha's parents had owned a house very similar to it once they retired from sheep farming. She took the seat next to Emeric on the sofa and clasped his hand in both of hers. Emeric gave her a desperate glance and went back to staring at the top of the coffee table. *Try not to look so guilty,* she wanted to say to him.

She had had Emeric on her suspect list simply because he had lied about his whereabouts that night. But she really couldn't imagine Emeric Scoville killing anyone. Even as she thought it, she could hear Inspector Rupert MacFarland's voice: *Always investigate! It's not what you can imagine, it's what you can uncover and prove!*

"I'm glad you're here, Father Selwyn," Constable Barnes said. "I have a few questions for you." Sister Agatha noticed that the constable completely ignored her presence. Well, if he wasn't going to pay attention, she might as well pull out her notebook and take some notes.

"First, do you mind telling me why you didn't mention your employee's criminal background on any of the several occasions that we talked about the death at your church?"

"Now see here," Sister Agatha broke in. "You needn't call him your 'employee.' Good heavens! You've been singing in Emeric's church choir for ten years. Call him by his Christian name."

The constable looked pained. "Alright then. When you hired Emeric as the church organist, did you know about his past?"

Father Selwyn glanced from Emeric to the constable. "What past?"

"His criminal past!" The constable almost exploded. Sister Agatha wondered if it really was good for his blood pressure to be this high. "Did you know that Emeric's real name is Michael Scoville?"

"Emeric is my middle name," Emeric said listlessly. "I started using it after the trial."

"Trial?" Father Selwyn said. "What trial?"

"You're telling me that you didn't know? You and the Sister here? All of your sleuthing and you didn't know that living right in the village with us is a man nearly convicted of murder?"

"I was acquitted. Twenty years ago." He turned to Father Selwyn. "I didn't think I needed to put it on my resume for the church musician job."

Father Selwyn looked at the constable. "How is all this relevant now?"

"After you left my office the other day, I had to ask, why would Emeric here lie to the police about being in the church? And when I couldn't think up a good reason, I had Parker run a check on him. Lo and behold, he was arrested once for nothing other than murder," Constable Barnes said, his voice almost squeaking. Again, Sister Agatha wondered if the constable was in perfectly good health. He seemed to be a candidate for a heart attack himself.

"Arrested or convicted?" she asked. "There's a big difference."

"Acquitted. But the facts are shaky."

"I didn't do it," Emeric said, looking from Father Selwyn to Sister Agatha.

"I believe you, Emeric," Father Selwyn said.

"And do you know *how* the murder was committed?" Constable Barnes looked as smug as Sister Agatha had ever seen him. And Constable Barnes' smug was not an attractive look for him.

"Well, of course we don't know," she said, annoyed both at Constable Barnes' attitude and at the fact that she hadn't discovered Emeric's past record herself. She should have looked into his background as soon as Bevan told them that he had lied. Why hadn't she? She knew why. Because she had broken the cardinal rule of the amateur detective. She had let her feelings get in the way of her investigation. The problem was she liked Emeric. Always had. "Well, are you going to tell us?" she said. "How was the murder committed—the one that Emeric didn't do?"

"Poison." The constable sat back and looked at Sister Agatha and Father Selwyn. "And not just any poison. He used aconitine."

Sister Agatha let out a low whistle. "*Aconitum napellus,*" she said. "The Queen of Poisons."

"You know it?" The constable looked surprised. And a little deflated, she thought.

"Of course I know it. Wolfsbane was one of Agatha Christie's favorite poisons. Not her very favorite—that was foxglove. But a favorite, nonetheless. It's a common plant found in most English gardens. Ingestion of aconitine makes it look as though the victim has died of a heart attack and . . ." Her voice trailed off. She and Father Selwyn looked at Emeric and then back at the constable. "But you didn't run a tox screen. So you don't know if there was any poison in Tiffany's system." Constable looked so self-satisfied, she could hardly stand it.

"Dr. Beese collected a blood sample, which she has sent away for a tox report. Upon receiving that report, we will know more about the cause of death. And Mr. Scoville's involvement." Sister Agatha sat back stunned.

"Dr. Beese collected blood?" she asked.

"She did." Constable Barnes hesitated. "Apparently, that's not entirely uncommon when the medical director is also a licensed physician. She thought that there was some potential for the death being considered suspicious. So, she drew blood before the body was embalmed."

"Well, then," Sister Agatha said to Father Selwyn. "I have new respect for Dr. Beese. Even if she is a little young to be a doctor."

"Do you have a warrant?" Father Selwyn asked.

"Of course I have a warrant. And it wasn't hard to get after I'd described Emeric's police record."

"Even so," Father Selwyn said. "All you have is conjecture. There are no actual facts. You can't arrest a man on circumstantial evidence."

"Unfortunately, he can," Sister Agatha said, flipping through her notebook and locating her notes from one of Inspector MacFarland's podcasts on the subject. She uncapped her Sharpie as she scanned the page. "An arrest can be made on probable cause, and probable cause can be based on circumstantial evidence even if it only indirectly indicates that a crime has occurred," she read from the page, trying not to look smug herself. "According to Inspector Rupert MacFarland, that is. However, as to holding him longer than forty-eight hours—that will prove tricky." She snapped her notebook shut and looked up. "Right, Constable?"

Constable Barnes sighed. "Right, Sister."

"Should Emeric get a solicitor?" Father Selwyn asked.

"That's up to him," the constable replied. "We're here to

search the house and see what we find. Even if we find nothing, don't forget that he lied to us, which interfered with a murder investigation."

Sister Agatha interrupted. "You weren't even investigating until Father Selwyn and I went to see you yesterday."

"In truth, Constable Barnes," Father Selwyn said, "you have nothing except a past acquittal."

"He was acquitted on a technicality. A goof-up in the courtroom concerning evidence. And the case went unsolved. The killer is still out there. And for all we know, the killer is sitting here in this house with us."

"Preposterous!" Father Selwyn boomed in his pulpit voice. Sister Agatha always noticed that it was hard to ignore Father Selwyn's pulpit voice. "You have next to nothing on Emeric. Not even evidence that Tiffany died of poisoning."

"And," Sister Agatha said, thinking quickly, "if you arrest Emeric, who will play for the St. Anselm's Christmas cantata? It's in three days and the choir's been practicing for weeks. Everyone loves the cantata. It won't seem like Christmas in Pryderi without the Christmas cantata."

It was true. The entire village turned out and filled the pews in St. Anselm's. For one moment, Sister Agatha thought she saw the constable waver. He had the solo in *O Holy Night*.

"That makes no difference, Sister. You know that."

"You would arrest a church organist during the last week of Advent? A good person like Emeric? Who has served this community faithfully for more than a decade? What about the children who take piano lessons from him? They have their annual Christmas recital coming up. Are you going to tell them and all their families that you've arrested their piano teacher?"

"What do you think they will say when they find out that their beloved teacher murders people with poison?" The constable's face had grown red and splotchy again. Perhaps, thought Sister Agatha, he hadn't thought through what it might be like to arrest someone so well-liked by so many people. She also realized that she felt annoyed with Emeric. It didn't look good that he just sat there staring. Just when the tension had grown almost unbearable, Parker Clough stepped into the room.

"Here you go, Guv," he said holding up a dried and shriveled plant with a bulb of frozen soil still clinging to its roots. He held it carefully, Sister Agatha noticed. Even in the midst of a murder investigation, the young officer was careful not to drop dirt on the carpet. "It matches the photo from the plant book. Wolfsbane. There's a whole patch of it in the back of the garden."

The constable stood up. "Can you identify that plant, Mr. Scoville?" he said.

Emeric seemed to shrink back into the couch. He looked at the plant and then buried his head in his hands. His long, delicate fingers, so adept at Bach and Vivaldi, entwined his unruly red hair.

"Please, Mr. Scoville." The constable's voice had lost its gruffness. "Emeric. Identify the plant."

Emeric sat up and looked into the fireplace. "Wolfsbane," he said. "It's Wolfsbane."

* * *

"But it doesn't mean he used it to murder anyone." Sister Agatha gripped the dashboard of Father Selwyn's 1968 BMI Mini as he sped past a lorry. The vicar was notorious for his white-knuckle driving. "It isn't illegal to grow Wolfsbane in your back garden."

"Did you see Emeric's face when the constable put handcuffs on him?" Father Selwyn said. "He was devastated. As soon as he can have visitors, we need to get to the jail and talk with him."

"And the tox screen isn't back yet, so we don't know for sure that Tiffany even died of poison. Have you given any thought to . . ." She couldn't bring herself to say it. Father Selwyn and Emeric had worked together for more than a decade. The relationship between vicar and church musician was often tenuous, but Father Selwyn and Emeric truly enjoyed each other and saw themselves as a team. She hated to say it, but what if it *was* Emeric? The evidence against Kendrick Geddings was stacking up. If she could make some progress on that end of things, it could prove Emeric innocent. If Emeric *was* innocent.

"Are you saying you think it could have been Emeric?" Father Selwyn twisted around in the front seat and looked at her directly.

"Eyes on the road, Father, *please.*" She clutched her seatbelt strap. "No. Of course not. But why did he lie about his whereabouts the night of the murder?"

"No idea. That's why we need to talk with him. Sooner rather than later."

"We need to meet with Emeric but also continue to build

up the case against Kendrick Geddings. I think the tox screen will show that no poison was involved. Emeric will be released in time for the cantata. And that will force Constable Barnes to take the case against Kendrick seriously."

Father Selwyn braked just in time to miss a flock of sheep crossing in front of him. "I do find your optimism encouraging." He paused. "Do you think that Emeric had any reason to want to . . . harm . . . Tiffany Reese? They certainly didn't travel in the same social circles. And I think that Tiffany, in general at least, was happy with the music at the church. Not that an organist would follow through with killing an unhappy church member."

"Tiffany was a soprano, wasn't she? In the choir? And that meant she would have been in the cantata, right?"

"Well, yes. But there weren't any problems. At least that had reached me. And are Christmas cantatas really that contentious?" They both looked at each other. *Yes. They were.*

Chapter Twelve

～

"I'm so sorry, Father Selwyn," Emeric said. Sister Agatha and Father Selwyn sat across from Emeric in the small jail cell. Father Selwyn had driven by the abbey and picked her up after evening prayers. Sister Gwenydd had wanted to send a tin of cookies, but Father Selwyn didn't think it would be allowed. "I've really let you down."

The atmosphere in the cell was grim. It echoed with a barren emptiness except for a gym bag tossed in the corner. The bag seemed full, with clothes and a toothbrush sticking out of it. "Constable Barnes went back to the house and packed it for me," Emeric said, noticing Sister Agatha looking at the bag. "And he brought over the score to the cantata. If they had a piano in this place, I would practice. I don't know when I will get back into the choir loft." According to Constable Barnes, Emeric wouldn't have a hearing until after Christmas, so he would spend the holiday in the village jail. The future of the cantata looked bleak. But Father Selwyn didn't seem concerned that Emeric wouldn't be back. Or maybe it was the least of his concerns at this point.

"I don't see how they could have any charges against you. You haven't done anything," Father Selwyn said. He sat on the wooden bench, leaning back against the cement wall. Sister Agatha half expected him to call out for tea. "And there isn't any evidence at this point that Tiffany Reese died from poison."

"When I lied about not being in the church the night Tiffany died and then also didn't report that I heard someone talking to the victim the same night, I interfered with a murder investigation. And that's enough to arrest me."

"Are you sure?" Father Selwyn asked. "That doesn't seem right."

"It is," Sister Agatha said. "Obstruction charges come into play when a person who is questioned in an investigation has lied to the investigating officers," Sister Agatha explained.

"Inspector Rupert MacFarland?" Father Selwyn asked. "Mystery Writer's podcast?"

"Inspector Barnaby," she replied. "*Midsomer Murders,* season six, episode two. However, at the time you lied, Emeric, it wasn't even a real murder investigation. The constable had declared that she had died of natural causes—a heart attack or stroke." Sister Agatha knew she was probably on shaky ground, but she couldn't accept the idea of Emeric as the murderer. "And what about the fact that Tiffany Reese's painting was missing? Constable Barnes can't blame that on you, can he? It's not like they found it in your house or anything."

"I don't know. I lied to the police, they found poison growing in my garden. And I was previously charged with murder by poison." They all sat in silence for a moment. The only sounds were the Christmas carols they could hear playing from the radio on the sergeant's desk down the hall.

Sister Agatha couldn't stand it any longer. "Why did you lie? Why not just say that you were up in the choir loft?"

Emeric hesitated a little long, in her opinion. She kept her eyes on him but opened her purple detective's notebook.

"I panicked. You know. After having been in a trial and all."

"Makes perfect sense to me," Father Selwyn said. "Panic can make people do all sorts of things." He paused for long moment and then locked Emeric in his direct gaze. "What I don't understand, though, is if you were accused of poisoning someone in the past, why would you grow the very same poison in your garden now? Wouldn't you want to distance yourself from poisonous plants completely?"

"Oh my God. You don't believe me either!" Emeric's eyes widened and his voice cracked. "I didn't plant it. I rent that house. The back garden was planted when I moved in and I've just let it grow. I barely knew what was back there. I'm not interested in gardening."

"OK. That's good. It's all you have to say then. That you had no idea it was back there." In Sister Agatha's opinion, Father Selwyn didn't sound convinced.

"I did say that. Very clearly. And yet here I am. Sitting in jail." Emeric's shoulders slumped and, blowing out his breath, he leaned against the wall of the cell. Suddenly, Sister Agatha felt sorry for him. But she knew that was a dangerous feeling. Empathy with a suspect was a slippery slope.

The bell in the clock tower had chimed ten times before

the three of them joined hands in a closing prayer. As she listened to Father Selwyn's comforting voice lifting up his petition for Emeric's safekeeping, she found herself wondering, just how innocent was he?

* * *

Sister Agatha pulled her woolly hat down over her ears. She and Father Selwyn had decided they needed to talk in complete privacy, and the church office was too busy on a Sunday afternoon. Privacy was hard to come by in a village as small as Pryderi, but one place it could be found was the footpath alongside the River Pwy. It was an especially private spot on a day when the temperature barely reached double digits.

The sun shone bright, but the air was bitter, and once again, she silently thanked Sister Winifred for her hand-knitted red jumper and matching mittens. Father Selwyn tromped along beside her in a long black duster that looked like it was left over from World War II. He had wound a bright-red woolen muffler around his neck. Sister Agatha thought he looked dashing and clerical and rumpled all at the same time. And more than a bit tired. She hated to see how depressed he had seemed after they left Emeric's jail cell the night before. If only she could do a little more sleuthing on Kendrick Geddings and so take Emeric off the suspect list. Kendrick still seemed a more likely murderer to her than Emeric. They walked in silence for a while, and finally she couldn't take it any longer. "What are you thinking?" she asked.

Father Selwyn stopped walking. He unwrapped his muffler and then, rewrapping it, gazed into the river, which was little more than a babbling brook. A mostly frozen babbling rook. "If you had asked me yesterday," he said. "I would have said that of course Emeric is innocent. Maybe I still think he is. But I did read the link you sent me about the trial. And, I have to admit, much as I don't like it, the whole thing wasn't as clear-cut as Emeric led us to believe."

Sister Agatha felt for her friend. If Father Selwyn was anything, he was a realist when it came to human sin. And murder was certainly a sin. In fact, it was up there in the top ten. Father Selwyn had been close to Emeric for years. And now it looked as though he had murdered someone in Father Selwyn's own church. If so, it was not just a horrendous act but a betrayal of friendship and trust. Tiffany, as annoying as she could be, was an active member of the church—the same church in which Emeric played the organ every Sunday. It was all very messy and, when word got out, would be devastating to the congregation. And a devastated congregation meant a lot of work for Father Selwyn as he struggled to shepherd them through it.

Sister Agatha said nothing, just stuffed her hands deep into her pockets. They turned into the wind and continued their walk. Snow blew up in gusting flurries and talking was almost impossible. But at least no one was listening in.

"What I can't figure out," she said finally. "Is *why?* What possible motive would Emeric have had to kill Tiffany?"

"Nothing that I can think of. Of course, Tiffany saw herself as an amazing soprano. And she wasn't. But a prima donna soprano is nothing new for a church choir director. And I hardly think that a difficult choir member warrants murdering."

"The sticking point for me . . . well, I have lots of sticking points with this murder . . . but the stolen painting doesn't make any sense."

"Are you sure it was stolen?" Father Selwyn took his hands out of his pockets and blew on them. "I need to ask Bevan if he has seen my gloves anywhere. I've misplaced them along with my hat."

"We have every reason to think that the painting was stolen. Lucy told me she had seen it on display in the parish hall late Saturday afternoon."

"Did the police find the painting in Emeric's house. Or were they not looking for it?"

"Interesting question." Sister Agatha stopped and, pulling a mitten off with her teeth, flipped through her notebook and managed to make a note without taking her other mitten off or letting the wind fling the notebook into the river.

"You would think that whoever killed Tiffany would have been who took the painting. And if Emeric is guilty, then the painting would be in his house."

"Not necessarily. He would certainly have pitched it. Incriminating evidence."

"But why?" Father Selwyn said, repeating her question. "Why would Emeric want the painting in the first place or, for that matter, want to kill Tiffany?"

"And a week before the cantata. Who murders their first soprano a week before the big show?"

"And what about all the strange things that happened at the abbey? The dognapping, your mysterious article in your desk drawer? Emeric couldn't have done any of that."

Sister Agatha thought Father Selwyn was grasping at straws. It was true that things at the abbey were a bit topsy-turvy, but that didn't prove Emeric innocent. In truth, she felt that Father Selwyn was striving to prove his friend innocent because he couldn't stand the thought of the alternative.

"My instinct tells me that it's all connected. But I have no actual evidence." She paused. Her mobile was buzzing and she retrieved it from her pocket, fumbling with her mitten. She glanced at the screen. "Reverend Mother. She says to return to the abbey." She looked at Father Selwyn. "And to hurry. It's an emergency."

*   *   *

For the second time in two days, Father Selwyn pulled the BMW Mini in behind the constable's police cruiser. They both jumped out and hurried into the kitchen. Sister Gwenydd met them at the door, her face nearly as white as the flour on her apron. "It's Lucy. They're all in Reverend Mother's office."

Sister Agatha and Father Selwyn ran up the stairs to the second floor and then down the wide hall, their footsteps echoing, and burst through the door. Lucy sat in the wing-back chair, Vincent van Gogh on her lap, her eyes red. Parker Clough sat across from her. He looked more perplexed this time than anything. Reverend Mother sat behind her desk gripping a basketball, her most effective stress reliever, second only to prayer, in both hands. Reverend Mother often tossed it from hand-to-hand during moments of anxiety. "Sister Agatha, good. You're here. And Father Selwyn. We could use a little pastoral care right now."

"What's going on?" Sister Agatha asked, looking from one to the other. Parker Clough handed Sister Agatha a small piece of paper. "This was found in Lucy's studio."

Sister Agatha took the note, prepared for the worst.

On it was typed in heavy type the words: *SURR/NDER DOROTHY OR DI/* Surrender Dorothy or die? And what's with the missing *e's?* She handed it to Father Selwyn.

"It's from . . ." he said.

"The Wizard of Oz." Reverend Mother said.

"I was going to say, 'My typewriter.'" Father Selwyn looked up. "I would know my Remington Rand anywhere." Sister Agatha noticed that Parker Clough was making a note. At least he was detective enough to recognize a clue when he saw one. She opened her own detective's notebook and, uncapping the Sharpie, wrote, "Check Father's Remington."

"Where exactly did you find it?" Sister Agatha, asked.

"I went into my studio—my *locked* studio—and it was taped to my easel." Lucy wrapped her arms around Vincent van Gogh. The dog was asleep, oblivious to the commotion around him.

"Didn't the Wicked Witch say just 'Surrender Dorothy,' but not the rest?" Sister Gwenydd asked.

"In the original screenplay, these were the exact words," Parker said. "They changed it for the final production." Sister Agatha made a note. Officer Clough a *Wizard of Oz* expert. Who'd have thought?

"It's not a joke, do you think?" Father Selwyn said, his brow furrowed. "I mean, if you want to scare someone, would you quote . . . who is that?"

"The Wicked Witch." Sister Agatha said, without looking up from her notebook.

"Of the West." Sister Gwenydd added. "That's important. I mean, it's not like its Glenda the Good Witch."

Parker Clough nodded. "No. This person is not Glenda the Good Witch. Not if they break into locked rooms on private property they're not."

"And if it is meant as a joke, it's not one I find particularly funny," Reverend Mother said, setting down her basketball. "Not in light of the fact that no one in the abbey would write it. And certainly no one would go into Lucy's studio—which all the sisters respect as personal space." Sister Agatha nodded her assent to that as well. The sisters at Gwenafwy Abbey took personal space very seriously.

"Are you sure you haven't rubbed someone in the village the wrong way? Gotten off on the wrong foot somehow?" Parker Clough said, turning to Lucy.

"No. I don't think so," Lucy said.

"What about when you went to the meeting of the Art Society?" Sister Agatha asked. "When you were guest speaker?"

"That went fine. I mean except for the one lady who didn't seem to like me. But I shouldn't have critiqued her painting. I thought she wanted advice, but she probably didn't."

"Which lady didn't like you?" Parker Clough asked.

"Tiffany Reese."

He looked at Reverend Mother and then back at Lucy. "When was this?"

"Last Friday night."

"The night Tiffany was killed," Sister Agatha added. She

kept her eyes on Officer Clough. He was thinking so hard she wondered if he was in pain.

He stood up and closed his notebook. "I'm sure the note is harmless. I'm not saying it isn't scary. And I don't like it that someone broke in. But usually anyone who writes a note isn't likely to follow through. Are you quite sure that you did indeed remember to lock that door?"

"The door was locked. I'm certain."

"Whoever left the note knew the abbey grounds. And they also had to have known when Lucy was in her studio and when she wasn't." Reverend Mother picked up the basketball and began to toss it from hand-to-hand again.

"Well, that's just the thing." At this point, the young officer looked decidedly uncomfortable. "It's nearly impossible for a complete stranger to have done this. And the dog kidnapping as well."

"What are you saying, Officer?" Reverend Mother's tone had gone frosty. She caught the basketball and sat holding it in both hands.

"Don't take this the wrong way, but it seems as though it might have been one of your nuns, Reverend Mother."

"Are you saying that one of the sisters placed a threatening note on Lucy's easel? That one of the sisters of Gwenafwy Abbey would have set out deliberately to frighten her with a ridiculous note from the Wicked Witch?"

"Of the West," Lucy said quietly.

"Are you actually suggesting," Reverend Mother continued, her voice rising slightly, "that a sister of Gwenafwy Abbey would have trapped a defenseless dog in a crate and left it out in the cold to die?" The room was now more than frosty. It was arctic. Perhaps, Sister Agatha thought, it was Parker Clough who should now surrender.

"I'm not accusing anyone . . ."

"You most certainly are. You are accusing one of us."

"I'm just saying that I don't think we should rule anyone out. Have a talk around, Reverend Mother. Ask a few questions about how people are feeling." He pulled on his parka and looked longingly at the door.

"Is Lucy in any danger?" Father Selwyn asked.

With one hand on the doorknob, Parker turned. "No. I wouldn't think so. A person who leaves an anonymous note, especially one quoting the *Wizard of Oz,* doesn't want a real confrontation. They just want to scare her off." He paused. "Although . . ." he started to add. "No. Ridiculous."

"What's ridiculous?" Sister Agatha asked.

"Well, think about it. The wicked witch in the movie does steal the little dog."

"Toto." Lucy said. "But Vincent van Gogh is a miniature pinscher. I forget what Toto was."

"Cairn terrier," Sister Gwenydd contributed. "And the witch puts him in a basket. Which is like a crate."

Sister Agatha stopped writing. *Good heavens, she thought. Why didn't I see that? Out-sleuthed by Sister Gwenydd.* She shook her head.

"Which was when Dorothy decided to run away," Parker Clough continued, looking directly at Lucy.

"Well, I'm not running away." Lucy said. "I'm freaked out a little, and this isn't what I signed on for when I came here.

But I am not going to be frightened by some creep who leaves cryptic notes and tries to hurt defenseless dogs."

"Good for you, Lucy." Sister Agatha found that she liked the young American girl more and more. She seemed to have a bit of spirit about her. Obviously Welsh by birth.

"You think it was the same person, then?" Father Selwyn said.

Lucy looked at him with surprise. "Yeah. Of course. Don't you?"

"I wouldn't jump to that conclusion." Parker Clough said. Sister Agatha rolled her eyes so hard it hurt. "There is no evidence that links the two."

"You just said that it was all from the movie. That certainly connects the dognapping and the note, right?" Sister Agatha's mind was racing. What about the letter in her desk? And the real question, did any of this have to do with the murder in the village?

"I'm just saying hold off a bit. We don't have a lot of facts here. Now, if you don't mind, I need to get back to the office." Parker Clough opened the office door. But before he stepped into the hallway, he turned back, "Father Selwyn, a word, please."

Sister Agatha waited while both men left the room, the door closing behind them. She turned to a fresh page in her notebook and, with her Sharpie poised, looked at Lucy. "Could you walk me through the whole thing, Lucy? Start at the beginning."

"There's not a lot to say. I came up to my studio after noon prayers. I thought I would attend. You know, the prayers."

"Why did you suddenly decide to attend prayers?"

"Well, I'm not big into prayer like all of you. But it seemed like it might focus me." Sister Agatha noticed that Reverend Mother smiled slightly.

"Actually," Sister Agatha said. "Start at the beginning of the day. Trace your steps for me from the time you got up this morning."

"Well, today was just a normal day. I got up early—around six. I know you guys get up earlier than that. Anyway, I got up. Took Vincent out for his walk.'

"Did anyone talk with you or see you on your walk?"

"I ran into Ben. He was at the barn. Vincent likes the meadow by the orchard for his morning walk. Since there aren't any sheep there, I let him off the leash for a few minutes."

"Did Ben say anything to you?"

"Not really. He always touches the brim of his hat—you know, in that old-fashioned way of his. But I don't think he actually spoke." Ben was known to be a man of few words.

"Then what happened?" Sister Agatha looked up from her notebook at the sound of Father Selwyn's voice on the other side of the door. She was so focused on Lucy that she hardly thought about it. Suddenly she realized that he was nearly shouting, something Father Selwyn never did. Except at the telly during the World Cup or maybe at Paul Hollywood on the Great British Bake Off. She forced herself to turn back to Lucy. Reverend Mother and Sister Gwenydd were staring at the door.

"Then I came back to my room. I put Vincent van Gogh

in his crate with a biscuit. It's his morning routine. Then I left to come down to breakfast. I know that I locked the door."

"Had you gone into your studio at all at this point?"

"No. After breakfast, I got Vincent out of his crate and took him over to the studio with me." Lucy paused. "I worked all morning with one break—a walk at about ten. Then lunch—he was back in his crate—and noontime prayer."

"Did you see anyone on the abbey grounds whom you didn't recognize?"

"No. In fact, I saw hardly anyone. Except Sister Gwenydd, because I stopped by the kitchen around ten in the morning just to say hello." It now was obvious that Father Selwyn and Constable Barnes were having a heated conversation. Reverend Mother looked toward Sister Agatha, her eyebrows raised. Sister Agatha shrugged.

"Has anyone been on the abbey grounds today, Reverend Mother? A workman? Plumber?" Sister Agatha asked, also looking at the closed door.

"No one. As far as I know. I was up here in my office all day. Dealing with paperwork, phone calls, the usual. The rest of the sisters have been occupied either in the cheese barn or in the village. A few were visiting at the care center. I believe Sister Harriet was at her drawing board.

Sister Agatha turned back to Lucy. "Then what? After noon prayers?"

"Then I went upstairs to my studio and the door was closed and locked. Like I left it." Sister Agatha nodded. Lucy was notoriously private about her work. "And there it was." She nodded toward the note in Reverend Mother's hand. "On my easel." Lucy looked down at the dog sleeping in her lap. She stroked his silken ear.

"And Vincent?" Sister Agatha asked.

"In his bed in the studio, totally fine."

Sister Agatha tapped her Sharpie on her notebook. The last thing she felt like doing was to agree with Parker. Yet it did seem pretty clear that only someone with access to the abbey, a master key, in fact, could walk around unnoticed—except maybe during noontime prayer.

"Reverend Mother, was anyone missing from the chapel at noon?"

Reverend Mother looked decidedly unhappy with the question. "I hope you are not following the officer's idea that it was one of the community?"

"Of course not. I just . . ."

"Well, Sister Winifred was in the cheese barn. And you were . . . where were you, exactly?"

"I was with Father Selwyn."

Reverend Mother frowned. "That only leaves Sister Callwen, and that thought is ridiculous."

"I agree. If Sister Callwen dislikes you, she tells you to your face. She would never leave a note."

Everyone turned as Father Selwyn came in the door, his face ashen. He looked at Sister Agatha and then at Reverend Mother. "What is it, Father?" Reverend Mother gestured to a chair. "Sit down. You look pale."

"The tox screen came back," he said, still standing. "They found traces of poison in Tiffany's system. *Aconitum napellus.* It causes death by ventricular arrhythmias or . . . ," he looked down at his notes. "Paralysis of the heart or respiratory center." He paused, looking truly ill. "The same poison that Emeric had in his back garden. And . . . ," his voice trailed off.

"And what?" Sister Agatha asked, not even opening her notebook.

"And *Aconitum napellus* is the same poison that Emeric was accused of using twenty years ago."

* * *

Sister Agatha sat at her desk staring out of the mullioned window. The clouds had hung low all evening, and now the night sky was black as pitch. A harsh wind rattled the pane. The words to the Advent hymn sung at compline echoed in her head.

> *In the bleak mid-winter*
> *Frosty wind made moan;*
> *Earth stood hard as iron,*
> *Water like a stone;*

The bell in the village clock tower chimed, its clear sound carrying across the cold night landscape. The meeting in the kitchen had ended badly. Father Selwyn had been nearly inconsolable. He had called Emeric's solicitor and then made plans to stop by the jail on the way home from the abbey. She wondered if it wouldn't be possible for Emeric to still play the cantata at St. Anselm's, but of course that was ridiculous. He had been accused of murder. She also tried to reassure Father Selwyn that there was little solid evidence against Emeric. Yes, Tiffany had been poisoned, but there was no solid physical evidence linking the poison she ingested to Emeric. Although they both knew that a good prosecutor could make the case.

Sister Agatha could not get Kendrick out of her head. Kendrick was at the church at almost the exact time of Tiffany's death—although the only witness, Emeric, was now accused of the murder. If she could only gather a little more evidence on Kendrick, she might be able to make a case that would help Emeric. And maybe even in time for the Christmas cantata. There had to be something she had missed. Her eye fell on the notes she had taken on Lucy. She sat back and thought for a moment, wishing desperately for a cup of tea but too tired to go down to the kitchen to make one.

She went over everything in her head: Lucy had had a negative interaction with Tiffany—but then so had half the village. Sister Agatha suddenly realized that Dorothy in the *Wizard of Oz* had also—in a manner of speaking—had a negative interaction with the Wicked Witch. And it was right before Toto was stolen just as Vincent was stolen. *Too much of a stretch? Maybe.* Then, less than a week later, a poison-pen letter left in Lucy's studio, Tiffany's murder, the kidnapped dog, the note, the wicked witch, poison, a church organist in jail, a mysterious article left in Sister Agatha's desk.

That article was especially puzzling. She had asked the other sisters, and no one claimed to have left it. Sister Gwenydd had shown the most interest. But if Sister Gwenydd had wanted her to read the article, she wouldn't have mysteriously left it in her desk. Someone from outside the convent left it. She was sure of that. But why? And who?

Suddenly she shivered. What if the same person who left her the article was the writer of the poison-pen letter? And the same person who kidnapped Vincent van Gogh? And maybe even the person who poisoned Tiffany? If that were true, then the murderer was slipping unnoticed into the abbey grounds and knew the nuns' schedule. Which meant the person was watching them. She shivered again and glanced at the closed door of the library. Between her and everyone else in the abbey was a long, dark stairway followed by a long, dark hallway.

She closed her eyes, her heart racing. *Lord, in Your mercy,* she finally whispered. *Protect all who dwell in this house.*

Chapter Thirteen

Sister Agatha breathed deeply as she stepped through the door of the Buttered Crust Tea Shop. Monday morning's baking had just come out of the large convection oven at the back of the kitchen. The fragrance of warm bread, mixed with the cheerful banter of the early morning crowd, was heartening. She had read an article in the *Huffington Post* saying that just the smell of freshly baked bread has such a profound effect on a human being that it has the power to make someone a nicer, kinder person. She believed it. The aroma of the Buttered Crust always left her with a small glimmer of optimism. And there was nothing like optimism to make you a better person. She pushed her way across the crowded room to the back booth, where Father Selwyn sat staring at an untouched cup of tea.

She had left Gwenafwy Abbey as soon as morning prayers were over and headed for the village to pick up supplies for Sister Gwenydd at Lettuce-Eat-Vegan. Walking into the village had always been a refreshing way to start the day, but now it was ruined by the devastation she felt as she walked past the construction site—mud frozen in jagged ruts, a deep gaping hole. The words of Devon Morgan came back to her every time she walked past it. "Development is just what North Wales needs," he had insisted in his smooth, politician's voice. Again reading the sign, DRM Industries, she had stopped at the edge of the Lane and, pulling off her mittens, made a note in her purple detective's notebook: *Check on DRM.*

Sister Agatha pulled off her hat and mittens as she slid into the back booth. Christmas music floated over the cheerful buzz of the breakfast crowd.

"My apologies," Father Selwyn said. "I didn't even order your usual."

"That's OK. Keenan just automatically brings it over when he notices that I'm here."

"Well, with Keenan, noticing a customer could be the problem."

"How are you?" she asked. He didn't look good.

"Worried. The constable is so set on the killer being Emeric he won't listen to reason. Or consider anyone else."

"I haven't given up on Kendrick. He seems guilty. Truthfully, Emeric and Kendrick both seem guilty. Constable Barnes is probably hoping to get a confession out of Emeric that will lead everyone to a discovery of hard evidence."

Keenan ambled over and they stopped talking as he slid a cup of tea and a Welsh cake in front of Sister Agatha. She smiled her thanks and scooped sugar from the sugar bowl into her tea. She liked it that the Buttered Crust Tea Shop still used sugar bowls and spoons. No little paper packets for them. She poured cream from the little pitcher. And none of that powdered business for cream either. Sister Gwenydd had tried to get Sister Agatha to switch over to soy milk for her tea. No chance.

Father Selwyn turned to the young waiter. "You know, Keenan, I think I will have a cranberry scone. With extra butter. A morning like this calls for pastry."

Keenan glanced at Sister Agatha then down at his shoes. They watched as he didn't move. Next his gaze went out the window. Finally he cleared his throat.

"What is it?" Father Selwyn said. "A cranberry scone. Don't tell me you don't have any today?"

"No. It's not that." Keenan heaved a great sigh. "You know, Father Selwyn, that Bevan is my cousin."

"Yes, I knew that."

"And that makes his mother my mother's sister."

"Keenan, I know your family tree. What are you getting at?"

"Bevan told me you're off scones and I could only bring you fresh fruit. So . . . today, it's banana slices with pineapple."

Father Selwyn sighed and, closing his eyes, slumped back in the booth. "Bananas with pineapple it is then."

Keenan turned and sauntered back to the counter, seemingly unaware of the customers still waiting to be noticed. Sister Agatha slid her oatcake across to Father Selwyn. He took half of it.

"Bevan's the best thing that ever happened to that church office, but I think it's time he and I have a talk about boundaries. Sicking the wait staff at the Buttered Crust on me is a bit over the line."

"Don't worry. I'll keep you well supplied with all things made of butter and cream." Sister Agatha did not believe in diets. "I have to tell you, I'm growing increasingly worried about the abbey. I mean, think about it. In order to kidnap the dog, leave the note, and stick the article in my desk drawer, you would have to know when the sisters are at prayer, or meals, or all working together in the cheese barn. The dog was stolen during breakfast and the note left during noontime prayer. I don't know exactly when the article was left in my desk."

"I hate to ask . . ."

"No. It can't be. What member of the abbey would do any of these things?"

"Ben?"

"Maybe. But I don't think so. I can see why he might not like the little dog. Though an act of cruelty seems way out of character. But why would he care that Lucy is here at the abbey? And would Ben ever leave a note quoting the Wicked Witch of the West?"

"That is pretty preposterous, I agree."

"This whole thing has gotten way out of hand. A week ago, everybody but me thought that Tiffany had simply had a heart attack in the parish hall—upsetting and tragic, but not dangerous. A week later, the abbey is being threatened and it is pretty clear that Tiffany was murdered."

Keenan walked up and slid a bowl in front of Father Selwyn. It contained six or seven rather pale-looking pineapple chunks.

"I thought you said you had bananas."

"Out of bananas."

"These pineapples are from a tin."

"They say tinned's just as good as fresh. Only it's . . . you know . . . tinned."

They watched as Keenan turned and walked away. Father Selwyn sighed and picked up his spoon.

"And if all of that isn't bad enough," Sister Agatha went on, "DRM Industries seems intent on continuing to dig up the meadow. It's on a temporary shutdown, but there were several guys out there yesterday walking around with clipboards. It didn't look like they were planning on moving out." Sister Agatha took the last bite of oatcake and stood up. "I saw that snake-in-the-grass Devon Morgan on the news last night. He was talking all about his family values campaign."

"I saw it too. I hate these candidates who go on and on about the moral decay of society. It's as if they just discovered man's sinful nature and somehow electing them to office will change everything."

"I thought Sister June was going to implode when he said that he was bringing family life into accord with biblical law."

"He said that?" Father Selwyn frowned into his teacup. "I don't mind a values-driven campaign. We need values in Wales. But not his so-called values."

Sister Agatha squashed her hat over her short gray hair. "He's not even Welsh."

"So you've said," Father Selwyn looked into his fruit bowl and sighed.

"I need to get back to the abbey," Sister Agatha said, pulling her mittens out of her coat pockets.

"And I'm going to have some lovely tinned pineapple."

"Go easy on Bevan," she said, smiling at her old friend. "Good help is hard to find."

* * *

Sister Agatha set off toward the abbey, walking quickly in the bright, late morning sun. She had to get back to help out with the cheese orders. With Christmas four days away, yet more orders had poured in.

The ten-minute walk back to the abbey was the perfect time to really think through the case. The most significant and troubling piece at the moment was that someone was targeting Lucy. But why? Who even knew the young artist from America? She realized with a start—*how well did any of them really know Lucy?* She was sure that Reverend Mother had done at least some vetting of the new tenant. But she also knew that the abbey was fairly desperate to bring in revenue and that Reverend Mother might have taken anyone with decent credit and the promise to put the abbey on auto-pay. On top of that, the nuns at the abbey were notoriously trusting. Hadn't they blindly embraced Sister Gwenydd even after she'd told them that she thought she had killed her boyfriend? In any case, she needed to talk to Lucy again, and sooner rather than later. And maybe digging deeper into the events at the abbey would shed some much-needed light on the events in the village.

As she started up the long gravel drive that led off Church Lane to the abbey, she felt her phone vibrate. Reluctantly pulling off her mitten, she fished the mobile out and read the text. It was from Reverend Mother. *Where are u? Cheese barn! ASAP.*

* * *

Sister Agatha had barely stepped through the door of the cheese barn before Sister Winifred thrust a dustpan into her hands. "Wax explosion," she said shortly. "Start scraping." The orderly cheese barn with its gleaming stainless-steel counters, shining tile floors, and meticulously organized shelves looked like a war zone. Spatters of red wax covered nearly everything, including a patch on the ceiling above the stove. Even the small crucifix on the east wall was covered in red wax. Wielding every sort of metal object to serve as scrapers, the sisters were tackling walls, floor, and cheese equipment. Peeling off her hat and mittens and tossing them in a corner, Sister Agatha stepped up next to Sister Callwen, who was busy applying a metal spatula to the wall closest to the outside door. "Good heavens! What happened?"

"What does it look like? That cantankerous stove finally lost it. The heat must have shot up and the entire vat of wax exploded like Vesuvius."

"Was anyone hurt?" Sister Agatha began to vigorously scrape the dustpan along the wall. She felt as she had in primary school when she had had to help scrape chewing gum out from under the desks.

"Amazingly, no. Sister Gwenydd was supposed to be in

here, minding the wax as it melted. She says she had turned the heat down and then left just for a moment—to go into the aging room. At least that's her story. She ran back in when she thought she heard gunshots. I guess exploding wax is pretty loud."

Sister Agatha was horrified. "What if all the nuns had been in here?"

Sister Callwen stepped back and looked at the wall. "Well, it would have been bad. But they weren't. So that's something to be thankful for. Reverend Mother has everyone in here scraping and cleaning up. We've been at it for nearly an hour and it still looks just the same as when we started."

"Are you sure that the temperature just shot up on its own?"

Sister Callwen sighed. "I've said for years that that ancient stove was going to do this. And now it has. I only hope we can get cleaned up and back to making cheese. We have sixty-three more orders to fill this week."

"Sixty-three? Holy Mother!" Sister Agatha surveyed the red spatters that seemed to cover everything. "Can we do that? Fill that many orders?"

"Oh, we'll do it," Sister Callwen said. "And we might just bring in enough revenue to buy a new stove."

The door opened, letting in a gust of cold wind. Lucy slipped in and, shutting the door behind her, looked around, her eyes wide. She pulled off her ski jacket and accepted a scraper from Sister Winifred. "Good God!" she said to Sister Agatha and Sister Callwen. "When Reverend Mother texted me that you needed help with the wax, I didn't know she meant this."

"Can you work here beside Sister Agatha while I see how Sister Gwenydd is doing?" With that Sister Callwen hurried across the room where Sister Gwenydd was toiling away on the stove top, which seemed to be one solid layer of hardened wax.

Sister Agatha and Lucy fell into sync with one another, scraping the wall around the door to the aging room. Sister Agatha wondered if this wasn't a good time to bring up her concerns about Lucy. The other sisters were occupied, and the room was loud with the noise of scraping. She and Lucy might actually be able to talk without anyone noticing.

"So how have you been?" Sister Agatha asked, wanting to break the ice without diving in completely. She usually just dove, but something told her Lucy was more reticent than most.

"You mean since the note? That was only yesterday. No more notes, if that's what you mean."

So much for reticence. "Well, any thoughts about it?" Sister Agatha tackled a particularly stubborn bit of red wax as she listened. For the hundredth time she wished she had her suspect in an interrogation room. She could picture it. A small, white-walled room, its only illumination coming from a single harsh lightbulb. Lucy seated on a rickety wooden chair across from her. She sighed as her scraper dragged across the wall, peeling off only a thin layer of red wax. She needed to resign herself to having to do interrogations in less than ideal places. Like the cheese barn, surrounded by nuns scraping wax off plaster walls.

"You know, thoughts about where the note might have come from? Or why someone would put it on your easel."

"How would I know?" Lucy shot back.

Sister Agatha felt a little surprised at Lucy's tone. She sounded almost defensive. But she had nothing to hide—or did she? Sister Agatha took a different approach.

"I meant, did you perhaps remember anything from that day? Like . . . someone that you might have seen? Or just anything out of the ordinary."

"I already told you everything that happened that day."

Lucy stepped back and looked at the plaster wall. "The wax is coming off but it's leaving a red stain."

"I know. I'm guessing we'll be painting next." Sister Agatha focused on the red wax on the wall. "Have you had any encounters with anyone in the village that seemed strange to you? Other than Tiffany?" Sister Agatha turned and regarded Lucy. The young woman stood only a few feet away from her. She was entirely focused on the wax on the wall, her red hair pulled back in a ponytail. Her pale skin seemed even paler. Sister Agatha thought that she detected just the tiniest hesitation before she responded.

"No. I'm never in the village."

"Have you run into Millicent again?"

"Not since that day on the beach. Look, I came to Wales to focus on my art, not get involved with people."

"But you paint people."

"So?"

"So . . . I would think that you would be constantly observing people. In fact, I think you are." Sister Agatha decided to take the plunge. "I know that as a writer I'm always paying attention. You know, to what people are saying, how they respond, their mannerisms. And I think you're the same. I think that as an artist, you're always watching."

Sister Agatha hesitated, then kept going. "And you told me once that you painted portraits because you were looking for someone. I was thinking that if you're looking for someone, then you would probably always be paying attention."

Lucy froze, staring at the wall, her scraper motionless against the splattered plaster. Sister Agatha waited. Lucy was hiding something. She was almost sure of it.

Lucy looked directly at Sister Agatha. "Sorry to shatter your illusion about me, Sister Agatha, but I'm not a tortured artist. And I probably don't pay half as much attention to the world around me as I should." She turned to the wall and applied her scraper to a stubborn red splatter. "And anyway, I don't think I said *exactly* that I was looking for someone. I paint portraits because I can sell them for money and pay my rent." She stepped back and surveyed the wall. "That's a little better. If you don't mind, I'm going to go see if Sister Gwenydd needs help. It looks as if the stove went through a natural disaster." Sister Agatha watched as Lucy began to walk away, then stopped and looked back. "Don't get me wrong. It's not that I don't appreciate your interest. It's just that I am only here to pursue my art. Nothing else."

"Sorry," Sister Agatha said with what she hoped was a warm smile. "But if you ever do want to talk, come and find me. I'm really good at problem solving."

"Thanks, but I don't have a problem." Lucy's voice caught, and for one second, her casual attitude wavered. Then it was back in place again, so quickly that Sister Agatha wondered if she had imagined it. "At least no problem that I can't solve myself."

She watched as the young woman made her way across the long room to join Sister Gwenydd. The two of them were soon engaged in taking apart the stove top, laughing as they did it. Sister Agatha turned back to the red-spattered wall. A young woman far from home. Her dog kidnapped. A threatening note left in her private room. Sister Agatha shook her head. If Lucy didn't have a problem, then no one did.

*　*　*

Father Selwyn must have had his talk with Bevan, because when Sister Agatha slid into the back booth at the Buttered Crust Tea Shop on Tuesday morning there was half a cranberry scone sitting on a plate next to a pot of Glengettie tea in front of him. He looked up from the theological journal he was reading and smiled. "Good to see you, my friend. A cup of tea?"

"No time, Father Selwyn. I was expected back at the abbey an hour ago. But when I saw you through the window, I had to come in. I heard Emeric is out of jail?"

"Yesterday, late afternoon. Constable Barnes finally admitted that he couldn't keep him locked up. Still, he insists that he is going to prove it was Emeric. But at least he's out in time for the cantata. Truthfully, I think the constable's solo during

O Holy Night had something to do with it. Not that he's ever going to admit it." He pushed his half-scone toward her, and she took an absent-minded bite.

Just as Sister Agatha was considering ordering some tea, Lewis Colwyn came in and looked around for an empty seat. Sister Agatha was again surprised at his appearance. The schoolteacher was always so put-together. This morning he looked like he had been dragged through a hedge backward. She remembered Sister Matilda remarking that he had missed their last meeting to work on organizing the community garden in Pryderi. Sister Matilda had been disturbed, because he didn't just cancel, he simply didn't show up and then didn't respond to her text. She was worried that something had happened to him.

"Is Lewis Colwyn still doing work at the church?" she asked Father Selwyn.

"Yes. He's filling in a bit during school holidays. Why?"

She nodded in Lewis' direction. "Don't you think he's looking a bit rough these days?"

"Well, now that you mention it, yes. I've been meaning to ask him if everything is all right. But whenever I see him at the church, he hurries off."

"He's avoiding you?" She looked over at Lewis. He was sitting slouched over at a table near the door. He stared out the window not even having ordered anything. He looked as though he hadn't slept or bathed in days. Certainly hadn't run an iron over his shirt.

Father Selwyn shrugged. "That might be overstating it."

"Anyway," she said, turning back to Father Selwyn. "What do you think of Millicent Pritchard?"

"Millicent? Nice young woman. Terribly shy, a bit awkward. Nothing wrong with that, of course. Keeps to herself." He thought for a moment. "I'd hoped she might find a spot for herself in the activities of the parish."

"Has she?"

"Not really." He poured some tea into his cup. "Why?"

"Do you remember that morning right after we discovered Tiffany's body in the parish hall?"

"Yes. Millicent came in. I forget why."

"She was delivering flowers and she had heard that someone had died."

"Oh right. And I had to tell her it was Tiffany."

"Do you remember that I asked her if she was an artist?"

"I do. Because you noticed that she had paint on her sleeve. I remember thinking how very clever you have become at noticing details."

"Yes. Well. Thank you. Anyway, she told us she was *not* an artist. But she is. Lucy ran into her on the beach a few days ago, painting. She had an easel set up and everything."

"Wasn't it awfully cold to be doing anything on the beach?"

"She's young. Lucy said that not only was she painting but she was very good."

"Why lie about being an artist?" He took a sip of tea. "Any progress on the dognapping or the note?"

Sister Agatha sighed and took the final bite of cranberry scone. "No. Nothing. But I'm not giving up. Not yet." And with that, she stood up and pulled on her blue woolly hat. "If you'll excuse me, Father. I need to get back to the abbey. You wouldn't believe our cheese orders. And I think I need one more conversation with Lucy."

* * *

Sister Agatha had been in Lucy's studio only once before and she had found it pleasant—sunny, filled with color and a comforting smell of acrylics and coffee. Lucy had purchased a coffee maker almost the first day she arrived and had placed it in the corner of her studio. Sister Agatha shook her head. Americans apparently did not understand the power of a good cup of tea. Though Sister Agatha had to admit, coffee *smelled* delightful. And for some reason it made her hungry.

Sister Agatha had felt as if the conversation while they were cleaning wax had gone badly, and she hoped to reestablish some of Lucy's trust. She also needed to get more information about Millicent from her. Sister Agatha couldn't let go of the fact that Millicent Pritchard had been in the church the night of the murder. She had lied about being an artist, and the whole murder was tied to art. Admittedly, Millicent Pritchard was a weak suspect, and getting more information about her to solve the mystery seemed a long shot. But, as Inspector Rupert MacFarland would say, *Don't ignore your long shots. They may be the only shot you get.*

When Lucy answered Sister Agatha's knock, she seemed reluctant to let her in and even asked her to wait on the landing. Lucy had closed the door. After a moment of loud moving and dragging, the door opened, and Lucy, dressed in jeans and a T-shirt with an oversize burgundy cardigan, invited her in. Whatever had been moved wasn't obvious in the crowded studio. Remembering Lucy's previous reticence about revealing her paintings, Sister Agatha tried not to look too closely at the canvases scattered around the small room. But it was difficult. Lucy was talented, and Sister Agatha could see half-finished paintings with likenesses of the people of the abbey and a startling image of Treven, owner of the Lettuce-Us-Eat-Vegan grocery in the village.

"When you do a portrait, I thought people had to sit for long hours?"

"No. That's pretty old school. I sometimes paint from memory or from a photo. Or even a quick sketch that I do when I'm with the person and then bring back to the studio. We don't really live in a world where people can sit for hours or days while you paint them."

"True. Our world is moving faster and faster," Sister Agatha said. "Which is both good and bad, I suppose."

"I think it moves pretty slowly. Especially out here." Lucy gestured her to a chair. "Sit down. Do you want a coffee? It only takes a minute to make. I'm sorry I don't have any tea. I should get some tea K-cups. Then I could have made you tea."

"A tea K-cup? Never mind. I'm fine, thank you." Although Sister Agatha could have certainly done with a good cup of Welsh Brew. Hot, with a bit of cream and extra sugar. She sighed and opened her notebook. *K-cup, indeed.*

The studio had a sagging but comfortable-looking loveseat, over which Lucy had flung a heavy bedspread, and an equally slouchy wing chair. She seemed to have replaced the flimsy canvas chairs of Sister Agatha's last visit. She chose the wingback chair, and Lucy sat on the loveseat. Sister Agatha noticed that she sat with a brush in one hand and a longing glance at the canvas resting on the easel. Sister Agatha felt badly that she had interrupted a working morning. She knew what it felt like to have one's precious time of creativity taken up.

"I was hoping you could help me out with something," she said, getting right to the point. "I wondered what more you could tell me about Millicent Pritchard, the young woman you met on the beach?"

"Why? Do you think she killed Tiffany?"

"Good heavens, why do you ask?"

"Sister Gwenydd told me that you are like a nun-detective, and if it hadn't been for you, the abbey wouldn't even be here and she would be in jail. And that you caught a murderer last summer."

"Well, Sister Gwenydd is very generous in her assessment. The events of last summer, including Sister Gwenydd's own personal dilemma, were solved by the help of a great number of people." Sister Agatha paused. "Although I did jump in and solve it all in the end. Nun-detective isn't completely inaccurate." Modesty was not Sister Agatha's long suit. She uncapped her Sharpie. "Which brings me to the matter at hand. I'm curious about Millicent Pritchard. And she's a hard one to get to know."

"Millicent? I'm having a coffee if you don't mind." Lucy got up and poured water into her coffee machine, then inserted a K-cup. The machine gurgled and coffee burst out in a steady stream into the green mug she had placed at the front.

"So that's how that works. What happened to grinding coffee beans and watching it perk?"

"I don't know. I've never done it that way."

Sister Agatha suddenly felt old. "Oh dear." She picked up her Sharpie. "Tell me everything that you remember about the day when you saw Millicent on the beach."

Lucy settled back on the loveseat holding the coffee cup in both hands. She slipped off her shoes and folded her feet under her on the couch, pulling one of Sister Winifred's prayer shawls onto her lap. This one was blue and purple. Obviously from her Advent collection.

"It was really cold that day. I was just walking along the shore with Vincent van Gogh thinking that it was too cold for me out there and that I needed to turn back. I mean we were both bundled up, but still."

Sister Agatha had seen the dog in his little coat and hat. Royal Stuart tartan, if she knew her tartans. Lucy's own sense of fashion was a bit more hit-or-miss, but Vincent van Gogh always looked like he had just stepped out of a bandbox.

"Anyway, when I saw that someone had set up an easel and was painting, I was impressed. That takes true dedication or . . ." Lucy paused and took a sip of coffee.

"Or what?"

"Or they really want privacy. Nothing is more private than the beach in December. And when I walked up, she wasn't thrilled to see me."

"Why did you think that?"

"Just a feeling."

"What did you think of her painting?"

"Stunning. Not what I do, but beautiful."

"Can you describe it to me?"

"Sure. A bird. A seabird. Not a seagull but one of those little birds you see running across the sand. And the ocean behind it."

Sister Agatha noticed that the American girl just called the beautiful Irish Sea an ocean. *Americans.* She reached into her book bag and pulled out a file. "This is a clipping from the Pryderi Art Society contest last year. It's the winning painting." Sister Agatha waited a moment while Lucy looked at the article. "You saw all the entries didn't you? Friday night when you went to the Art Society meeting."

"I did . . . and. . . ." Lucy looked up and handed the clipping back to Sister Agatha. "The woman who was killed. Her painting was very similar to the one I saw Millicent working on. Lucy thought for a moment, taking another sip of coffee. "Tiffany was clearly the more established artist. She even had an art dealer interested in her work and an offer of a gallery-showing in Cardiff."

"If Tiffany Reese was well-known in the art world . . . or at least having a show . . . then maybe Millicent was copying her. You know, trying to learn from her. It's a small village. I can't imagine that Millicent didn't notice Tiffany's work. Especially if she won the Art Society Show last year."

"Did Tiffany give lessons to Millicent? It's easy to start painting like your teacher." Lucy hesitated. "Although . . ."

"Although?"

"Well, Millicent had the better painting in my estimation. I would assume that Tiffany would enter her best work in the

Art Show. And yet, Millicent's half-done sketch on the beach was already better."

Sister Agatha stood up to leave. "Thanks, Lucy. I'll let you get back to work."

"Any progress on who left the note on my easel?"

"Sorry, no. But I'm definitely pursuing it. Just keep your doors locked."

"My door was locked the day the note was left."

"Right . . ." Sister Agatha was reaching for the door handle when she turned around. "Have you ever heard of Margaret and Walter Keane?"

"No. Are they people in the village?"

"No. Margaret Keane was an artist in the 1960s."

"Oh, sorry." Lucy stood up and put her coffee cup on the small table next to her easel. "Before my time. I was born in 1994."

Sister Agatha sighed and stepped out onto the landing, closing the door behind her. That was the year she had bought her blue woolly hat.

*　*　*

Father Selwyn leaned forward in the wingback chair and looked directly at Sister Agatha. "You think what again?" he asked.

"That there is something fishy about the paintings. I need to get into Millicent's and Tiffany's studios. I need to see both artists' work and compare them."

"What could you possibly learn that would tell you anything about the murders?"

"What if Millicent copied Tiffany, learned from her, and then exceeded her as an artist?"

"Well, Tiffany wouldn't have liked that. At all. But if that's the case, why is Tiffany dead and not Millicent?"

"I know. It doesn't make sense. That's why I need to get into the studios of both women. And I want to take Lucy with me."

"How?" Father Selwyn looked at her quizzically. "Tiffany is dead and her house sealed off until the estate is settled. And Millicent is exceedingly private."

"For once, I've decided to start with the police. Instead of my usual avoidance pattern."

"Constable Barnes?" Father Selwyn eyebrows shot up.

"Please. I'm confused enough over this case. I don't need Constable Chaos. No. I am going to see if the young officer Clough will help me out."

Chapter Fourteen

~

Sister Agatha couldn't help noticing that Officer Clough's eyes lit up when she introduced him to Lucy. Parker had met the two of them at the Buttered Crust Tea Shop in the back booth, which was fast becoming Sister Agatha's office away from the abbey. She realized that there probably weren't a lot of single young women in the village of Pryderi. Or young people at all, for that matter. A lack of jobs and nightlife seemed to be the contributing factors—or at least according to Sister Gwenydd, who rolled her eyes and snorted when she was asked why twenty-somethings weren't settling in the village. Lucy was certainly single as well as talented, well-spoken, attractive, and, from what Sister Agatha could tell, entirely uninterested in Officer Clough. In fact, she was uninterested in the entire venture. She didn't like the idea of sneaking into someone's studio, nor was she at all keen on leaving her own studio early in the morning to sit in a tea shop and talk to a cop about another artist. And, as she told Sister Agatha, police officers, in her experience, were not people who cared about things like the arts. In other words, the abbey's young artist-in-residence was in a grumpy mood.

"Officer Clough. So glad you could join us," Sister Agatha said. She cast a sidelong glance at Lucy, who sighed and looked out the window. "Would you like tea? Or a Welsh cake perhaps."

"A cup of tea would be lovely, Sister." He smiled at Lucy. "I have heard you are very skilled as an artist."

Sister Agatha was not at all sure where he might have heard that, as almost no one had seen any art produced by Lucy. But she did notice that Lucy stopped staring out the window and turned to him. "Thanks," she said coolly.

"Are you liking Wales?" he asked, as Sister Agatha poured him a cup of tea.

"I'd like it better if all sorts of weird things weren't happening to me. But, yes. It's beautiful. Far lovelier than I would have thought."

"Someday I would like to hear more about what brought you here to our little village." *Wouldn't we all like to hear that, thought Sister Agatha.* She noticed that Lucy stiffened and turned back to the window. Officer Clough looked down awkwardly. She wondered if he knew who Armand Gamache was. It might help him with Lucy if he read a little more Louise Penny.

"What we were hoping for, Officer Clough, is permission to enter Tiffany's house. To take a look around for . . ." Suddenly she found she didn't have a great argument to put forth.

Officer Clough leaned forward. "For your investigation?" he said in a quiet voice.

"I didn't think your office approved of my investigation. As you put it."

"Well, Constable Barnes doesn't. And he wouldn't be too happy if he knew we were here, having this conversation."

"Do you mean you would be in trouble with your boss if he knew you were here talking with us?" Lucy interjected. Sister Agatha thought her interest in Officer Clough might have gone up a bit.

"Well, he's actually out of town today. In Cardiff, at a department meeting. So I guess it's not going to do any harm if we talk." He took a sip of tea. "Tell me why you want to get into Tiffany Reese's house."

"I want to see the room where she painted. According to Vonda Bryson, she did all her painting at home in a specially built studio. It was apparently very elaborate and expensive and modeled after a famous artist's. And no one was ever allowed inside it."

Sister Agatha ignored the snort that came from Lucy, who covered it by taking a quick drink from her mug of coffee. Until this morning, Sister Agatha hadn't known you could buy coffee at the Buttered Crust Tea Shop. It seemed wrong somehow.

"I think I could learn a lot about Tiffany if I could just spend some time with her paintings. See how she organized herself. Look at what was finished, what was in progress."

"You think that somehow her art would give you a hint about who poisoned her?"

"Yes. Who and why."

"Interesting." He dug into the Welsh cake that sat in front of him. "What do you think, Miss Pennoyer? Do you think an artist's studio is a window into the soul?" Sister Agatha noticed the tiniest spark awaken in Lucy.

"I do," she said, offering him the smallest of smiles. "One's studio is the place where it all happens. Where you are the most experimental, the most vulnerable, the most . . . the most . . . *you.*" She paused. "So, yes. I guess you could call it a window into the soul."

"There's one problem, however," Officer Clough said, draining his cup of tea and setting it with a clatter into the saucer.

"What's that?" Sister Agatha felt her hope fading. *What would be the harm in letting her walk through the studio? It's not as though it was the crime scene.*

"There *is* no studio. We turned her house upside down once the tox screen came in. And I can tell you for certain— there is no artist's studio in that house. You would never have known that Mrs. Reese was an artist at all."

* * *

Sister Agatha usually enjoyed a late night at her desk in the attic library. But tonight, even with a steaming cup of Welsh Brew and one of Sister Gwenydd's chocolate-covered Advent pretzels in front of her, she only felt stress. Officer Clough's revelation that Tiffany wasn't an artist had made Sister Agatha almost frantic to get into Millicent's studio and see if she could figure out exactly what was going on.

Taking a sip of tea, she sat back and thought. When she had first begun the investigation, she had been quite certain that Millicent had been copying Tiffany's art. That the younger artist had even perhaps seen Tiffany as a mentor, though Tiffany Reese was certainly not the mentoring type. Millicent wore Tiffany's cast-off clothes, painted the same subjects in the exact same style. And then, she had thought that perhaps Tiffany had gotten tired of the younger woman. Or perhaps, as Millicent's skill and expertise improved, that Tiffany began to feel threatened by her.

But now, it seemed unlikely that Tiffany had been Millicent's mentor at all. Instead, Sister Agatha had started asking who was copying whom? Was the article on art fraud simply a nudge by Millicent to figure things out? But when would Millicent have had access to her desk in the library? Or how would she even know that she had a desk in the abbey library? It was impossible to imagine Millicent Pritchard sneaking into the abbey, climbing three flights of stairs, hiding the letter in Sister Agatha's top desk drawer, and then sneaking out again. But if not Millicent, then who? Who else knew what was going on?

She bit into the Advent pretzel. *Nothing as good as salty and sweet.* There was altogether too much sneaking onto the abbey grounds and making mischief. The dognapping, an article left in Sister Agatha's desk drawer, the poison-pen letter. Who and why? And were they done yet? Or was there more dangerous mischief to come?

More tea. Another bite of pretzel. *She had to get into Millicent's apartment.* And talk to her. And this time, to be more direct. Maybe not a full-blown Bates Melanchthon interrogation, but something a little more to the point than what she had been doing.

She looked down at the chocolate pretzel. It had a generous sprinkling of candy stars on it. Sister Gwenydd and Lucy had made them together. She had overheard them laughing in the kitchen while the rest of the abbey watched the season finale of *Midsomer Murders*. The nuns loved John Nettles as Inspector Barnaby. They could overhear Sister Gwenydd telling Lucy about how the pretzel represents the folded arms of prayer and the three circles represent the Trinity. And that monks in the sixth century ate them during Advent and Lent to remind themselves of the expectation of prayer and penance. Although covering them in chocolate and candy stars was Sister Gwenydd's idea; Sister Agatha didn't suppose that the early monks had a lot of melted chocolate and candy stars on hand.

Taking another bite of the pretzel gave Sister Agatha an idea. *Recruit Sister Gwenydd and Lucy to work together.* They always seemed ready for adventure. At least Sister Gwenydd did, and perhaps she could convince Lucy to come along.

Chapter Fifteen

~

Sister Agatha had parked the abbey's aging minivan under the elm tree on the corner of Main Street and Bishop's Walk. Millicent rented a small apartment above the Just-for-You Florist shop, and from under the tree she could see the light in her upstairs window. The ancient tree had stood on that corner for as long as anyone could remember. The parish council had debated cutting it down for years, and every time gave it a reprieve. Sister Agatha was of the opinion that the tree should stay. It had survived Dutch elm disease, a collision with the Blackthorne Dairy milk truck, and half the village carving their initials into its smooth bark. And, as everyone knew, it was bad luck to cut down an elm tree.

Sister Agatha turned off the dome light in the minivan and glanced down the length of Main Street. *They certainly rolled up the sidewalks in Pryderi.* Eight o'clock on a Thursday evening and the downtown was deserted. She unscrewed the top of the thermos of tea she had brought along and poured a cup. The fragrant steaming Welsh Brew revived her energy. This was a little bit like a true Stephanie Plum stakeout. All she needed was a bucket of chicken and for the minivan to blow up.

Lucy and Sister Gwenydd had been in Millicent's apartment for an hour. They had planned to drop in on her under the pretense of just stopping by to say hello and then talk with her while looking around to see what they could figure out about her paintings. Reverend Mother had handed Sister Agatha the keys to the minivan without comment after the Sister had explained what she needed and why—conveniently leaving out the part about deceiving Millicent into thinking it was a casual social call.

Sister Agatha said a quick prayer of gratitude for Reverend Mother's generosity and turned her attention back to the window of the apartment. It was just down the street from St. Anselm's church, which meant that Millicent could have murdered Tiffany and then easily slipped back home before anyone was the wiser. Sister Agatha wondered where Father Selwyn was right now. She didn't have to wonder long, as the side door facing the rectory opened to a pool of light and Father Selwyn stepped out. She smiled as he walked over to her. Stakeouts were more fun with company.

"Sister," he said, as she cranked down the window. "Are we doing a good old-fashioned stakeout? Like Stephanie Plum? Where's your bucket of fried chicken?"

"Sadly, there is no bucket of chicken."

"May I join you?"

"Of course. Get in."

"So what are you doing, exactly?" he asked, settling into the passenger side.

Sister Agatha launched into an explanation of her idea of recruiting Sister Gwenydd and Lucy to collect information on Millicent and had only just finished when her mobile buzzed. It was a text from Sister Gwenydd.

"*We have to talk.*"

"*Come down to the van?*" she texted back.
"*U come up.*"
"*With Millicent there?*"
"*Ys. Now.*"
"*Can I bring Father Selwyn?*"
"*Ys. We may need him.*"

* * *

Millicent's apartment was at the top of a narrow, steep stairway. Her door had a cheerful bird painted on it with a bubble issuing from its beak containing the word "welcome." It was decidedly more cheerful than Sister Agatha would have expected. Millicent was always so serious. Perhaps here, in her own space, she was more comfortable.

Sister Agatha knocked and then pushed the door open. Millicent was sitting on the couch, her plump face pale and drawn. Sister Gwenydd sat next to her, holding her hand, and Lucy was in the tiny kitchen to the right of the living room. It looked like she was trying to make tea. Sister Agatha's eyes took in the entire scene, including the fact that Lucy did not have a single K-cup at her disposal. *I hope she knows what to do with a tea bag, she thought.*

"Good gracious. What's going on?"

Sister Agatha pulled off her hat and tossed it in the corner. She sat down on an ottoman in front of Sister Gwenydd and Millicent, slipped her notebook out of her jumper pocket, and uncapped a fresh Sharpie. Father Selwyn, shrugging off his coat, sat in the only sturdy-looking chair in the room. He leaned forward, his hands clasped, concerned eyes on Millicent.

Before anyone could speak, Lucy came into the room bearing a tray of cups, a teapot, a bowl of sugar, and a pitcher of cream.

"I may be American, but even I know when a cup of tea is needed, she remarked," and set the tea things on the coffee table.

Lucy looked at Millicent. "Tell them."

"I don't know where to begin," Millicent said, taking a deep breath.

Apparently, no one was questioning the stakeout-coverup-fake story about dropping by to say hello. Sister Agatha reminded herself to stay quiet. She noticed that Father Selwyn didn't say a word either. He was much better at listening than she was.

"If I tell you everything, it'll sound like I killed Tiffany. Which I didn't. But I just don't think I *can* tell you everything. . . ." She looked at Lucy and then at Sister Gwenydd.

"Tell them. It never helps to hide things. I learned that the hard way," Sister Gwenydd said.

Lucy brought a kitchen chair into the tiny living room and sat down, cradling her teacup in both hands. Sister Agatha added cream and sugar and took a sip, never taking eyes off Millicent. *Not a bad cup of tea, she thought. For an American.*

"It doesn't make you look entirely like a murderer," Lucy said. "Just sort of."

"OK. Well. Everything started about a year ago," Millicent began, haltingly. "I hadn't ever shown anyone my art. I didn't think it was worth anything. And truthfully, I've improved a lot since then so it's a lot better now. Anyway . . ."

"One second. How old are you?" Sister Agatha asked, Sharpie poised.

"Twenty-one."

The room went silent. Millicent seemed older. Perhaps because she dressed older. No skinny jeans and boots for her, like Lucy. Or bright-pink hoodies pulled over a nun's habit, like Sister Gwenydd. "So you were barely twenty when this story starts, right?"

"Yes. And I was . . . well . . . alone."

"Your mother died that year, didn't she?" Father Selwyn asked.

"The year before. Anyway, I was on my own and I had just started at the florist shop—they let me have this apartment really cheap. I was at work one day when Tiffany came in. She sort of *swept in*, if you know what I mean. She started giving me orders about flowers. But not in a bad way. In an impressive way. I was sort of blown away by her."

"Did she talk to you?" Sister Agatha asked.

"Yes. In fact, she went out of her way to talk to me. Which made me feel important. I know that sounds stupid."

"You're not stupid. It's easy to feel important when important people take a special interest in you. The problem is when their interest is more about them than it is about you."

Lucy yanked her hair out of its ponytail holder, pulled her hair back, trapped the messy red curls back in the ponytail holder again. Sister Agatha looked at her as if for the first time. Lucy sat on the kitchen chair, her long legs crossed, a young woman at ease with herself, sure of who she was. Sister Gwenydd as well. Both of them were ready to take on the world. In contrast to Millicent, whose eyes were never sure, voice was often trembly, and who was always swathed in layers of mismatched clothes.

"Well, anyway," Millicent continued, "that day in the florist shop I had been doodling on an order blank. And it was a really slow day so my doodle was pretty elaborate. I know because I saved it."

"You saved a doodle from more than a year ago? Why?" Then Sister Agatha wished she had just waited and listened.

"Because it was the whole reason Tiffany noticed me. It was the thing that brought her to me." Millicent stood and walked over to a round table against the wall. She opened a small decorative box on top of the table and removed a slip of paper. She handed it to Sister Agatha.

A doodle indeed. Drawn in faded blue ink, but beautiful. It was of a swan floating across a lake. Even faded and done with a ballpoint pen, it captured the tranquility and majesty of the large bird, the stillness of the water, the gentle breeze. Sister Agatha looked up.

"Lovely. So when Tiffany saw this, what happened?"

"She asked me to come by her house for a glass of wine. And I'm embarrassed to tell you how much that meant to me. Tiffany was older, smart. And I thought that she wanted to be friends with me. And she did. In a way."

"When did she ask you to start painting for her?" Sister Agatha asked.

"How did you know?" Millicent looked at Sister Agatha, her eyes wide.

"I didn't until right now."

"Well, it was soon after the glass of wine at her house." Millicent lifted her teacup off the coffee table but set it back down without drinking. "She showed a lot of interest in my art. Which no one had ever done before. My mother had liked it, but never thought it was something I could pursue. But Tiffany thought it was brilliant. Or that's what she said at first. Anyway, she told me that she was the new president of the Village Art Society. And when she said that, I thought . . ." Millicent's voice caught. "I thought she was going to ask me to join. But then she said that I had a unique opportunity as an artist. That she would enter one of my paintings under her name. As hers. She told me that no one would believe I had done it."

Lucy drew in her breath but didn't speak.

Millicent looked at the floor. "She said that if people thought it was her painting, they would be impressed, and it would get far more attention." Millicent paused again, and this time she did take a sip of tea. "And that at the next art show she would tell everyone it was done by me and I could enter my own painting."

"Why didn't you tell her to bugger off?" Sister Gwenydd said sitting on the edge of her kitchen chair. "Sorry," she said with a glance at Sister Agatha and Father Selwyn. "But seriously. Why didn't you?"

"I understand why," Lucy said quietly. "She offered you two things you wanted more than anything. Friendship and recognition of your art. Unfortunately, she tied the two things up in a tangled knot. A stranglehold."

"I feel like an idiot," Millicent said.

"Don't. Artists get used all the time by rich, powerful people who can hold their livelihood in their hands. What she did was despicable, but your response to her is not that surprising."

"Especially considering the difference in your ages." Father Selwyn interjected. "I am particularly appalled at that aspect. We should be nurturing the young talent in this village." He shook his head. "Despicable that a prominent member of our community, of the parish, would do something like that. Bugger off indeed."

"Millicent," Sister Agatha said. "Keep going. I want to hear all of it. Right up until last Friday night."

"You think I killed her, don't you?"

No one spoke.

"I didn't. Not that I didn't think about it a hundred times. She never did tell anyone that the painting was mine. She won first place with it. And then, this year, she wanted another one."

Millicent paused and took a breath.

"This time she came into my apartment and chose it herself."

Lucy rose to her feet suddenly, eyes blazing. Sister Agatha thought that Tiffany was lucky she was already dead. Everyone watched as Lucy took a deep breath and then sat back down again.

After a minute Millicent continued.

"So when she wanted to choose the painting for the next show, I reminded her how she had said that she would tell everyone I was the artist."

Millicent picked up her teacup, but her hand was shaking so much that she set it clattering back on the saucer.

"She stood in this apartment, and I remember looking at her thinking that she was so stylish, everything about her was perfect. Her hair, nails, clothes. I remember feeling dowdy and . . . and fat." Millicent paused. "Anyway, she laughed. And said that it was too late to tell anyone because no one would believe me. And that I couldn't go back on my commitment."

Millicent stopped. No one spoke.

"She looked around the apartment and then just plucked a canvas off the easel. I had worked on it for weeks. 'Melyn yr Ei thin,' *Yellow Bird of the Gorse.* I managed to capture it just as it landed on the beach, wings outspread, toed-claws touching down and creating the tiniest puff of sand. Tiffany slid it into her bag and left."

Those in the room sat in stunned silence. Lucy frowning, Sister Gwenydd sitting perfectly still, Father Selwyn as grim as Sister Agatha had ever seen him.

Millicent took a breath. "The problem also was that, even though she was usually really nice—especially in public—she had an ugly, angry side. Scary, like a flying monkey."

"A what?" Sister Agatha asked.

"A flying monkey. You know, from *The Wizard of Oz.* I'm just saying that she could be really intimidating."

"You like *The Wizard of Oz?*" Sister Agatha asked.

"Doesn't everyone?" Millicent said.

"Lots of people like *The Wizard of Oz,* Sister Agatha." Father Selwyn said, shooting Sister Agatha a wide-eyed glance.

Millicent stood up and went into the tiny bedroom. Through the doorway Sister Agatha could see an easel and paints and canvases stacked on the floor. She watched as Millicent rummaged around for a moment and then selected four paintings. She lined them up along the kitchen counter, leaning one against the wall, another propped up by the toaster, another against the teapot, and the fourth against a stack of cookbooks. They all stared at the detailed and exquisite paintings of birds in the wild. One of the birds was brilliantly yellow and was shown landing on the sand. Sister Agatha let out a breath. *The missing painting!*

"They are all taken from life somewhere in North Wales. I only paint wildlife, and always in Wales. My dream is to be an illustrator for nature books." Millicent blushed with pride as the room sat in admiring silence.

"And you will be!" Father Selwyn exclaimed. "They are amazing. Lovely." He leaned forward. "Lucy, give us your professional opinion."

"They're good. Really good. You're both an artist and a craftsman. Which is an awesome combination in today's market." Lucy walked over to the paintings and leaning closer, examined each one. "You could certainly be an illustrator."

Sister Agatha cleared her throat. "You have the painting that was in the Art Show?"

Before Millicent could respond, Lucy jumped in.

"Good for you!" she said. "I'm glad you got it."

"After more than a year of her stealing your art, you stole it back. What gave you the courage?" Sister Gwenydd asked. She poured tea into Father Selwyn's teacup and held the teapot up in Sister Agatha's direction. But Sister Agatha was too stunned at Millicent's admission even to respond.

"Wait a minute, Millicent. Are you saying . . ."

"It was the art dealer, wasn't it?" Lucy said, cutting her off. "Tiffany had been going on and on about an art dealer being interested in her work. She must have mentioned it ten times at the Art Society meeting. And it was that particular painting that had caught his eye—the yellow bird."

Millicent nodded. "Tiffany didn't tell me, but I heard about it from someone in the florist shop."

Millicent stood up and walked over to the canvases on the counter. She picked up the one of the yellow bird and gazed at it.

"And so, I confronted Tiffany and told her that entering my stuff in the village show was one thing but telling a dealer that it was hers went too far."

"How did she react?" Father Selwyn asked. Sister Agatha wondered if he was hoping Tiffany might have shown some remorse. *Fat chance,* she thought.

"She laughed at me. And said that if I told everyone now, I would be implicated in fraud. That I had used her and her reputation to make it this far. That I owed her. So I went down to the parish hall at night and stole it back."

Father Selwyn set his teacup down and sat up very straight. Sister Agatha looked at him and then back at Millicent.

"So when you saw us that morning in Father's office, you knew all about Tiffany having died?"

"Sorry," Millicent said. "But it was my painting. I had a right to it. Tiffany was already dead when I went down there."

"Are you telling me you stepped over her body to remove the painting? You didn't think to call the constable or an ambulance? I mean, did you know for sure she was dead?" Father Selwyn was straying toward his pulpit voice.

Or did you kill her yourself? Sister Agatha and Father Selwyn exchanged a glance.

"I honestly didn't notice her at first. I thought the room was empty. You know, except for the paintings that were hung there for the show. I didn't turn on a light. I was just going to take the painting off the wall and then deliver the flowers upstairs. And leave."

"You had the flowers in your hands?"

"I came straight into the hall from the van. The floral delivery van. I parked it outside."

"So let me get this straight. You're standing in the parish hall, flower vase in hand, then what?"

"Like I said, I didn't turn on any lights, that's why I didn't see Tiffany at first, I suppose. You know, until I was right there. And then I just . . . well . . . I just let her lie. It was pretty obvious she was dead."

"*Pretty obvious?*" Father Selwyn said. "You didn't check? Feel for a pulse? Drop everything and call an ambulance?"

All four of them stared at Millicent, no one wanting to say what they were thinking: *Did you kill her or simply help her die?*

"I wanted my painting. More than anything. I wanted to take it to the dealer and show him that it was mine."

Millicent turned to Lucy.

"You're a real artist. Do you think he'll still be interested? You know, now that Tiffany is . . . out of the picture."

Lucy appeared speechless. "Uh . . . sure," she finally replied. "I don't see why not."

Sister Agatha had a sudden thought.

"You left the article in my desk drawer, didn't you? Were you hoping I would investigate?"

Millicent looked genuinely perplexed. "What article?"

"About the art fraud in the 1960s?"

"The sixties? Sorry. Before my time."

Sister Agatha couldn't even write in her notebook for a moment. If Millicent hadn't left the article, then who had? She had another sudden thought.

"Do you think anyone else knew about the fraud?"

Millicent turned red. "Yes. One person." She reached forward for her teacup but put it back down without drinking.

"Who?" Sister Agatha asked.

"Tiffany's brother. Kendrick."

Millicent didn't seem to notice that Father Selwyn and Sister Agatha went completely still at hearing this.

"I went to him for help. I thought he would—you know—would stand up to his sister and get my paintings back."

"What did he say?"

"He said to leave him out of it. That his sister was difficult and he didn't want to get involved." Millicent looked up. "He was nice, but he didn't help me at all."

Father Selwyn turned to Millicent.

"You are aware of how this looks, right?"

Millicent stared back at him, her large eyes unblinking.

"What do you mean? It was my painting. I had every right to take it."

"Did you touch the crime scene at all?" Sister Agatha asked.

"No. I don't think so. I mean, I didn't think of it as a crime scene at the time. I figured that Tiffany had just keeled over."

They all sat in silence. The bell in the clock tower chimed, and down the street a dog barked. Father Selwyn took a deep breath and looked straight at Millicent.

"My dear," he said. "I'm going to ask you a question, and whatever your answer is, we will go from there. As your vicar I will stand by you. But I need to know. Right now. Did you kill Tiffany Reese?"

"No," she said. "I'm not sad that she's dead. But I didn't kill her."

* * *

"I don't believe her," Sister Agatha said, stepping off the curb and walking toward the van parked under the elm tree. Lucy and Sister Gwenydd had gone on ahead and were waiting for Sister Agatha in the van. They had missed compline. Reverend Mother would understand. She hoped.

"I don't know what I think," Father Selwyn said. "At least not for sure. But I am certain that if we don't take this new evidence to the constable, we will be considered accessory to murder."

"Agreed." But Sister Agatha noticed that neither of them made a move.

"We should go immediately to the police station." Father Selwyn said, buttoning his long coat against the cold.

"Yes. Absolutely." They still didn't move. "Or, we could sort things out a bit first. There are a few missing pieces that I want to find."

"And for some reason, I want Millicent to be innocent." Father Selwyn shoved his hands down into his pockets.

"You want Emeric to be innocent. And didn't you just say you didn't believe her?"

"Well, I know. But hope springs eternal." She watched as he turned and walked toward the rectory.

*　*　*

As soon as Sister Agatha got into the van, Sister Gwenydd, who was riding shotgun, reached into the apron pocket of her habit and handed her a small paperback. Sister Agatha held it up to the dome light. *4.50 From Paddington* by Agatha Christie.

"When I excused myself to use the bathroom, I saw it. On her night table."

"You took it from the apartment?" Sister Gwenydd would make a good detective. Although her methods might need a little refining.

"Is that bad?"

"Constable Barnes might have some problems with it," Sister Agatha said. "But I don't particularly. This is the book in which Agatha Christie kills off her victim with monkshood. Also known as wolfsbane. Also the poison that killed Tiffany Reese."

Lucy leaned forward. "*4.50 From Paddington* was the first Agatha Christie I ever read." She paused, her brow furrowed. "The active component in the plant was aconite And it makes its victim go into cardiac arrest."

"A lot of people have read *4.50 From Paddington*. It's never gone out of print since 1938." Sister Agatha said slowly, thumbing through the book.

"Yeah, but don't you think it's a little weird that it just happens to be her bedtime reading?" Sister Gwenydd said from the backseat.

"Did you happen to notice what page it was open to when you picked it up?" Sister Agatha asked.

"Page 137."

Sister Gwenydd would indeed make quite the amateur sleuth.

"Excellent. I'll check it out as soon as we get home."

Sister Agatha drove slowly. She needed a few minutes before she got back to the abbey to think through her next actions. She and Father Selwyn had left it that they were not going to call Constable Barnes that night. Neither felt completely convinced, however, that that was the right decision. On the other hand, what solid evidence did they have that Millicent had killed Tiffany? True, she stole the painting, which was certainly a crime that Constable Barnes would be interested in. But as it was her painting, could she really be said to have stolen it? Sister Agatha knew the answer to that was yes, at least in the eyes of the law, especially as Millicent had stepped over a dead body to get to the painting. But did that make her a murderer? She also harbored great resentment toward the victim. OK, that was troubling. Throw in the fact that she loved *The Wizard of Oz*—though of course, as she said, who doesn't? The two attacks on Lucy seemed to have involved someone who had watched the movie one too many times. Things were not looking good for Millicent. But call in Constable Barnes? She wasn't ready yet to see Millicent behind bars.

"What did you make of that *Wizard of Oz* comment by Millicent?" Lucy asked, almost as if she could read Sister Agatha's thoughts.

"It bothered me." Sister Agatha said, slowing as she took the curve heading up Church Lane.

"But it *was* pretty generic," Sister Gwenydd said. "I worked with Tiffany on the parish dinners—it's probably not the first time she'd been called a flying monkey."

"True," Lucy agreed. "Assuming that the same person who poisoned Tiffany is doing all the scary stuff to me—you know, stealing Vincent, leaving the note—then it doesn't really make sense that it's Millicent." Lucy paused. "Although I can see that she had reason to hate Tiffany and even cause her harm, but why would Millicent hate me?"

"Well, you're an artist. It could be that she has transferred her anger at Tiffany onto anyone or anything artistic," Sister Gwenydd said.

"Did it bother either of you when she said that . . ."

Suddenly Sister Agatha clutched the steering wheel and pulling hard on it swerved to the right as another car slammed into the side of the minivan. Both young women screamed, and for a moment all went black as the van toppled sideways and bounced to a halt in a ditch.

They spent the next few moments reassuring each other that they were all right and untangling themselves from their seat belts. Sister Agatha felt a sharp twinge in her left shoulder.

Then they heard gravel crunching as a vehicle backed up alongside the van. A man's voice shouted: "There's no place like the ditch, Dorothy! There's no place like the ditch!" And with a squeal of tires and spray of gravel, he sped away. Sister Gwenydd had just gotten the window open and was able to lean out and watch the car leave.

"Did you see the license plate?" Sister Agatha called from the depths of the front seat where she was still trying to unfasten her seat belt.

"No, I think it was a Subaru though. An old one, like my dad had." Sister Gwenydd turned back and, giving Lucy a hand, added, "But you know what?"

"What?"

"That guy is one creepy dude."

* * *

Reverend Mother poured tea for Sister Agatha and Sister Gwenydd.

"I'm sorry, Lucy," she said when she got to where the young woman sat at the long kitchen table. "I know you prefer coffee. But I'm afraid I make a terrible cup of coffee."

"That's OK. I'm fine." But Lucy's hands trembled as she

pulled her hair out of her ponytail and then stuffed it back again. Sister Agatha added sugar and cream to her tea and then cupped the tea mug in both hands. The kitchen was warm as toast, but she still couldn't stop shaking. Only Sister Gwenydd seemed unfazed by their roll in the ditch. Sister Agatha had always admired the young nun. Nothing was ever too much for her.

"It is a miracle that no one was hurt," Reverend Mother said, pulling a bag of frozen peas out of the freezer and handing it to Sister Agatha. "Put that on your shoulder and see if it helps."

"I'm fine. I just fell against the door when the van went down. Sorry I lost control of it like that. Between getting hit from the side and then spinning on the gravel, I couldn't get it back on the road."

"It was a good thing you were driving so slowly, Sister Agatha," Sister Gwenydd said. Sister Gwenydd was known to complain that Sister Agatha drove like an old-age pensioner. To which Sister Agatha replied that it was in reaction to riding with Father Selwyn, who zipped around in his BMI Mini as though it was the last lap on the international raceway.

"The driver really yelled, 'There's no place like the ditch, Dorothy?'" Reverend Mother asked.

"I know, right? How creepy was that?" Sister Gwenydd took a long gulp of tea and glanced around. Sister Agatha hoped she was about to bring out a cake tin.

"First, they kidnap Vincent van Gogh, which is the min-pin-stand-in for Toto. Sister Agatha smiled into her tea. *Min-pin-stand-in*. Only Sister Gwenydd.

"Then the note, 'Surrender Dorothy,' and now, 'There's no place like the ditch,' which, of course, is, 'There's no place like home.'"

Sister Gwenydd stood up and, turning around, reached up to the top kitchen shelf. *Bingo. Cake tin.* "The guy is deranged."

Reverend Mother poured Lucy a cup of tea. "Try it, dear. With lots of cream and sugar, tea can be very comforting. A good cup of tea has seen the Welsh people through everything since the Norman invasion."

"Or the guy just really loves the cinema," Lucy suggested. "A hit man who loves old movies."

"A hit man? In Pryderi?" Reverend Mother looked skeptical.

"Well, I don't know. But it wasn't Millicent, right? I mean, I thought maybe it was Millicent who was sending all *The Wizard of Oz* threats to me. But we were just at her house, and unless she jumped into a waiting blue Subaru, followed us up the hill, and then disguised her voice as a man's, it wasn't she." Lucy replied.

"I wouldn't dismiss her so quickly," Sister Agatha said. "Whoever hit us knew where to find us. And only Millicent knew that we were heading back to the abbey in the minivan."

"Unless we were being followed," Sister Gwenydd said. Sister Agatha noted a slight thrill of excitement in Sister Gwenydd's voice. Too much *Midsomer Murders* with the sisters on Sunday nights.

"Do you think Millicent is that scheming? To set out after us or, rather, to send some man in a Subaru after us?" Lucy asked. "After all, she's this shy thing who paints birds."

The silence around the table answered Lucy's question. The shy and hesitant Millicent had let a woman lie on the floor without calling for help and then stepped over her body to steal a painting. She had lied about where she'd been and claimed that she wasn't an artist. The fact that Tiffany had manipulated her and stolen her work could have been enough to make an unrecognized artist angry enough to kill. Sister Agatha took a sip of tea. *You never knew what could drive someone to murder.*

Reverend Mother took the slice of almond cake offered her by Sister Gwenydd. "Have you told me everything," she asked, stabbing a forkful, "about Millicent and Tiffany? I don't want to look uninformed when Constable Barnes gets here. He just texted that he was at the site of the accident, and the wrecking crew should be done soon."

"I don't think we left anything out," Sister Agatha answered. "Did we?" She looked at Sister Gwenydd, who looked back at her with an open expression.

Lucy picked up her tea and peered over the cup at Sister Agatha. "Nope. Not that I can think of."

Sister Agatha noticed that her voice, though both casual and confident, was matched by the slightest quiver of her teacup. Shakiness was a sure sign of a suspect who was lying. Although, she reminded herself, Lucy is not a suspect at all, but a victim. And why would a victim lie? Had a victim ever lied to Miss Marple? Armand Gamache? Inspector Barnaby? Uncapping her Sharpie, she made a note to check.

"I only ask, Sister Agatha," Reverend Mother said. "Because on occasion—not often, of course but on occasion—you have withheld information from me when I really ought to have had all the facts."

"I think I have been very open with you, Reverend Mother. Yes. Absolutely, I have."

She folded her hands on her lap before there could be even the slightest chance of a tremor. A good detective keeps a few things up her sleeve. Although most detectives only had to answer to a mere lieutenant, not a Reverend Mother.

"And anyway, I feel as if I know less and less every day about the murder of Tiffany. Not to mention the weird things at the abbey. The weird *Wizard of Oz* things."

"Well, I understand, but . . ." Reverend Mother was cut off by the sound of boots stomping in the hallway. Constable Barnes and Parker Clough came into the kitchen pulling off hats and gloves. "Ah. Nice and warm in here," Constable Barnes said. "It's brass monkeys out there in the ditch." He nodded to Sister Agatha. "You laid that van in nice and easy, Sister Agatha."

"I was going slowly," she said.

"No one hurt, then?" Parker Clough asked, looking only at Lucy.

"No. Thankfully no one was hurt." Reverend Mother set out two teacups. "How does the van look? Reparable?"

The two men exchanged a glance. "Sorry, Reverend Mother, but I would be very surprised if you could drive it again. Looked totaled to me."

Constable Barnes slid out of his anorak and draped it over a chair. Sitting down, he pulled out a black notebook. "Take a seat, Parker," he said.

Sister Agatha noticed that the young officer sat across from Lucy and smiled at her. She also noticed that Sister Gwenydd gave the slightest smirk in the direction of Lucy, who looked down at her tea and sighed. Apparently, young Parker wasn't making a lot of progress in raising the estimation of either young woman.

"Start at the beginning, if you will."

During the heavy silence that followed, Sister Agatha and Sister Gwenydd looked at each other. The beginning? How far back to go?

Constable Barnes looked up. "Well, what happened? Your van is in a ditch and you say someone ran you off the road. You must have something to say?"

"It is just that the *beginning* is a little difficult to identify."

"How about when you got hit by the other car? That seems like a pretty good start to me." Constable Barnes looked toward Reverend Mother and back to Sister Agatha. "Did it start before then? Did you notice the car when you were in the village?"

"I'll tell you where it began," Lucy said, sitting up straight and pushing away her plate of almond cake. "It began a year ago with a despicable example of emotional manipulation and artist abuse. And it has ended with a kidnapped dog, a wrecked van, a stolen painting, and a dead woman." She drew a breath. "Actually, it hasn't ended at all. Because we have some crazy Judy Garland fan out there who is targeting me. Probably because I'm an artist."

She stood up. "Sorry, but this calls for coffee. Tea might

have gotten Wales through the Norman invasion, Reverend Mother, but coffee got me through art school."

Lucy stood and reached for a dusty tin of coffee that the nuns kept for the rare visitor who didn't want tea.

Taking Lucy's outburst as her cue, Sister Agatha launched into the long and detailed description of everything Millicent had told them. Constable Barnes sat silently taking notes in his notebook. When she got to the part about the painting being Millicent's and that Tiffany Reese wasn't an artist at all but a thief, Constable Barnes stopped writing and tossed his pen onto the table. Then, when she told him that Millicent had been at the crime scene and stolen back the painting, he nodded to Parker Clough, who got up and left the room. Sister Agatha noticed that Reverend Mother picked up her mobile and began to text. She hoped Reverend Mother was texting Father Selwyn. If Millicent was about to be arrested, she was going to need some pastoral care. And Father Selwyn wasn't expecting the story to be told to the constable tonight. On the other hand, he didn't know that they had been run off the road either.

When the long saga was finished—ending with the man yelling out the window "There's no place like the ditch, Dorothy!" the constable looked at Reverend Mother and then at each woman at the table in turn.

"That's it, then? Nothing else?"

No one spoke. Sister Agatha felt exhaustion creeping into her very bones. A fatigue that even almond cake wasn't going to fix. Constable Barnes opened his notebook and read aloud:

"Tiffany stole art from Millicent. The only one who knew was the brother, Kendrick Geddings. The victim of the theft was at the crime scene, stole from the victim, says she hated the victim, but insists that she didn't kill anyone."

He closed the notebook and tossed it on the farmhouse table. "Then, after you get all this out of her, you drive home and someone in a Subaru runs you off the road." He paused and looked from one to the other. "That's it in a nutshell, right?"

"You left out all the stuff about *The Wizard of Oz*," Sister Gwenydd pointed out. "Remember, Millicent refers to 'flying monkeys' and the guy yelled, 'There's no place like the ditch, Dorothy.'" Sister Agatha noticed that Constable Barnes looked as if he were in pain.

"Right. *The Wizard of Oz* bit again."

"Don't you think it's odd, Constable, that the person who is threatening me has this obsession with *The Wizard of Oz?*" Lucy waited, and when he didn't respond, added, "Weird, right?"

Constable Barnes picked up his notebook from the table and tucking it into his front pocket fixed his gaze on Lucy.

"Why are you in Wales, Miss Pennoyer?"

"Excuse me?" she said, sounding surprised.

Everyone looked at Constable Barnes. Seldom did you hear him use a voice like that. For one fleeting second, Sister Agatha was reminded of Armand Gamache. She sat up straight. Could she have underestimated the constable all these years? Thinking he was an amiable middle-aged man counting the years to retirement when all the time he was Chief Inspector Gamache come to Wales?

"Why do you ask?" Lucy said.

"Well?" Constable Barnes sat back without moving his eyes from Lucy.

Sister Agatha noticed that even Reverend Mother had stopped pouring tea into her cup and was staring at the constable.

"I came here to rent a studio and pursue my art."

"You came all the way across the Atlantic to North Wales for studio space in a convent?" He leaned forward. "There aren't any good art studios in the United States?"

Lucy's pale skin turned splotchy red starting at her neck and climbing up to the roots of her red hair. And Sister Agatha noticed that Sister Gwenydd was staring at the table top, outlining a groove in the pine top with her finger. Did Sister Gwenydd know something that she didn't know? *Good gracious! This was getting complicated.* She longed to open her purple notebook, but Constable Barnes/Inspector Gamache would probably find that suspicious.

"Constable Barnes," Reverend Mother said, setting the teapot down. "Lucy is our guest here at the abbey."

Sister Agatha looked inquiringly at Reverend Mother. Lucy wasn't exactly a guest. She was a paying tenant who had signed a lease. She also noticed that Reverend Mother looked quite put-together for a midnight interrogation in the abbey kitchen.

"I just find it interesting," Constable Barnes said, "that at the same moment a young woman from America shows up in a tiny village in the North of Wales, suddenly a person is murdered and then all sorts of strange things begin to happen."

"Constable Barnes!" Reverend Mother bridled. "That is entirely uncalled for. Certainly you are not saying that you think Lucy had anything to do with any of this?"

"My apologies, Reverend Mother," he said. "It's late. But tomorrow morning, when we've all had a chance to think things through, I would like Miss Pennoyer to pay me a call at the station. We need to have a talk."

He stood up, his heavy frame seeming to fill the kitchen.

"If any of you think of anything," he said, looking directly at Lucy, "that you think might contribute to figuring out this tangled mess, call me straight away. I'll stop by the rectory and see if Father Selwyn can give me his version of what happened."

Pulling on his anorak, he tipped his head to Reverend Mother. "Stay in touch." Then he fixed Lucy in a steady gaze. "And if you don't mind, Miss Pennoyer, don't leave the village."

With that the door closed behind him and the group sat in a stunned and exhausted silence. Reverend Mother was the first to speak.

"I think it's time you told us, Lucy."

"It's a long story," Lucy said quietly.

Without moving her eyes from Lucy, Sister Agatha opened her notebook and uncapped her Sharpie. *She knew it.* Lucy did have a secret. And Reverend Mother had figured it out. Reverend Mother. A regular Miss Marple.

"Tonight seems to be the night for long stories," Reverend

Mother observed. She turned to Sister Gwenydd. "I think we will need something to see us through beyond your wonderful almond cake. Anything in the larder?"

Sister Gwenydd stood up, pushing back her kitchen chair. "Savory or sweet?"

"Well, I for one am hungry. How about you Sister Agatha?"

"Starved."

"Lucy?"

"Famished."

"Savory, then, Sister Gwenydd."

"I've got just the thing." She lifted her long kitchen apron off the hook next to the larder. "Keep talking, I can listen while I cook."

"I'm thinking that you might already know most of Lucy's story already. Am I right, Sister Gwenydd?" Reverend Mother and her youngest nun exchanged a long look. Sister Gwenydd didn't say anything, just stood there with her apron half-tied.

"So, Lucy. Tell us everything," Reverend Mother said. "I'm dying to hear. And I have a feeling so is Sister Agatha."

Lucy looked at Sister Gwenydd, who shrugged and smiled. "Alright then. Have you heard of Bernardo's Children's Home?" Lucy asked.

"Of course," Reverend Mother replied. "Bernardo's is well known in Wales."

"And very respected," Sister Agatha added. "They've taken care of the children of Wales for more than a century. Bernardo's took in children back in the day when we still called them orphans.

"Well, my parents adopted me from Bernardo's when I was just a few weeks old," Lucy said. "My parents are Welsh, which I've told you. But as soon as the adoption was final, they moved to the United States. They both had fellowships at Stanford."

This was all information that Sister Agatha knew already. She wondered when the secret stuff was to be revealed.

"I'm sure your adoptive parents were thrilled to get an infant," Reverend Mother said.

"And a Welsh baby, at that," Sister Agatha added. Sister Gwenydd grunted from the stove.

"You may protest all you want Sister, but Welsh children *are* superior." She looked at Lucy. "It's common knowledge. Everyone knows it."

"Well, superior or not," Lucy said. "They took me home, and I grew up in New York City, which was a very cool place to be a kid."

"Sounds exciting to me. Living in New York City," Sister Agatha said. "All that crime."

"Most people don't like the crime aspect of New York."

"I suppose not. But there must be so many murders to investigate."

"Sister," Reverend Mother said, shaking her head. "Please."

"I just mean, it would be great for my writing."

"Lucy, could you keep talking or it'll be time for morning prayer before you tell them," Sister Gwenydd said, sliding a platter of Welsh rarebit onto the table and taking her seat at the table. A fragrant, cheesy steam rose up from the toasted bread.

Reverend Mother and Sister Agatha looked expectantly

at Lucy while each picked up a slice of the Gouda-covered bread.

"First, I want you to know that I love my parents. I don't think of them as 'adoptive parents' but as my real parents."

"Of course they are, dear." Reverend Mother said, biting delicately into the thick, crusty slice. "Sister Gwenydd, you really take Welsh rarebit to new heights."

"But here's the thing," Lucy said. "My dad's a neuroscientist and my mother's a biochemist." She looked around the table. Sister Agatha wondered if Lucy felt she had made her point. "Don't you see?" she said when no one responded.

"See what?" Sister Agatha said. "Your parents sound very accomplished."

"They're not artists," Lucy stated emphatically.

"No, they're not," Sister Gwenydd said. "Which means they're able to earn a living from what they do."

"Very funny. The problem is . . . I'm an artist, and so I've always wondered, were my birth parents artists? I mean is it in my DNA or did I just grow up with enough privilege to have the money for art lessons?"

"Why would having artist parents mean anything? I'm a nun. My parents were sheep farmers. Sister Gwenydd is a brilliant chef, and neither of her parents is a chef." Sister Agatha looked at her.

"My mother can't boil water." Sister Gwenydd added. "And it's doubtful that my father ever made his own tea."

"But isn't art different? Shouldn't it be at least a little *inside* of you? The artistic temperament and all that." Lucy said.

"That's the problem with artists," Sister Gwenydd said. "You think you're special. I'm surprised art school didn't cure you of that. I went into cooking school thinking I was amazingly talented. But I learned pretty quickly that I'm no better than anyone else."

"Sister Gwenydd, please," Reverend Mother said. "We are all entitled to our own insecurities. And you *are* very talented. At least to us, here at the abbey. Before you came along, we were ordering takeaway twice a week."

Reverend Mother looked at the plate of Welsh rarebit. "Split one with me, Sister Agatha?"

Sister Agatha held out her plate.

"What I think Lucy is telling us," Reverend Mother said, pushing her knife into a piece of the thick, crusty bread oozing with toasted cheese. "Is that she would feel more legitimate, or validated, if her parents were also artists."

"You want to feel that you're for real." Sister Agatha said. "I feel that way as a writer sometimes. And then I kill someone off and it helps." She ignored Reverend Mother's quiet sigh.

"Yes." Lucy agreed. "I want to feel like I'm for real."

"I've seen your work, Lucy, at least some of it. I can't imagine it being more *for real* than some of your portraits," Reverend Mother said. "The painting you have done of Ben Holden is striking. And anyway, aren't we all here on earth to see where God takes us?"

"That's right," Sister Gwenydd affirmed. "You were created in God's image. Think of it that way."

"Well, that argument only works if you believe in God. I don't." Lucy said.

"Then I see your point." Reverend Mother said. She chewed a bite of Welsh rarebit thoughtfully. "Atheism does seem to throw a monkey wrench into things."

"OK. Let's forget about God for a moment," Sister Agatha said.

"I beg your pardon," Reverend Mother said, picking up her teacup. Sister Gwenydd noticed that she smiled into her tea.

"You know what I mean. Just think of it as a wonderful thing that two such non-artistic people—scientists—would be willing to raise an artist. In a lot of families, you only would have been encouraged to go into the sciences and nothing else. Especially not to art school, which I understand doesn't come cheap. Nor is it, as Sister Gwenydd has pointed out, a quick path to gainful employment."

"Well, anyway. I needed to know. So I contacted Bernardo's and they sent me a letter identifying my birth mother."

"It's that easy?" Sister Agatha said. "I thought those things were kept a secret?"

"Not since 2002 with the Adoption and Children Act," Lucy said.

"So Bernardo's told you who your birth mother was. What about your birth father?" Reverend Mother asked.

"His name isn't on the birth certificate. I inquired, and they said that either no one knows who he is or he left his name off deliberately."

"So the woman signs, takes all the legal responsibility, and the man just disappears?" Sister Gwenydd said, placing a tray of lemon squares on the table. "Typical."

"No kidding," Sister Agatha said. "I guess things don't change that much after all."

"Are you saying that your birth mother is in Wales and you came here to find her?" Reverend Mother asked.

"Yes. When I heard from Bernardo's, I started trying to think of ways to get to Wales. So I was googling stuff, like, you know, art opportunities in the UK, and your ad on Craigslist popped up. You were looking for an artist-in-residence to rent your studio. And since it was North Wales, it was perfect."

"You mother is in the North?" Reverend Mother asked slowly.

Sister Gwenydd coughed, and then stood up abruptly and moved over to the window, looking out on the dark night. Sister Agatha wasn't sure, but she thought her shoulders were shaking.

"Well, once I knew my birth mother's name, I found her on the Internet. In fact, she's all over the Internet."

Lucy glanced at Sister Gwenydd, who had turned around and stood leaning against the sink. Her head was bowed and she held the bridge of her nose pinched between thumb and fore-finger, as if she had a headache. Not a good sign, Sister Agatha thought.

"Really?" Reverend Mother said. "And right here in North Wales? How intriguing. That's lovely."

Reverend Mother's enthusiasm sounded a bit forced to Sister Agatha.

"Have you contacted her yet?"

"No," Lucy said hesitantly. "She's not exactly what I expected. Or hoped for. I wanted to observe her from a distance first."

"You wanted her to be an artist. And it sounds like she's not." said Reverend Mother.

"No. Not an artist. Not even close." Lucy frowned.

"Good heavens, just tell us. Who is she? *What* is she?" Sister Agatha had had enough.

"She's a bishop in the Church of Wales."

The room fell silent. The bell in the village clock tower chimed once. Sister Agatha thought that she could feel time itself slowing down. She was vaguely aware of Sister Gwenydd pulling a chair out and sitting down next to her and that Sister Gwenydd was staring at Reverend Mother.

"Not . . ." Sister Agatha said. She couldn't continue. She looked at Sister Gwenydd. "She doesn't mean . . . ?"

Sister Gwenydd nodded. "She does."

"Your birth mother is a bishop in the Church of Wales?" Reverend Mother said. Her voice shook slightly, but overall Sister Agatha thought she was holding up admirably.

"Which bishop?"

"Reverend Mother, there is only one female bishop in all of Wales," Sister Agatha said quietly. "As you well know."

"I want to hear it from Lucy. It could be that there is a misunderstanding."

Talk about hope springs eternal, Sister Agatha thought.

"My birth mother is the Reverend Suzanne Bainton, bishop of Saint Asaph." Lucy sighed and took a lemon square from the blue platter. "A religious person. Like you guys." She bit into the lemon square. They watched as she chewed and swallowed. "Not an artist at all."

Chapter Sixteen

"Suzanne Bainton is Lucy's birth mother? She has a child? Who is twenty-three years old?" Father Selwyn sat down heavily on the sofa in his office, staring at Sister Agatha.

The morning sun filtered through the stained-glass window, casting squares of warm light on the worn carpet. Sister Agatha pulled off her blue woolly hat and mittens and tossed them into the corner. Running her fingers through her short hair, she sat down in the wingback chair across from Father Selwyn.

"I'm speechless," he said, still staring at her.

Before Sister Agatha could respond, there was a knock at the door and Bevan came in. "Would you like tea?" he asked. Bevan paused. "Father Selwyn, are you all right? You don't look so good."

"I'm fine, Bevan, and yes to tea. If there ever was a time Sister and I needed tea, it is now. Thank you."

"I'll put the kettle on," Bevan said, shutting the door behind him.

Father Selwyn looked at Sister Agatha. "So what happens next?"

"Reverend Mother is talking with the bishop this morning. She left right after breakfast. She felt that too many people knew and she didn't want Suzanne to hear it through the grape vine."

"Good heavens, no." Father Selwyn shook his head. "Can you imagine what a shock this is going to be for her?"

"Actually, I *can't* imagine. Our bishop doesn't like to be blindsided."

"This is about as blindsided as it gets."

"And once she's dealt with a problem, she doesn't like it to resurface."

"Certainly not." They both sat in silence for a moment, considering the bishop and her somewhat overwhelming personality.

Bevan came in with the tea tray and set it on the little coffee table between them.

"Everything OK in here?" he asked, this time looking at Sister Agatha.

"Depends on how you define 'OK.'"

She watched as Bevan poured a cup of tea for Father Selwyn. She noticed that he emptied white powder from a little pink packet into the tea and then followed it up with milk so weak and thin it was nearly blue.

"Don't worry, Sister Agatha," Bevan said. "I've brought a pitcher of real cream and a bowl of real sugar for you."

Just as he was about to leave, Bevan turned back.

"Is it true that Millicent Pritchard is in jail?"

"Good heavens!" Sister Agatha exclaimed. In all the excitement and shock about Lucy, she had forgotten about Millicent. She'd started to speak when Father Selwyn said, "Yes. I'm afraid so."

"Does Constable Barnes really think she killed Tiffany? I can't quite picture it."

"I pray it was not Millicent, but . . ." Father Selwyn's voice trailed off and he looked at Sister Agatha. They sat in silence for a long moment. Sister Agatha wished she had something comforting to say about Millicent. But she really didn't.

"All right then. Call me if you need something."

Bevan stood in the doorway looking at both of them. After a minute he stepped out and closed the door behind him.

"In all the excitement about last night, I forgot to tell you—on the way home the van was sideswiped."

"Constable Barnes told me. He said you were run off the road."

"We were, and in the process of explaining it all to him for his report, the whole story about Millicent came out."

"I'm relieved he knows. We were wrong not to go directly to him last night. If we had, we might have kept the accident with the van from happening."

"Well, maybe. *The Wizard of Oz* stuff, the dog, the murder, the article in my desk—I still think they're all related, but for the life of me I can't figure it out." She accepted the cup of tea he handed her. "It's all a big muddle. I keep trying to think of what Inspector Rupert McFarland would say. And really I have no idea."

"What about your go-to folks? Agatha Christie, Inspector Barnaby? Jessica Fletcher? And what's-his-name? The guy in Quebec."

"Chief Inspector Armand Gamache." Sister Agatha took another sip of tea and looked thoughtful. "What *would* the chief inspector do?" She looked at Father Selwyn, who still seemed a bit in a state of shock. "You know what?" she said, putting down her teacup. "He would slow down. He would have a chocolate latte and a licorice pipe and just *think*."

"Are you saying we need chocolate and licorice?"

"Well, chocolate and licorice are always helpful. But we need more than chocolate and licorice. I'm saying we need to *really* think. We've been rushing too much. It's time we pulled together all the facts and looked at the big picture. The forest, not the trees."

Sister Agatha paused, and then her face brightened. "I know what the chief inspector would do. We should have done it a week ago." She stood up and reached for her book-bag. "It's time we set up an incident room."

* * *

"I don't think the kindergarten Sunday School was actually meant for solving murders, but I do have to admit, this giant white board and all these colored markers are perfect." Father Selwyn was standing in front of the Noah's ark play set, resting a hand on the head of a small giraffe. "And having Noah here is quite cheerful."

"Don't forget the yarn for connecting one suspicious incident to another." Sister Agatha looked around with satisfaction.

They had just listed all the players on the huge floor-to-ceiling white board in the children's room, attaching photos with magnets shaped like the letters of the alphabet. Lengths of yarn connected individuals to events and to each other. It was quite impressive, Sister Agatha had to admit.

"The only drawback is that we have to remove everything before Sunday morning. I don't want the children to walk into their classroom with the words *murder, poison,* and the names of their parents' friends written in bright purple. You know, where they are used to seeing pictures of Jesus, Moses, and Abraham."

Father Selwyn unscrewed the lid from the thermos he had brought along and poured two cups of tea. "My goodness, these Sunday School rooms are cold."

Father Selwyn stepped back, surveying the white board. In the center was a huge pink oval. The oval was empty, and radiating from it were five arrows made of pink yarn connecting to nine names. Vonda, Millicent, Kendrick, Ben, Lucy, Vincent van Gogh, *Wizard of Oz* guy, Judy Garland, Suzanne Bainton.

They stood silently studying the diagram until Sister Agatha broke the silence. "I wonder what's going on with the bishop. Not the morning she expected."

"Is Reverend Mother is at the bishop's office right now?"

"At this very moment. I keep watching for a text from her. But nothing." Sister Agatha took a step back and stared at the pink oval. "All of these events have to have one thing in common. Right? And that one thing is what we'll put in the pink oval."

"That's the theory." Father Selwyn pulled up one of the

children's chairs in front of the board. When he sat down, his knees came up to his chin. "I did have one thought. Do you think anyone else knows about Lucy and why she came to Wales?"

"Well, she told Sister Gwenydd."

"Which means that she could have told someone else."

"And remember, she's from the city; she may not realize how word travels in a small village. She probably has no idea that in Pryderi everyone is connected in some way to everyone else. So if she told one person, she probably thinks that person doesn't know anyone connected to her or the abbey."

"Good God!" Sister Agatha felt her stomach heave. "She told the Art Society when she was their guest speaker."

"The Art Society? Why would she tell them about Suzanne?"

"No, she didn't tell them about looking for her birth mother. But I know she told them that she was adopted."

"So Tiffany heard her say she was adopted?"

"Yes. And the next morning, Tiffany was dead."

Sister Agatha stared at the white board as if something might jump out at her. She picked up the purple marker and twirled it in her hand. *Just like Jean Beauvoir in* Three Pines, *she thought.* She uncapped the marker and noticed it smelled like grape. "Did you realize these markers are flavored?"

"I heard that. One of the teachers told me after I inquired why all the children had blue tongues."

"Why blue?"

"I guess blueberry is a favorite among the seven-year-old set."

Sister Agatha moved the blue marker from the white board tray to the sand table on the other side of the room.

"If Tiffany heard Lucy's story, then the two of them are connected." She drew a grape line between the two of them. "And their connection is knowledge of the adoption, but not knowledge of the birth mother's identity. I have an idea," Sister Agatha said, capping the marker. The grape aroma mixed with the kindergarten smells of construction paper, glue, and wax crayons—a smell that was both nostalgic and nauseating. "We need to consider every name on this board and see if we can connect them with Lucy."

"With Lucy? Why?"

"Because I think Lucy is the one who belongs in the pink oval."

* * *

Sister Agatha sat at her desk peering out the window at the front door of the dovecote three stories below. She expected Reverend Mother to emerge from Lucy's studio at any minute. Sister Agatha did not have a good feeling about the whole fact of the bishop finding out that the daughter she had given up long ago had suddenly reappeared and that she was living at Gwenafwy Abbey. On the other hand, Father Selwyn had all confidence in Suzanne Bainton, and he knew her better than Sister Agatha did. So why was Reverend Mother still in the art studio talking with Lucy nearly an hour after getting home?

Sister Agatha opened her purple notebook. The events of the night before raced in her head and she needed to make some sense of them. Looking back, the entire evening seemed surreal: Millicent's admission that she had been in the parish hall and stolen the painting, stepping over Tiffany's dead body to do it. The van being run off the road and totaled. And then Lucy's revelation that Bishop Suzanne Bainton was her birth mother. Yet, as disturbing as the last twenty-four hours had been, she kept coming back to one image—the pink oval on the white board in the kindergarten incident room. *Lucy's name belonged in the pink oval.* The one common thread running through everything from Tiffany's death to all the weird things that had been happening at the abbey was Lucy. But why?

Time to review the evidence. Sister Agatha pulled the broken teacup out of her drawer and sat it in the middle of her desk. Next to it she placed the tiny nail, and then the bag of Welsh Brew. Was the teacup the vessel for the poison—the extract of aconite, the Wolfsbane? And if so, what if anything could Lucy have had to do with it?

She thought back over the crime scene. Tiffany slumped on the floor, leaning back against the wall. The empty spot above her head where the painting had hung. The teacup on the floor. She had clearly just finished a cup of tea when she suddenly died. According to Dr. Beese, she had had a heart attack. Sister Agatha opened her laptop and clicked into the Medline database. There were some advantages to being a librarian and one of them was access to some of the best databases available. She typed *poison* and then *Aconitine* into the search function.

Several articles popped up, and she clicked on one and began to read quickly. Aconitine was the key toxin in Wolfsbane. But she knew that without going into Medline. *The estimated lethal dose of aconitine, 2 mg which can cause death within 4 hours.* How much was two milligrams? She googled it. *Tiny.* And therefore easily concealed. She switched back to Medline. *The taste of aconitine is so bitter that it is seldom actually ingested. Most people spit it out.* If it tasted so bad, how was it that Tiffany ingested enough to kill her? Tea with cream and sugar. The tea in Tiffany's Queensware canister was Welsh Brew. But hadn't Vonda insisted that Tiffany only drank Radiant Infusion from Harrods? So why was there Welsh Brew—an inexpensive workingman's tea—in the canister? Had someone mixed aconitine into the Radiant Infusion that Tiffany had used to make a cup of tea that late night at the parish hall, drunk it, and died? Then did the person come back, throw out the expensive tea, and just refill the canister with the first tea they found on hand? But who?

She pulled Christie's *They Do It With Mirrors* off the shelf and flipped through the pages until she found what she wanted. "Poison has a certain appeal. . . . It has not the crudeness of the revolver bullet or the blunt weapon." Miss Marple knew that not everyone wants a messy death. Something nice and neat. Civilized. What was more civilized than a cup of tea?

If only she had thought to check the tea canister or searched the kitchen while the crime scene was still fresh! Sister Agatha sighed. The disadvantage of being an amateur sleuth and not a real one. She made a final entry in her notebook—*Was anyone seen at the church that night?*—then answered her own question. Emeric was up in the choir loft practicing, Millicent was in the parish hall stepping over Tiffany's dead body, and Kendrick was at least in the vicinity of the church, as the race took place close by. She thought for a moment. Bevan had told them that he had ridden by on his bike. She started to write his name and then crossed it off. *Not Bevan.*

Sister Agatha tapped her Sharpie on the desktop and looked out the window. The door of the dovecote had not opened. Reverend Mother was still in there. She sighed and turned back to her notes. *Vonda.* She had looked so promising in the beginning but had turned out to be irrelevant. She sighed. Getting rid of a suspect was a little like the day she realized that chapters three through thirteen of her murder mystery no longer worked and had to be cut. It was painful, but she had done it; she had hit delete. So she did it again. Only this time she uncapped her Sharpie and drew a heavy line through Vonda's name.

Next, she divided her list into two columns: *Actual Suspects* and *Weird Events: The Dogs, People, Objects, and Movie Stars Involved.* In the *Actual Suspects* list she wrote: Millicent, Kendrick, Ben, Suzanne Bainton, Emeric, and Lucy. In the second column, she wrote: Vincent van Gogh/Toto, Judy Garland, Blue Subaru, teacup, bird painting. She thought for a moment and added *4.50 From Paddington.*

She began with Millicent, who was, at the moment anyway, both at the top of her suspect list and in jail for the murder, although Constable Barnes didn't have anything on her worth a charge of murder. No weapon at least, and it wasn't a crime to read murder mysteries, even if Millicent's choice of reading seemed suspicious. But Millicent had admitted to being at the crime scene and she had removed evidence. She admitted hating the victim, but she wasn't the only one, and that didn't mean she was the killer.

Emeric was still a suspect, though not a very strong one. At the moment, focus had shifted away from the choir director. Which was a good thing considering it was a few days before Christmas and there was a cantata to perform. Although Emeric had lied to the police and did have a questionable background, the only thing that tied him to the murder was a dried-up plant in his back garden.

What about Kendrick? He certainly had motive to kill Tiffany as he was next in line to inherit her share of their parents' wealth. He was also the only other person who knew about the art fraud, although when Millicent reached out to him, he put her off. He and Millicent had one thing in common—they had both been abused by Tiffany. Sister Agatha couldn't shake the image of Tiffany clutching Kendrick by the throat. But would it have driven him to kill her? Also, there was the fact that Kendrick seemed to be an extraordinarily nice person.

Sister Agatha's turned the page to her second column, *Weird Events: The Dogs, People, Objects, and Movie Stars Involved*, and next to Judy Garland wrote "Millicent." Did her flying monkey comment indicate that she was the one targeting Lucy? Whoever was harassing Lucy was also obsessed with *The Wizard of Oz*. Was Millicent obsessed? And would Millicent steal the little dog? Or leave a sinister note? Whoever did those things had to have access to the abbey. And how could Millicent have chased down the minivan and run it off the road? What if she was working in tandem with someone else?

But if Millicent was the one threatening Lucy, then why? Perhaps she felt threatened by Lucy, a talented art school graduate. Maybe Millicent had projected her anger at Tiffany onto Lucy. Was that enough reason to threaten her? And to do it in such a whimsical and weird way—through references to *The Wizard of Oz?* Which was a bit strange. But then, Sister Agatha had to admit, it could be said that Millicent was a bit strange. And did Millicent have the means to kill using an extract from Wolfsbane? Sister Agatha wrote, *Open copy of 4.50 From Paddington on bed table.* She needed to reread that book. Who knew what Agatha Christie still had to teach her?

She flipped back to her suspect list.

Ben Holden. Aside from being someone who didn't like small dogs, Ben was pretty much off the suspect list. There was one anomaly, though, that could possibly tie him in. He was Millicent's great-uncle and had a small painting of hers in his workshop in the back of the cheese barn. Sister Agatha had seen it before—many times, in fact—whenever she was out giving Bartimaeus his weekly currycomb. It was a little canvas propped up on his worktable. At the time she had thought nothing of it—a slightly faded and crude painting of a bird. But that morning after the long night in the abbey kitchen, Sister Agatha remembered it and had gone back for a closer look. She realized that it could have been done by Millicent, but years ago, when she was a child. When asked, Ben was very open about it. "My grandniece, Millicent, painted it when she was at school," he had said with some obvious pride, while dumping feed into Luther and Calvin's trough. *So Ben was Millicent's great-uncle.* But would that link him to Tiffany's murder? Maybe. Ben was an enigma. He seemed like a quiet elderly gentleman who kept to himself and worked with sheep. On the other hand, his taste in reading material ran to romance. She left his name on the list of suspects.

It was the Lucy connection that was really puzzling Sister Agatha. Kendrick certainly had no connection to Lucy. Millicent's connection was more obvious—they were both artists. Perhaps the insecure Millicent resented Lucy. But to systematically scare her with weird *Wizard of Oz* references? Also, whoever was threatening Lucy was very good at sneaking around. They had been on the abbey grounds at least three times: the dognapping, the poison-pen note, and the article left in her desk. And then whoever it was also had the ability to run them off the road. Which didn't sound like Millicent but did sound like Kendrick. Or at least possibly. The problem with Kendrick was if he killed Tiffany for the money why was he so exceedingly charitable in every other aspect of his life? Don't you need to be greedy and feel entitled to kill someone to keep an inheritance all to yourself? And with everything she uncovered, Kendrick Geddings had been proven over and over again as nothing but generous and kind.

Sister Agatha tossed her Sharpie on the desk. She had no idea. The moon broke through the clouds and she took this as an encouragement. She turned back to her notes.

Blue Subaru. Nothing. The car looked familiar for some reason, but she couldn't place it anywhere. She started to cross it off and then left it, placing a question mark after it. She couldn't quite bring herself to eliminate it altogether.

Looking up from her notebook, she saw the door to the

dovecote open. Reverend Mother slipped out and walked across the garden. Her step was slow, and she bent her head into the cold wind. Sister Agatha watched her until she was out of sight. Closing her eyes, she said a quick prayer.

Several minutes later, her mobile pinged. A text from Sister Gwenydd.

Saints and Sinners pub. ASAP.

Chapter Seventeen

～

Sister Gwenydd and Lucy sat across from Sister Agatha at a small table near the fireplace where a fire burned. Christmas music played in the background. Each had pint in front of her.

"Tell me again exactly what Reverend Mother said." Sister Gwenydd took a long sip of her pint.

"She said that Suzanne Bainton wasn't interested in meeting me." Lucy's voice trembled.

"Why not?" Sister Agatha asked.

"I guess she told Reverend Mother that the past is the past and she doesn't want to stir things up."

The three sat in silence for a moment. Then Sister Agatha spoke up. "Maybe she just needs time to get used to this. I mean, it would be a lot to take in."

Lucy nodded. "Yeah, I know. I just thought that she would be more interested at least in meeting me. It's sort of like she's rejected me twice."

"But think about it. Your coming back is a total shock. The bishop was only twenty when she got pregnant, which means she was younger than we are now. For her, it was another lifetime," Sister Gwenydd said. "And if she was only twenty, she must have been in seminary. That would have been more than awkward. Pregnant and training for the priesthood."

"Especially as women were just entering the priesthood back then. The first woman wasn't ordained until 1997, which was almost exactly twenty years ago," Sister Agatha added. She didn't like how miserable Lucy looked.

"So the year she entered seminary and found herself pregnant was the first year a woman had ever been ordained?" Lucy asked.

"Every woman would have been heavily scrutinized and judged," Sister Agatha said, shaking her head. "They probably had to be better than any man around."

"And then the future bishop—unmarried—gets pregnant." Sister Gwenydd took another drink of her pint. "But she stuck it out. And now she's the first woman bishop in the Church in Wales. Your birth mother might not be the artist you wanted her to be, but she's pretty amazing. Although I've met the bishop. She's a little scary too."

"If nothing else, I wish she would talk to me just so I could hear her story. As it is, I'm never going to meet my birth mother. I came all the way to Wales for nothing."

"You're not giving up, are you?" Sister Gwenydd asked.

"What else can I do? Even Reverend Mother told me to stay away. That it was a very painful time for Suzanne and that it wouldn't be respectful of her needs. And she's right. I guess. I'm just super-disappointed." They all sat in silence for several minutes. *Frosty the Snowman* came over the speaker.

Finally Sister Gwenydd spoke up. "I'm not saying that I

disagree with Reverend Mother entirely. And she is usually right in these kinds of situations. However, you really can't come all this way and not at least *see* your birth mother."

"What are you saying?"

"I'm saying that it's time to stalk her."

"Stalk her? Reverend Mother seemed very serious about not doing that."

"Reverend Mother isn't your authority. You're not a nun, remember?" Sister Gwenydd took another long drink of her pint.

"And I never will be." Sister Agatha noticed that Lucy's miserable mood lifted for one moment. "That cop finally asked me out."

"Parker Clough? Are you going?" Sister Gwenydd said.

"I don't know. I'm thinking about it. This whole thing with my birth mother seems more important."

"Now you really can't leave Wales," Sister Gwenydd said. "You have to go out with him at least once."

"He asked me to go to a Christmas concert. A highbrow sort of choral event at a church."

"Really? How very Welsh of him. Whatever happened to grabbing a pint together?"

"I told my parents. They got all excited." Lucy rolled her eyes. "I was dragged to that kind of thing all my life."

"What's the event exactly?" Sister Agatha wondered about how quickly the mood could shift from devastated to optimistic. All because of a possible date. *Youth.*

"Handel's *Messiah*." Lucy took a sip of her beer. "It's kind of romantic. In a way. On the other hand, do you know how long the *Messiah* is? It's hours, and the only really good part is the Hallelujah Chorus. Which actually does make all the sitting there worthwhile."

"Never been," Sister Gwenydd said. "Until I became a nun, Christmas meant paper crowns, crackers, and drinking a Buck's Fizz for breakfast." Sister Gwenydd munched on some crisps from the bowl between them. "It sounds sweet though. Christmas music and all." She thought for a moment. "Where's the concert?"

"I don't know," Lucy said, digging into the crisps. "It's put on by the Saint Asaph Choral Society. I didn't ask Parker. I didn't want to look too interested."

Sister Gwenydd took out her phone. "If it's at Saint Asaph Cathedral, you can bet Suzanne Bainton will be there. It's just the kind of thing she would go to." She looked up from her phone. "It's Saturday. As in tomorrow. You should go. Parker seems like a nice guy—you could do worse. And he's cute enough. Especially in his uniform. And if you just happen to run into Suzanne Bainton while you're there, it's not your fault, right? You'll be on a date."

Sister Agatha just hoped Reverend Mother didn't ask her too many questions.

* * *

Lucy realized that she hadn't been on an actual date in almost a year. Between finishing graduate school, tracking down her birth parents, and moving to Wales, she hadn't really had time for men. And much as she loved the art community in Providence, it didn't really offer the kind of men she wanted for a long-term relationship. As she had tried to explain to her parents, being a starving artist was one thing, marrying one was quite another. And now, her first real date in forever was in church.

She breathed deeply and only half-listened as Parker explained how the St. Asaph Cathedral was built in the thirteenth century and was the smallest ancient cathedral in Great Britain. She nodded and scanned the front pew for anyone who looked like a bishop.

"It's the home of the William Morgan Bible," Parker said, pulling at his tie. "Which interconnects Welsh religion with Welsh literature."

"Right," she said. She had almost told him the real reason for wanting to go out with him—to get a glimpse of Suzanne Bainton. But he had seemed so happy when she called and said she would accept his invitation to the Choral Society's concert that she couldn't bring herself to tell him. And Reverend Mother had asked her to be very discreet in whom she talked to about the bishop.

As Parker continued his history and architecture lecture, she looked around. The cathedral was resplendent with evergreens, purple and white candles, gold bows. It would have been nice to sit here, to finally perhaps feel the nostalgic pull of Christmas. Even though her family wasn't at all religious, they always attended Christmas Eve Lessons and Carols at the Cathedral of Saint John the Divine. The songs, the incense, the candlelight—for her that was Christmas.

Even the nativity story tugged at her imagination and heart. She was hoping perhaps to recapture a bit of that Christmas feeling tonight. But the fact that she was on a date with a man she was pretending to like so that she could catch a glimpse of the woman who had given birth to her—well, that put a damper on things.

She smoothed her short wool tunic and looked down at her tasseled high-heeled leather boots. She had carefully selected her outfit for the event. Attractive and sharp yet a little casual. But what *was* the event? A date with a guy who was cute, even if he did talk too much. Or was the event finally meeting her mother? She harbored a fantasy that she would see Suzanne Bainton and somehow intercept her. But how would the bishop react?

"St. Asaph Cathedral is the mother church of the diocese of St. Asaph," Parker was saying. "Although since you live at the abbey, you probably already know that." He looked at her and she knew that he probably wanted her to say something, but she was more preoccupied with watching the empty chair in the front row. At the top of the program were the words *Opening remarks, the Right Reverend Suzanne Bainton.*

"And as I am sure you know," Parker continued, "St. Asaph is one of the six dioceses of the Church in Wales."

"Interesting," she said.

"And what is a really interesting tidbit of history is that Saint Kentigern built the church here originally in AD 560 and then, right before he died, made Asaph his successor. That was in 573. Which is why the cathedral has been dedicated to Saint Asaph and the diocese has his name." Parker's voice trailed off. "I can quit talking if you're getting tired of history," he said with a weak smile.

Lucy felt like a jerk. He really was a nice guy. And he had gone to a lot of effort tonight. She found out that tickets to the event were expensive. So the fact that she was completely preoccupied and anxious really wasn't fair to him. And she hated women who led men on. But she wasn't really leading him on. It was more like she was using him. She felt a rush of guilt, but it was quickly replaced by a staggering anxiety.

She had just reassured Parker that she was truly interested in the history of the cathedral when she heard high heels clicking down the long aisle in the middle of the sanctuary. She turned and saw her—as tall and strikingly beautiful as she looked in the photos that Lucy had found on the Internet. Her birth mother had perfect posture, perfect hair, and perfect poise. Her chic black dress, mid-length and close-fitting, was both elegant and simple, and it all somehow worked with the clerical collar. Certainly expensive. Lucy watched as Suzanne Bainton brushed past, laughing on the arm of none other than Father Selwyn, who twisted around and looked at Lucy, his eyes wide and his normally ruddy face pale. Lucy gave a little wave and then watched as Suzanne took her seat in the front row.

"That's the bishop of St. Asaph," Parker said. "She always says a few words at these things. Have you met her?"

"Met her?" Lucy squeaked.

"I'll introduce you at the reception after." If he noticed her dumbfounded look he didn't let on.

"Sure," she said, "that would be nice." *Holy mother!* as Sister Agatha would say. She looked up just as Suzanne Bainton stepped into the pulpit.

"*Croesus,*" she said. "Welcome to our annual Advent Choral Society Concert. Advent is both somber and joyous as we journey to Bethlehem. Part of my journey every year is this wonderful concert just a week before Christmas."

Lucy could barely focus on what she was saying. She hadn't expected the rush of emotion that she felt. Suddenly, with her birth mother standing in front of her—in a thirteenth-century pulpit no less—she realized fully why she had come to Wales. Not just to find out if her parents were artists, not to feel "real," as she told Reverend Mother and Sister Agatha. It was more than that. She had always felt as if a part of her was missing. And yet, her real parents, the ones back in New York City who were probably worrying about her right now, had been so good to her that she never could really explore that feeling of emptiness. But now, as she sat here in this beautiful cathedral listening to the woman who gave birth to her, it hit Lucy. She felt as if a question had been answered. *This was her mother.* And yet, she wasn't. All at once, she needed air. She felt dizzy and overwhelmed and suddenly glad that Parker was there. He seemed like the kind of guy who could handle anything.

"I've got to get out of here," she whispered. The bishop had stepped down from the pulpit and taken her seat. The conductor walked to the front, tapped his baton on his music stand.

"Are you ill?" he whispered back as the choir launched into the opening lines of *Comfort Ye My People.*

"Yes," she said, unable to explain. She barely understood it herself. When she and Sister Gwenydd planned this evening, it had seemed like an adventure, not an emotional onslaught.

"Follow me." Parker stood up and, taking her arm, guided her down the crowded row and into the middle aisle where he hurried her toward the back door. They stepped out into the clear winter night. "The car is right over here," he said. "Get in and I'll turn the heater on."

"No," she said. "I need to breathe."

And then to her horror, she began to cry—not small, sniffling crying, but deep sobs that wracked her body, making breathing hard and talking impossible—tears flowing, nose running. She noticed that Parker stood perfectly still, with one hand placed gently on her arm. He didn't make a big deal or even insist that she tell him why she was having a meltdown in the car park of St. Asaph Cathedral. He simply waited, offering her a neatly folded, pressed handkerchief from his pocket. *A man who carries a handkerchief.* She was astounded, and for one moment jolted out of her crying jag.

"I can't believe you carry a pocket handkerchief," she gasped between hiccups. "That's so nice."

"I actually carry two. One for me and one for a lady."

"You're joking." Lucy blew her nose more loudly than she had meant to and, folding the handkerchief, wiped her eyes.

"No. I do. You're not looking like you want to go back into the concert."

"Would you mind?"

He grinned. "No. I'm only here for the Hallelujah Chorus and it takes forever to get to it." He opened the car door for her. "Fancy a pint?"

* * *

Parker's phone buzzed just as Lucy finished telling him the whole story about why she was in Wales. The sounds of the small pub they had found near St. Asaph went on around them. They hardly noticed. He was staring at her with such surprise that he ignored his phone until she pointed to it. She watched him as he read the text. "I have to respond to this. I'm not on duty, but everyone's at a barn fire in Wrexham. There's been a minor accident on the A5."

"Isn't the cathedral on the A5?"

"It's about a mile this side of the cathedral." He glanced at this watch. "The concert must have ended. Although the reception is probably still going on." He stood and held her coat for her. "Coming with me, or shall I drop you at the abbey? It's on the way."

"I'm coming," she said sliding into her coat. Parker Clough was more interesting than she had given him credit for. And as Sister Gwenydd would be quick to point out, he wasn't bad looking.

In less than ten minutes, they were pulling up next to a car at the side of the road, its flashers blinking. From where she sat, Lucy could see that the back tire was blown out.

"You stay here," Parker said. "I'll keep the car running so the heat stays on."

Lucy watched as Parker walked to the car. He leaned in and talked for a few moments, then she saw him open the car door and a tall, thin woman stepped out. Lucy knew who it was even before she moved into the headlights of the cruiser. The Right Reverend Suzanne Bainton.

* * *

"It isn't that I didn't wonder about you over the years. I have often thought of you and what you might be like."

Suzanne and Lucy sat in Parker's backseat while he changed the tire on Suzanne's car. Lucy was glad it was dark. She didn't want to betray too many emotions. She certainly didn't want to have a repeat of her car-park meltdown. She had imagined this meeting with her birth mother ever since she had decided to come to Wales, and now it was here.

"It's not that you don't have a mother. You have a wonderful mother. And I am immensely grateful . . ." Here Suzanne Benton's voice caught and she cleared her throat, "immensely grateful to her for all that she has been to you. She has been everything to you that I couldn't have been. I hope you understand that."

"I do. Totally. It isn't that." Lucy paused, unsure how to continue.

"Unmarried and pregnant in the late 1990s wasn't easy. Nor was it the usual path to ordination."

"I can imagine. You were actually younger than I am now."

"And now I feel old," Suzanne said, smiling.

"And you should know that I'm not looking for the love and security one gets from parents. I have that. My parents are great. It was just that . . . I was hoping . . ." Lucy's voice trailed off.

"Hoping what?" Suzanne looked out the front window and winced as Parker swore at a stubborn lug nut on her flat tire. "What did you hope?"

"For one thing, that you would be a famous artist."

"I collect art, if that's any help."

"Well, it is. Sort of. I guess you don't have to be an artist. I mostly just wanted to see you. You know, in real time and space."

"And now that you have, how are you doing?"

"I'm OK."

"Is there anything you'd like to ask me?"

"Who is my birth father?" At this, Lucy noticed that Suzanne Bainton stiffened.

"That is the one question that is off-limits." Suzanne Bainton looked directly at Lucy. "I can't . . . won't . . . tell you."

"Why? I thought maybe he wasn't on the birth certificate because . . . you know?"

Suzanne's eyebrows shot up. "You thought perhaps I didn't know who the father was? It's not that, he's a dangerous man. He wouldn't want to know that you have . . . surfaced."

"So he is around? In the area?"

"Lucy, I'm not telling you anything about him."

"You have to. I haven't come this far to not even be allowed to know his name." Lucy hated the whine in her voice, but she couldn't seem to stop it. "Really, shouldn't it be up to me whether or not I know who he is?"

"I could not be your mother then and I'm not replacing her now—but I know one thing—no mother would put her daughter in that kind of danger. And I simply won't."

Just then a car pulled up to the side of the road and slowed almost to a stop. Lucy tried looking in the window of the driver's side, but it was too dark to see anything. Parker, who had been crouched behind the left side of Suzanne's car working on the flat, stood up. The driver hit the accelerator and roared off. As the car pulled away Lucy thought it looked like the same blue Subaru that had run Sister Agatha off the road two nights earlier.

Chapter Eighteen

꩜

Sister Agatha thought a hot cup of Welsh Brew and a crispy oatcake would make the perfect Christmas Eve afternoon tea. She had been dispatched to the village to purchase a small bottle of brandy for Sister Gwenydd's Christmas pudding. What good was Christmas pudding if you couldn't light it on fire? She settled into the back booth and sent Father Selwyn a quick text. *At the Buttered Crust. Join me?*

She looked around her. The tea shop was doing a slow trade on this late afternoon. Most people were probably already home with their families preparing for the Christmas Eve celebration and then for Christmas day itself. As a child, Sister Agatha had been convinced that animals could talk on Christmas Eve and, deep down, she still wondered. Of course, she knew they couldn't, but the magic of Christmas, especially Christmas Eve, was still alive for her. The long, dark dreariness of Advent would end in the celebration of the birth of the Christ child.

She turned as the bell above the door jangled and Father Selwyn's voice boomed "a blessed Christmas Eve!" to

Keenan behind the counter. She wondered what kind of tinned fruit Keenan might bring them. Was there a holiday tinned fruit?

"Are the sisters all coming to St. Anselm's for Lessons and Carols tonight?" Father Selwyn asked, sliding into the booth across from her. He had left his hat and long coat on the rack at the door.

"Of course. We wouldn't miss the cantata for anything."

The Christmas cantata was originally scheduled for the week before Christmas, but with Emeric in jail, the choir had fallen off its tight schedule. Add in the problems of Constable Barnes being occupied with the murder of Tiffany and the arrest of Millicent, and the bass section was sorely under-rehearsed. Not to mention the fact that Tiffany had been first soprano. Father Selwyn had suggested that they incorporate it into the Christmas Eve service at St. Anselm's instead to provide a few extra nights of rehearsal. The choir enthusiastically agreed, and so it was tonight at eight o'clock. All the residents of Gwenafwy Abbey, including Lucy and Ben, were attending.

"We're having our own candlelight service earlier this evening. We're calling it Christmas Evensong. And Lucy says she has a surprise for us—at five o'clock—so I need to get back."

"A surprise during the service? I didn't think Lucy concerned herself much with worship?"

"She says she's an atheist, but I don't believe her. Anyway, I think it's something she's painted." A large sheet-draped canvas had been placed at the front of the chapel, to be revealed at the Christmas Evensong. It had added an extra bit of anticipation to the day. Although the recent events of the murder, the dog-napping, the crash of the van, and the menacing note had all taken their toll on the sisters, especially Reverend Mother, Christmas was still Christmas at the abbey. When she left that day and headed out, she could hear Sister Gwenydd's Bose speaker blasting Frank Sinatra in the warming room and smell the delicious fragrance of Christmas cookies drifting from the abbey kitchen. There was definitely a day-before-Christmas buzz in the air that no amount of murder and intrigue could diminish.

Keenan stopped by their table and Father Selwyn ordered a pot of Welsh Brew for both of them, and an oatcake—extra crispy—for Sister Agatha. A bowl of fruit for himself. "You'll share your oatcake, right?" he said to her.

"Of course. How is Millicent?"

"Not good, really. It's Christmas Eve and she's sitting in jail. There's no hope of a hearing until after the holiday, so she's stuck there."

Sister Agatha said nothing, thinking of the pink oval on the whiteboard. She opened her notebook and flipped through a few pages.

"I've been thinking about something. "It's that blue Subaru. The first time I saw it was when I walked into the village the day Tiffany was killed. It nearly knocked me into a gorse bush."

"Did you get a look at the driver?"

"No. I was too busy picking myself up out of the ditch. And then, when I was looking for clues about the dognap-ping, I noticed that there was blue paint residue on the stone wall in front of the abbey as if a car had sideswiped it and tire treads that were not those of the minivan. I'm thinking it was the same car."

"Or not," Father Selwyn said. "It could have been any car."

"True . . . but it was definitely a blue Subaru that sideswiped the minivan—may it rest in peace." She turned the page and scanned down. "It was a blue Subaru—or at least Lucy thinks so—that drove past them the night of the flat tire. Whenever the blue Subaru shows up, Lucy is in the area and suspicious things happen. Except for that first time, when I was walking into the village." Sister Agatha thought for a minute. "Actually, Lucy *was* in the village that day. I heard her tell Sister Gwenydd she would help with the shopping if they could run to the art store in Wrexham. And the car came up the hill from the village. I wish we were in our incident room where we have all this drawn on the white board."

"Alas, our incident room has turned into the St. Anselm's annual Santa's workshop. The Sunday school teachers are at this very moment assembling stockings to hand out at the cantata."

"All of our hard work gone? That would never have happened to Armand Gamache and Jean Beauvoir. Fortunately for us, I took a photo of the white board and have it on my phone."

Keenan came by the table with their order.

"Sorry it took so long," he apologized. "We're shorthanded on Christmas Eve."

Keenan continued to stand there for a minute. Father Selwyn looked at him. "It's just that you usually drink Glengettie tea, Father Selwyn. And this is Welsh Brew."

"True, Keenan. You are a good man to notice. But today, I guess I was just in the mood for something else."

"You know who else drinks Glengettie?" he said placing their order on the table.

"If you don't mind, Keenan, Father Selwyn and I are . . ."

"That big politician."

"Devon Morgan?" Sister Agatha asked. Would that scourge on humanity not leave Pryderi alone? Especially the day before Christmas?

"About an hour ago, I guess. With Mr. Colwyn. Mr. Colwyn didn't order tea though. He didn't order anything. Who goes to a tea shop and just sits there with nothing?"

"Mr. Colwyn?" Sister Agatha looked at Father Selwyn. "Lewis?"

"He was my botany teacher. Nice but really tough. Funny too. For a teacher he had a real sense of humor." Keenan looked toward the window. A gaggle of teenaged girls walked by, and even though they didn't look his way, Sister Agatha noticed that he turned red.

"Mr. Colwyn didn't even say anything, which was weird, because in class he talked and talked. He's sort of a comedian. On the last day we got to watch one of his old movies instead of doing work."

Keenan began to amble away, then turned back. "He wanted to know about that girl with the red hair. Lucy."

"Lucy?" Sister Agatha spoke slowly. "What did they want to know, Keenan?"

"Just if I'd seen her in the village today."

"What did you say?"

I said, "'What do you think she is? My girlfriend?' I mean, seriously, like I could get a girl like her?" Keenan smiled shyly. "She's hot, you know? No offense, Sister."

"None taken, Keenan. Although she isn't just 'hot.' She is also an extraordinarily talented artist." Sister Agatha began to gather her things together and shove them into her book bag. Her hands began to flutter with nervousness. Why was Devon Morgan asking about Lucy?

"Has Devon Morgan been in here before?" Father Selwyn asked. "The politician?"

"No," Keenan said, looking out the window again. "I've only seen him at the Pryderi Hotel. I valet there. Midnight Saturday till seven on Sunday mornings. I park his car for him. A Mercedes. Nice. That's why I'm never at mass, Father."

"Worship doesn't start till ten. I bet you could make it."

Keenan shrugged.

"When did you last see Devon Morgan at the hotel?" Sister Agatha asked.

"Not for a month or so. He used to go there with Mrs. Reese."

Father Selwyn spewed his tea across the table. "With whom?"

"Mrs. Reese. You know. The artist lady. The one who died. Which is sad. Of course."

Sister Agatha watched as the young waiter drifted back to

the front counter. Father Selwyn had gone pale. "Late nights at the hotel with Tiffany?"

"Do you think they were having an affair?"

"Well, not to cast aspersions, but if they were arriving after midnight on Sunday morning it seems a little obvious. I do recall Emeric saying that Tiffany had been missing choir. And because she was our best soprano, that was a big deal."

"Devon Morgan was having a relationship with a woman who is found murdered the day after she meets Lucy for the first . . . and last . . . time?"

"And now Devon Morgan is asking about Lucy? And why was he with Lewis Colwyn?"

"Tell me again what Suzanne Bainton said to Lucy about her birth father?"

"That if he knew that Lucy was in the area, it could be dangerous for her."

"But she didn't say his name?"

"No. Just that he was a powerful figure and . . ." Sister Agatha's eyes went wide. "You don't think . . . ?"

"I do." Father Selwyn stood up and grabbed his hat.

"But what's the Tiffany connection?"

"I have no idea. But I think it's time for Suzanne Bainton to give us some answers."

Sister Agatha and Father Selwyn pulled their coats on and hurried across the room. Just as they were about to leave, Sister Agatha turned and looked at Keenan. He stood behind the counter staring at his mobile.

"Keenan," she said. "Did you say Mr. Colwyn let you watch a movie on the last day of class?" Keenan nodded yes.

"What was the movie? Do you remember?"

"Sure, I remember," he said. "*The Wizard of Oz*. It's like his favorite movie. He was always quoting it in class."

Sister Agatha and Father Selwyn left the tea shop at a run.

*   *   *

"This is my fault," Suzanne said. She sat behind her massive desk in the diocesan office. Her voice trembled and her hands shook as she clutched a file folder in front of her. Sister Agatha had never seen the bishop so rattled.

"What is your fault?" Father Selwyn asked. Sister Agatha glanced at the clock on the wall. The nuns' Christmas Evensong started in exactly one hour. She knew that Reverend Mother was expecting her to be there for the service, which was to be followed by a traditional Welsh dinner and gift exchange, rounding off the evening with the cantata at St. Anselm's. She especially didn't want to miss the unveiling of Lucy's surprise.

Suzanne Bainton sat back and stared at the top of her desk. "Oh my God. Devon."

"Are you saying that it's true, then? That Devon Morgan is Lucy's birth father?" Sister Agatha asked.

Suzanne Bainton nodded but didn't speak.

"Holy mother!" Father Selwyn breathed quietly.

"I was in seminary. My first year. And I met Devon at a food kitchen, of all places. He was serving the homeless dinner. I later found out he did things like that just for the publicity—it made for a great photo op. He was nearly twenty years older than I, and at the age of twenty-three I found a man in his forties intriguing. Especially one as charming and wealthy as Devon Morgan—handsome, nice car, always paying me compliments. We were together for three months when I found out I was pregnant."

Suzanne Bainton shook her head. "I was ecstatic. I actually thought he would marry me and we would live happily ever after."

She paused, and Sister Agatha thought perhaps she wasn't going to keep talking, but she did.

"I knew he was married. But he told me he was unhappy, and he was going to leave her, and that I made him happy. I actually believed him. Of course, he ended our relationship as soon as I told him I was pregnant. I left his apartment that night for the last time and I think I grew up about ten years on my drive home."

Suzanne Bainton walked over to the window and stood with her back to them, looking out. A gentle snow had begun to fall. *A white Christmas.* They all sat in silence for a moment. Then she turned back.

"At first, I wanted to keep the baby. But common sense—and panic—kicked in. I was a graduate student with no money. I lived in student housing. And if I told the seminary that I was pregnant, would I even have a job in the future? The Church in Wales has come a long way in twenty years since the first woman was ordained, but . . ." The bishop paused. Sister Agatha resisted looking at the clock. "He tried to pressure me into an abortion, but there I drew the line. I'm not saying a woman shouldn't have that choice, but it wasn't for me. In the end, I agreed to . . ." Suzanne Benton's voice broke, but she immediately regained her composure. "I agreed to take the baby to Bernardo's and tell them that I didn't know the name of the father."

Father Selwyn nodded. "A wise decision. All around."

"Thank you. A hard decision." Suzanne Bainton paused again. "There's something that I am not telling you. That I am ashamed of."

"Why ashamed?" Sister Agatha said. "You were brave. And you did the right thing."

Suzanne Bainton snorted. "You say that because you don't know."

"Know what?" Father Selwyn asked.

"That I accepted money from him. He paid me to lie about his name. I feel that was shameful. It's as if I made money off the baby and now . . ." Suzanne Bainton looked at Father Selwyn, her eyes bright with tears.

"My dear," he said. "We all regret our younger selves. Extend to yourself the grace and forgiveness that you so readily extend to others."

Sister Agatha wasn't sure that Suzanne Bainton did extend grace and forgiveness readily to others, but nonetheless her heart broke for the bishop.

"Look what you have made of yourself?" she interjected. "The life you have lived has more than made up for any lack of judgment you had as a twenty-year-old. I for one would not like to be held accountable for everything I did in my youth."

Suzanne Bainton plucked two tissues from the box on her desk and wiped her eyes. Sister Agatha noticed that the bishop even cried with self-control. And her mascara didn't smudge.

"I suppose. And there is certainly nothing I can do now to change the past."

"What did C. S. Lewis say? 'No one can change the past, but anyone can change the present.' Or something like that," Father Selwyn proffered. He could always be counted on to pull out a good C. S. Lewis quote in a moment of crisis.

"And it's the present, not the past, that I'm worried about," Sister Agatha said. "I'm certain that somehow Devon knows about Lucy. And has some weird *Wizard of Oz* guy out to get her." Sister Agatha still couldn't get her head around the idea that it might be Lewis Colwyn.

"Did you say, '*Wizard of Oz* guy?'"

"A guy in a blue Subaru keeps doing increasingly dangerous things to Lucy. And he seems to be channeling Judy Garland. Listen, do you think Devon would murder someone if he thought they knew about his past with you?" Sister Agatha asked.

"I think he might. He has his eyes on being First Minister of Wales. And nothing stands in Devon's way. He gets what he wants. Imagine if his constituents found out that their candidate for First Minister had paid a woman to keep his name off the birth certificate, washing his hands of his newborn daughter? Especially now with his ridiculous family-values campaign. What if I leaked to the press that he pressured me to have an abortion? His political aspirations would be ended. Or at least seriously threatened. It's not a chance he would be likely to take." Suzanne looked from one to the other. "Why are you asking about murder?"

"I'm not certain, but I think he murdered Tiffany," Sister

Agatha said. "Tiffany somehow knew about Lucy. Or at least I think she might have. And she was in an intimate relationship with Devon. Maybe *he* told her about Lucy. And then Lucy shows up at the Art Society meeting."

"Let's go," Father Selwyn said, getting to his feet. "We have to find Lucy before Devon does."

* * *

Suzanne Bainton rose in Sister Agatha's estimation when she wordlessly and without hesitation—in high heels, pencil skirt, and cashmere coat—climbed into the tiny backseat of Father Selwyn's 1968 BMC Mini.

"You ride shotgun, Sister Agatha." she said. "I've driven with him before. The people in the front die first."

Sister Agatha nodded. Turning back around, she clutched the dashboard as Father Selwyn, palming the wheel, shot out of the diocese car park.

"The Christmas evensong at the abbey starts in twenty minutes," Sister Agatha said, as she checked her seatbelt. "The good news is that Lucy should be there. Not much harm can come to her in a chapel full of nuns. She's planning some sort of surprise for us, and whatever it is, I know she was going to spend the afternoon getting it ready."

"I feel so responsible. I should have gone straight to Constable Barnes as soon as I knew Lucy was in the area," Suzanne said, clinging to the backseat as Father Selwyn careened around a lorry. "Selwyn, please. It won't help Lucy if we meet our end on the A5."

"Sorry," he said, laying on the horn and then going into

the breakdown lane to pass a car that was merely observing the speed limit. "I've never gotten a speeding ticket yet."

"That's only because your collar has gotten you off the hook." Sister Agatha twisted around in her seat again and faced the bishop.

"Tiffany Reese was found dead the morning after the Art Society meeting. The meeting where Lucy was the guest speaker. It's possible that she told enough of her story that Tiffany figured it out. Would Devon have told someone like Tiffany about you and the baby?"

"I wouldn't imagine that he would." Suzanne thought for a moment. "On the other hand, I do remember that Devon was a very chatty drunk. Enough bourbon, and he blurts out anything."

"We have reason to think that he was having an affair with Tiffany Reese. So it's possible that she had at some point heard him say something about Lucy and then let him know that Lucy had resurfaced."

"She would have to be a horrible person to do that. Anyone who knows Devon Morgan knows that he's ruthless."

"Lucy offended Tiffany about her art," Father Selwyn added. "And you didn't do that to Tiffany Reese."

"Art that wasn't even hers," Sister Agatha interjected.

"So she outed Lucy to Devon just because she was offended? She sounds as unethical as he is."

"I doubt she really thought it through," Father Selwyn said.

"I don't know about that," Sister Agatha said. "Tiffany was pretty nasty when she wanted to be. Flying monkey, remember?"

"You think that Devon had Tiffany killed because she knew about Lucy?" Suzanne asked.

"It's possible. I think he hired someone—who drives an old Subaru—to kill Tiffany and to scare Lucy off. You have to give Devon a little credit. He did balk at killing his own offspring, only scaring her. Although Lucy doesn't scare easily."

"So he hired someone to kidnap her dog, send her a threatening note, and run her off the road?" Suzanne Bainton paused. "I'm sure you see the pattern here, don't you Sister Agatha?" she asked.

"That each action against Lucy has grown progressively more dangerous and frightening?"

The two women looked at each other. Suzanne Bainton leaned forward. "Selwyn, I never thought I would say this to you, but . . . *drive faster!*"

* * *

Father Selwyn skidded to a halt in the driveway of the abbey. The three piled out and began to run toward the chapel. Sister Agatha noticed how very silent the evening was. Just past twilight, not quite pitch dark, that gentle, hushed moment on a winter evening as the light fades from the sky. But there was nothing gentle or peaceful this evening. Where was everyone? Why were all the lights off? Father Selwyn pulled open the heavy door of the chapel and the three of them tumbled in. It was then that she remembered, it was Christmas Eve and the nuns were about to start the candlelight service.

"Good heavens!" Reverend Mother said from the pulpit. "What's going on? Bishop Bainton, why are you . . . ?"

"Lucy," Sister Agatha interrupted her. "Where's Lucy?"

"Sister Gwenydd just left to find her. We didn't want to start without her. Or you, for that matter." Reverend Mother gestured toward the large veiled canvas that sat off to the side of the chancel. "Apparently we are to sing 'Away in the Manger' as she pulls off the sheet."

The other sisters already in the pews turned and looked inquiringly at the three of them. Sister Callwen stood up. "Has there been a development?"

"You can say that." Father Selwyn said hurrying to the front of the chapel. "If Lucy is fine, then all is well. However . . ."

All heads turned as Sister Gwenydd pushed through the chapel door. "Call Constable Barnes. Now! I saw Lucy." Sister Gwenydd was gasping for breath. "A man in a car. Blue. Shoved her in the trunk. And Vincent van Gogh."

Reverend Mother grabbed Sister Gwenydd by the arm. "Take a deep breath and tell us exactly what you saw."

"Lucy was out by the lane walking Vincent. One last time, you know, before the service. And I started down the drive to meet her and tell her to hurry, that we were waiting for her. And that dented blue car pulls up and a man jumps out and he . . . and he . . ." Sister Gwenydd seemed suddenly overwhelmed.

"What? What happened?" Reverend Mother asked.

"He opened the trunk of the car and just pushed her in. She had Vincent van Gogh with her too. I saw her shove him under her parka, and then the man tried to grab the dog and, like half in and half out of the trunk, she kicked him in the . . . well, you know where she kicked him. But he shoved her back in and slammed the trunk shut."

"Did you see which way they went?"

"Down Church Lane. Toward the village."

"Sister Gwenydd, do you think the man saw you?" Sister Agatha asked, and was only slightly relieved when Sister Gwenydd shook her head and said, "No."

Reverend Mother turned to Sister Agatha. "Where do you think they're taking her? Do you have any idea?"

Sister Agatha forced herself to think calmly. Inspector Rupert McFarland always said that hiding a dead body is far trickier than you think it will be. *Kill your victim as close as possible to the site of disposal* was his advice. What better place to kill someone and hide the body than where there are lots of holes, earth-moving machines, and piles of dirt?

"Let's go," she said, running toward the door. "We can't wait for the constable."

"Go where?" Sister Callwen said.

"The housing development. It's the perfect place to dump a body."

* * *

"All I can say is that it's a good thing Sister Agatha crashed the van," Sister Winifred said from the driver's seat of the luxury tour bus, on loan from the insurance company, as she headed out onto Church Lane. The development site was less than a half-mile from the abbey, but it seemed better and certainly faster to load into the tour bus than for the entire contingent to take off running. "Or we wouldn't be able to transport the entire abbey to save Lucy and Vincent van Gogh. We could never have all fit into the minivan." Fortunately, Sister Winifred was comfortable with a stick shift, multi-person vehicle. In fact, Sister Agatha thought, she looked right in her element.

"For the record, I didn't crash the minivan," Sister Agatha said. "It was driven off the road by the same crazy man who is now holding Lucy hostage." She looked in the big rearview mirror at her sisters sitting in rows behind her. Pale, but determined. Even in her incredible fear, she had to admit that if you need rescuing there is nothing better than a group of determined nuns.

"I just hope you're right, Sister Agatha, and Lucy is at the development site." Suzanne Bainton said, her voice shaking. "Reverend Mother, did you reach Constable Barnes?"

"Officer Clough is on his way to the church to pick him up. He's at St. Anselm's at cantata practice."

"Oh, right. I had forgotten the cantata in all of this," Father Selwyn said. "Most of the police force is singing," he said to Suzanne. "It's an all-village ecumenical choir."

It only took a minute for them to reach the development site. Sister Winifred cut the wheel hard and bounced them over the frozen ground. In the shadows, the drills and earthmoving equipment looked like hulking monsters. The whole area was silent and apparently shut down for the holidays. There were a few spotlights scattered about, but no one seemed to be in sight. Maybe the security guard had been dismissed by Devon, Sister Agatha thought. Which couldn't mean anything good for Lucy.

Sister Winifred pulled the big coach to a halt. She looked up into the long rearview mirror, made eye contact with Sister Agatha, gave her a small smile, and then held crossed fingers up to her heart.

"Sisters," Reverend Mother said, standing and facing them. "Be careful. And stick together. But remember, we have God on our side. Of all nights of the year, this is the night we must remember the words of the angels, 'Fear not.'" And anyway, there are only two of them and twenty-two of us."

"It's my fault all this happened," Suzanne said. "I'm finding Lucy."

And with that, the bishop of St. Asaph hurried down the steps of the bus and jumped down onto the rough ground. The rest of the sisters followed. They moved as quickly as a solid group of nuns could across the meadow toward the earth-moving equipment and the giant, gaping hole.

Then Sister Agatha stopped them. "We need to think for a moment," she said. "If I were a criminal, where would I be?" Just at that moment, Vincent van Gogh came shooting across the field like a bullet.

"Vincent!" cried Sister Gwenydd. She knelt next to the little dog. "Where's Lucy?" she said in a high-pitched voice. "Where's Lucy?"

"Does she expect him to answer?" Suzanne said quietly to Reverend Mother. "You're so not a dog person, Suzanne," Reverend Mother quietly replied. They all watched as the little dog twirled around twice, barked once, and then shot off again.

Come on," Sister Gwenydd yelled, and in one motion all the

nuns of Gwenafwy Abbey picked up their habits and began to run, streaming after Vincent van Gogh and Sister Gwenydd.

Sister Gwenydd, who had gotten ahead of the others, suddenly screamed and ran toward the large blue storage tank. The others quickly saw why she had screamed. Vincent van Gogh was standing in front of the tank. He had both front paws on the metal wall and was barking frantically. Sister Gwenydd started pounding on the outside of the container. It was about twenty feet long and five feet high and had a large white pipe coming out of it. The pipe was more like a huge hose, and it was sealed off at the end. As far as Sister Agatha could tell, it didn't have any other opening.

"Good God!" Father Selwyn started pounding and calling Lucy's name. From inside came a faint voice. "Father Selwyn, is that you?"

"I'm here, my dear. We are all here. We will get you out. Are you injured?"

"I'm tied up. I can't . . . breathe."

"Oh my God! Where is that constable? I'm going in!" Suzanne Bainton ran to the white pipe. "Lift me up, ladies," she said. Sister Winifred made a step out of both her hands, and two other nuns hoisted Suzanne Bainton up. She hovered there for a moment, held up by nuns, and then said, "It's no use. We can't get in this way. This pipe is sealed to the opening."

"There has to be a way in," Father Selwyn said, as he skirted around the storage tank.

Sister Agatha frantically wracked her brain for what Armand Gamache or Inspector Barnaby or even Stephanie

Plum would do. *Nothing.* She began to panic. She knew that Armand Gamache would never panic. "Dear God," she prayed aloud. "Please. In your mercy."

"I think you'll need more than mercy, Sister Agatha." Devon Morgan stepped out from the shadows of the earth-moving equipment. Sister Agatha turned, and when she saw the Sig Sauer P226 pointed directly at her, slowly raised her hands.

"Sisters," she said not taking her eyes off the gun. "Reverend Mother. Everyone. He has a gun."

"That's right," Devon said. "And, if I chose, I could kill every one of you."

"Actually, you couldn't." Sister Agatha thought she could hear a slight groan from Sister Callwen. "A Sig Sauer P226 has fifteen rounds in the magazine. And as we are twenty nuns, one bishop, and a vicar, there is no way you could ever kill all of us."

"Everyone against the tank," Devon yelled, waving the Sig. "Your little Christmas Eve rescue is over."

"Let her out, Devon." Suzanne Bainton stepped forward out of the shadows.

"Suzanne Bainton. Well. Long time no see."

"Do you think you can get away with this? There are witnesses. Twenty-three of them in fact."

"Witnesses to what?" Devon asked. "What did you actually see me do?"

"Sister Gwenydd saw you shove Lucy into the trunk of your car."

"Sister Gwenydd? Do you mean the one arrested for killing her boyfriend? Who faked being a nun?"

"I didn't actually kill him," Sister Gwenydd interjected. "And I am a nun, truly."

"Let her out, Mr. Morgan," Reverend Mother interrupted. "I assure you nothing will happen to you if Lucy is OK. But if she's not, if she . . . if she dies, then this will be something from which you will never recover."

Father Selwyn began to pound on the side of the tank. "Lucy!" He turned, his eyes wide with fear. "She's not responding."

Suddenly, Devon grabbed Sister Agatha by the back of her habit. He forced her to her knees and put the gun to her head.

"Now all of you need to turn slowly and walk toward that bus of yours. When I see you on it and headed out the drive, I'll let Sister Agatha go. If not, then I'll do with her what I have already done to Tiffany and, pretty soon, Lucy."

"Tiffany?" Father Selwyn said, and he looked around wildly. "Where is Lewis Colwyn?" Sister Agatha noticed he was using his pulpit voice. "You were at the tea shop with him."

"Lewis Colwyn? He's safe at home with his family." But Sister Agatha thought that, in the spotlight of the construction site, Devon Morgan wavered for one second. "Don't worry about him. He's the least of your problems right now."

Devon pushed Sister Agatha down on her face. "All of you, go. Get in that stupid bus."

Sister Agatha heard the sirens coming up Church Lane. *Stall him,* the voice of Inspector Rupert McFarland said in her head. *When you're in the weeds, stall the bad guy and see what you can make happen.*

"You know, Devon," she said, twisting her neck and

shoulders upward. "On Christmas Eve it is said that animals can talk. Do you believe that? Because I . . ."

"Shut up! And why aren't you people moving? I said get on the bus."

"We're not leaving Sister Agatha here. Or Lucy." Reverend Mother said.

Suzanne stepped forward. "Look, Devon, your problem is with me. Let Sister Agatha go. Let Lucy out of that tank. And you can do whatever you want with me." Sister Agatha saw the two of them pass a long look. In the distance, she definitely heard the wail of a siren.

"What would I want with you?" Devon said. "I didn't want you twenty years ago, why would I want you now?"

"For God's sake, Devon. You are a horrible, despicable person." Suzanne's controlled voice had reached a near screaming pitch. She threw herself at him, knocking him slightly off balance, which allowed Sister Agatha to scramble to her feet. But her hiking boot caught in the hem of her habit and she fell down again. Sitting up, she saw Father Selwyn lunge at Devon. They both fell into a pile of pallets stacked next to the tank. Out of the corner of her eye she saw Sister Winifred hike up her habit and bring her size-ten Wellingtons down on Devon's wrist. She only hoped it was his gun hand. At the same moment, Sister Callwen, Sister Harriet, and Sister Matilda raced over and threw themselves on top of Devon in a jumble of parkas, habits, jumpers, scarves, and wooly hats. Just then, the police cruiser pulled off Church Lane and tore across the meadow toward them, headlights bouncing.

Constable Barnes was out the door, shouting for everyone to get down. Which was a little late, Sister Agatha thought, considering that half the convent had just landed on top of Devon. She heard a shot fired. Constable Barnes yelling. She thought she heard Parker Clough shouting Lucy's name, and then, as Reverend Mother helped her back up on her feet, she saw that Parker and two other officers were going hammer and tongs at the white pipe. It looked as if he had gotten a jimmy bar into the seal between the pipe and the tank and was using it as a lever. In a minute, and with a loud cracking noise, Parker had the pipe off and was shouting into the tank. And the next thing she knew they were pulling Lucy out and into a waiting ambulance. Devon was in handcuffs, and they watched as Constable Barnes shoved him into the back of the police cruiser. "Officer Clough will drive the bus back to the abbey," he shouted over his shoulder.

"I told Constable Barnes about Lewis," Father Selwyn said. "He's going to pick him up."

"Lewis Colwyn?" Reverend Mother asked, her eyes wide.

"We'll tell you later,"

The nuns fell silent. They stood together in the middle of the empty field, watching the taillights of the ambulance, its siren now blaring, as it pulled out onto Church Lane and raced toward the hospital.

Chapter Nineteen

⟡

"I wish I could have made it to the cantata, but they wouldn't release me till now—even though by the time we got to the hospital, I was pretty much fine," Lucy said. She sat next to Parker Clough on one of the comfortable couches in the warming room.

The spacious warming room, decorated with greens, a huge blue spruce in the corner, and a crackling fire in the fireplace, was filled with the laughter and conversation and the enticing aroma of Sister Gwenydd's traditional Welsh Christmas dinner. Sister Agatha looked at her friends gathered in the cheerful room and tried to wrap her head around the fact that the murder was solved with the perpetrator behind bars. Along with Lewis Colwyn, the amiable botany teacher, hit man, and *Wizard of Oz* guy. Sister Matilda looked devastated, and Sister Agatha felt more than a little embarrassed that despite all of her sleuthing, the real bad guy had been under her nose the whole time.

To everyone's surprise, when the cantata had ended and the applause died down, Reverend Mother had left her pew and stepped into the pulpit. She then invited anyone who wanted to come back to the abbey for a very late-night Christmas feast. The nuns had missed the wonderful dinner that Sister Gwenydd had spent the day preparing because they were away at the housing development rescuing Lucy and Vincent van Gogh. Then they had all gone straight to the cantata at St. Anselm's, as several of the sisters were singing in the choir. Constable Barnes had slipped in at the last minute and filled in the bass section. Sister Agatha was pretty sure he had pulled his choir robe on over his uniform.

Sister Gwenydd thought her Christmas Eve dinner could be reheated, and she and a few sisters were in the kitchen going hammer and tongs to get it on the table. All of the Gwenafwy Abbey nuns, Constable Barnes, Father Selwyn, Emeric, Millicent, Bevan Penrose, and Suzanne Bainton were gathered in the large warming room happily awaiting the meal of Welsh cawl, scallops with bacon, fish pie, freshly baked bread, and, of course, Christmas pudding. At the last minute, Sister Agatha remembered the small bottle of brandy in her book bag. Ben Holden, who had been in the far pasture with the sheep when they all left for the housing development, had returned early from the cantata to start the fire in the warming room.

"I'm fine, I think," Lucy said to Parker Clough, stroking the silken ears of her little dog. Or, as Sister Gwenydd now called him, *min-pin-stand-in*. "It was scary in there, though it was worse in the trunk of the car. I'm just really glad that Vincent ran off before they could shove him into the tank too."

"It's a good thing that tank was empty," Constable Barnes said. He looked at Reverend Mother. "It was brand new. If it had been used even once for waste storage . . ." Constable Barnes shook his head. "Well, let's just say we might not be celebrating right now."

"The little pup really did save the day then," Ben Holden said. "I can't say I like small dogs, but this one is a corker. He's a big dog in a little body." Ben reached down to scratch Vincent van Gogh's ears. Sister Agatha, who was sitting on the other side of the fire, felt a wave of guilt for thinking that Ben had kidnapped Vincent van Gogh when it had been Lewis Colwyn all the time. She suddenly had a thought. "Ben," she said quietly. "Why did you leave the article in my desk drawer?"

"You knew it was me?" the old sheep farmer asked.

"Not until right now."

"Millicent is my grandniece. And I didn't like her being cheated by that woman. I knew who the real painter was. Millicent showed talent when she was just a wee thing. No one encouraged her though. I thought she deserved better."

"Why didn't you just come to me directly?"

"You're the detective." Ben stood up and placed a log on the fire. "I knew you'd figure it out." He smiled and sat back down. "Just like you figured everything else out and now that tosser Devon Morgan and his lackey are behind bars. Where they ought to be."

"Hear, hear," Father Selwyn said raising his glass of Pimm's.

"It was Devon all along?" Lucy said. "When Tiffany was

so hostile to me at the Art Society meeting, I thought it was because I had insulted her art."

"Excuse me?" Millicent said.

"Sorry. Your art. And I didn't insult it. I critiqued it. I love your art."

"Thanks, and you may critique it anytime you want. Now that it's mine again."

"So that's why at the end of the meeting, when I had left to find the ladies room, I overheard Tiffany in the church kitchen. But at the time, what she said didn't make any sense." Lucy paused, her brow crinkled.

"What did you hear her say?" Sister Agatha started to reach for her notebook but then accepted a glass of Pimm's from Father Selwyn instead.

"She said something like, 'one click on Facebook and your past goes viral.' To be honest, I didn't really think about it."

"Did you hear anything else?"

"No, that was it. But then, at that point, I had no reason to suspect Tiffany of anything. Or Devon."

"It sounds to me as if Tiffany threatened Devon with putting on social media that he had an illegitimate daughter—who he deserted at birth—and that she was back in town."

"He must have panicked. Visions of you giving BBC an interview. 'Family Values Candidate Dumps Mother and Daughter'. No wonder Devon hired Lewis Colwyn." Father Selwyn shook his head and looked into his drink. "Sad, really."

"You saw Devon that night, didn't you?" Sister Agatha said. "As you left the meeting?"

"I did. He had pulled up in his big car as the Art Society meeting ended. And then I recognized him at the village meeting."

"You saw him?" Suzanne asked, her eyebrows up. She also was drinking Pimms. Sister Agatha thought she might have to trade out her cup of Welsh Brew for something more fitting to a celebration.

"When I came out of the meeting, there was this tall, handsome older guy with a really expensive car and a driver. I had dropped my portfolio on the sidewalk and he helped me pick it up and then offered me a ride. I didn't take it. Something about him creeped me out."

"Well, at least you have better judgment than I did at your age," Suzanne said.

"It's sort of weird to think that I was meeting my birth father and I had no idea."

"But why would Devon show up at the Art Show?" Sister Callwen asked.

"If Tiffany called Devon and he panicked, then maybe he came straight over. Perhaps he was campaigning in the area," Sister Agatha said. "Maybe he wanted to meet with Tiffany and convince her to keep his secret."

"I'm confused," Sister Harriet said. "How would Tiffany even know, though, about Devon being Lucy's birth father?"

"Well, Tiffany and Devon seemed to have had an affair not long ago. And . . ." Sister Agatha left off. She looked to Suzanne.

"And if memory serves, Devon is a very talkative drunk," Suzanne picked up. "So I'm thinking that he told Tiffany at some point, blurted it out, and then she used it against him when Lucy came to town. He had probably dumped Tiffany by then, and perhaps she wanted some revenge—Devon brings that out in a person. I would assume that Tiffany wanted to get back at him. So she calls him and says, 'your daughter is back and I am alerting the press.' Although it sounds as if, she threatened him with Facebook. Which today is probably more harmful than the front page of The London Times.'"

"The next day, Tiffany is dead, and the day after that, Vincent van Gogh is kidnapped," Father Selwyn filled in.

"But why all the intrigue—poison, threatening notes, the Wizard of Oz theme?" Bevan asked.

Constable Barnes cleared his throat. "Turns out that Devon Morgan doesn't do his own dirty work. He hired Lewis Colwyn to do it. Our family-values politician didn't want to kill anyone himself, but he wasn't opposed to hiring it out."

"I can't believe that Lewis Colwyn would do such a thing," Sister Matilda said, handing Sister Agatha a glass of Pimm's. "Really, Sister," she commented, "tea?" She settled her large frame into an easy chair. "When I think of all the hours we spent working together in the abbey greenhouse." She shook her head.

"Which was how he targeted Lucy. He was here at the abbey all along. So, in a way, it was an inside job." Sister Agatha was a little dismayed that she had missed the whole Lewis Colwyn connection. Armand Gamache would have picked up on it straight away.

"I got a confession out of Lewis Colwyn pretty fast. In

fact, he broke down right there at his house when we picked him up." Constable Barnes looked pained. "Turns out that Devon was blackmailing Lewis Colwyn over an . . . unfortunate incident in Lewis' past. He had been involved with an older student when he was a young teacher. He hadn't been fired, though he would be today, and Devon Morgan told Lewis Colwyn that he would go to the press with it. Lewis was desperate to keep his past a secret."

"Desperate enough to kill Tiffany and scare Lucy into leaving Wales?" Reverend Mother said.

"Desperate enough to put the extract from a deadly plant into the tea canister at the church. I guess Lewis Colwyn's background in botany came in handy."

"Never underestimate the power of a secret," Millicent spoke up from her seat next to the blue spruce. "It can make you do things you would never have imagined doing."

Sister Agatha and Father Selwyn exchanged a glance. *Like stepping over a dead body to steal a painting and not even considering calling for help?*

"I don't understand why Devon Morgan didn't just have me killed? Why steal my dog and send me notes and run us off the road? It seems like a lot of trouble for a hit man to go to. Even if he does enjoy drama."

"Much as I hate to defend Devon Morgan, I would say that even he didn't have it in his heart to kill his own flesh and blood," Suzanne said.

"No, but he did stuff her in a waste-storage tank to die," Reverend Mother pointed out. "So I wouldn't give him too much credit."

"True. Devon must have realized that Sister Agatha and I were getting close to figuring it out. And when he saw that Suzanne had appeared on the scene, he raised the stakes. Especially as he planned to run for First Minister. And you can't do that if you have fathered a baby, abandoned its mother and forced her to give it up for adoption," Father Selwyn said. "He knew his political career was in jeopardy if the story got out. Another secret."

"There is a silver lining here. Awful as everything is that has happened," Lucy said. "I may have been given up for adoption for not-so-great reasons, but I ended up having a wonderful childhood with great parents."

Suzanne Bainton looked down into her drink and used her cocktail napkin to wipe her eyes.

"And I've met my birth parents—well, perhaps they weren't quite what I expected." Lucy paused while laughter rippled through the room. "The friendship I now have with the woman who gave birth to me, and with everyone here at Gwenafwy Abbey, makes it all very worthwhile. And so I have created a special gift as a way to say thank you."

At that moment, the door between the warming room and the outside hall opened, and Ben and Parker entered, carrying between them the large sheet-covered canvas from the chapel. They set it down carefully in front of the fireplace.

"As you know," Lucy said, standing in front of it, "I am an atheist. But living here at the abbey has changed that a bit. No, I'm not going to become a nun. Like some people who drop in and then never leave." She looked at Sister Gwenydd, who laughed from where she stood in the door, her hands in potholders and wearing her long kitchen apron. "But I think there is something to be said for the love and companionship of this place. And I think, after being with you through all of this, that the love you have for each other and for the world comes from something greater. I'm not sure that I'm ready to say it is God. Or Jesus. But it's definitely something bigger than all of us." She took a deep breath. "So, this is for you." And Lucy swept the sheet off the large canvas.

At first, Sister Agatha thought it was a nativity scene. "Very well done," she was about to say, but then paused, looking closer.

For a moment, everyone stood silently, admiring the scene at the manger. But very quickly, a gasp went through the room, and they all broke out into laughter, and then applause. The nativity scene was peopled by familiar faces. At first, one of the shepherds at the side of the manger looked like any other shepherd in any nativity scene. But on closer examination, the tall figure with the kind eyes and gentle smile was recognizable as Father Selwyn. Kneeling next to a lamb on the other side of the manger was another shepherd, Ben Holden. Mary was Sister Gwenydd. Joseph was none other than Officer Clough. The three angels hovering above the manger each had the sharp eyes and ready smiles of Sister Winifred, Sister Matilda, and Sister Harriet. The wise men were wise women—Reverend Mother, Suzanne Bainton, and Sister Callwen. Holding on to the rope of a camel was Constable Barnes. And standing at the back, observing everything with purple notebook in hand, was an angel whose wings were slightly tilted—Sister Agatha.

The door to the kitchen opened, and Sister Gwenydd

entered with a steaming pot of Welsh cawl, followed by two sisters carrying fresh bread, cheese pie, and oatcakes, just as the bell in the village clock tower chimed midnight.

"Everyone," Reverend Mother said, "it is Christmas day. And a truly glorious Christmas. Let us all join hands and welcome the babe of Bethlehem."

As they formed a circle around the big room, a fire crackling in the fireplace and fragrant steam rising from the platters of food on the table, Constable Barnes' deep bass joined with Reverend Mother's soprano until the entire group raised their voices in the ancient hymn:

> *Come, Thou long expected Jesus,*
> *Born to set Thy people free;*
> *From our fears and sins release us,*
> *Let us find our rest in Thee.*

Acknowledgments

I would like to thank Stephany Evans, agent-of-my-dreams, for all her support and encouragement.

Many thanks to my publisher, Crooked Lane Books, for sending me such awesome editors who care so much about my manuscript, my characters, and my feelings.

To Jenny Chen and Sarah Poppe for their quick response to my questions and needs. And to Teresa Fasolino whose compelling cover art continues to capture so perfectly the world of Gwenafwy Abbey.

To Jane Gardner, always available when I needed her, especially during my social-media-learning-curve-crisis (and any other crisis I have).

To Dr. Anne Nafziger for her expert medical advice on how a person looks when dead and all events that might have led to their state of being dead.

To my friend and relentless copyeditor, Lanny Hilgar, who recently said to me, "Someday we need to sit down and talk about commas."

Acknowledgments

To the members of the First Congregational Church of Paxton who have embraced my writing life with boundless and characteristic enthusiasm making me the happiest pastor ever.

And to my husband, Don, who brings coffee in the morning, wine at night, and inspiration all day long.